THE ERIDANI CONVERGENCE

a novel of T-Space ™

Alastair Mayer

Mabash Books

THE ERIDANI CONVERGENCE

This is a work of fiction. Names, characters, places, and incidents are either the product of the author's imagination or are used fictitiously, and any resemblance to real people or incidents is purely coincidental.

Cover © 2019 by Mabash Books
Image credits:
      Spaceship crashed on the beach © lurii - Depositphotos.com
Image used by permission.

T-Space is a trademark of Alastair Mayer

For announcements about other T-Space books and special offers, sign up for Alastair Mayer's newsletter at
      http://www.alastairmayer.net/

A Mabash Books original.

Second Edition, July 2019

Mabash Books, Centennial, Colorado

Hardcover Edition: ISBN-13: 978-1-948188-128
Trade Paperback Edition: ISBN-13: 978-1-948188-159

For Jerry E. Pournelle, 1933-2017

Thanks for everything, Jerry.

A Few Words About Space and Time

Dear Reader:

The events here cover several months and many light years. The story follows characters separated widely within that space and time, converging on a single point in both. For best entertainment value, read it as written here, even if, from a universal, objective viewpoint (which Einstein tells us is nonsense anyway), the first few chapters may seem out of sequence.

With one exception—Carson's flash-forward in Chapter 1—the chapters for any given character (or their location in space) are in chronological order; it's just the threads that are braided.

If you *insist* on reading it in a non-Einsteinian, rigid space-time order, use the time-line given at the back of this book (or front, for the ebook). It lists the chapters in that order. (Although please note that, thanks to Alcubierre, the warp drive *is* Einsteinian.)

But to quote Steven Moffat writing for *Dr. Who*: "People assume that time is a strict progression of cause to effect, but *actually* from a non-linear, non-subjective viewpoint—it's more like a big ball of wibbly wobbly . . . time-y wimey . . . stuff." And who am I to disagree with a multiple Hugo Award winner?

Enjoy!

—Alastair Mayer

flight Paths, by Ship

(not all are explicitly referenced in the book)

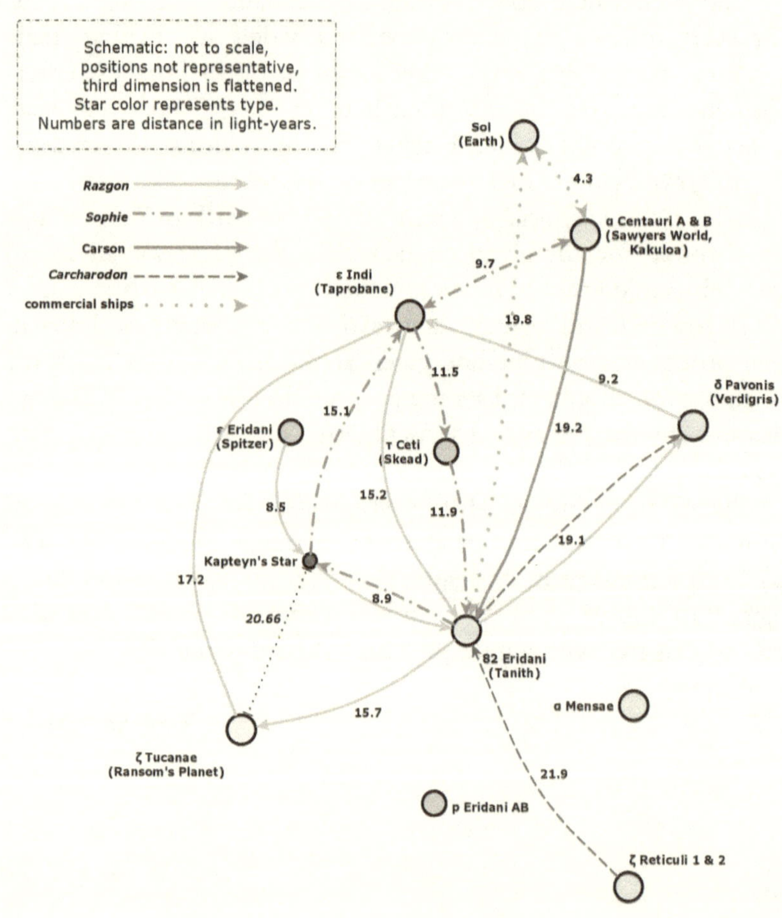

CONTENTS

PART I: A Scatter of Timelines
Prologue — 7
1: Taxi! — 9
2: A Rude Awakening — 12
3: Marten's Homecoming — 18
4: Findings — 21
5: The *Carcharodon* Arrives — 26
6: The White Hart — 28
7: Cuneiform — 34
8: Report Received — 35
9: Old Records — 39
10: Planet Skead — 44
11: Stirring the Pot — 49
12: Ducayne's Message — 52
13: Sawyer — 55
14: Dinner — 61
15: Going for a Ride — 63
16: Dessert — 67
17: Homeworld Security — 73
18: Departure — 76
19: Ducayne Has News — 81
20: Operation Jade Ribbon — 87
21: Approaching Tanith — 90
22: A New Artifact — 92
23: Harp City — 99
24: Carson's Other Ride — 106
25: The Whereabouts of Smith — 110
26: Rendezvous — 112
27: Approaching Convergence — 116

28: An Unexpected Caller   118

PART II: *Convergence*
29: Convergence   132
30: Vaughan   136
31: The Pickup   140
32: Vaughan Recalled   147
33: Catching Up   149
34: Carson and Burnside   160
35: Tevnar   167
36: Divergence   177
37: Packing It Up   182
38: Tevnar's Story   189
39: The Artifact   199
40: Meanwhile, Back at the Ranch   206
41: Change of Plans   212
42: Second Divergence   216
43: Kapteyn's Star   220
44: Toward Delta Pavonis   225
45: Kapteyn's II   227
46: Delta Pavonis   235
47: Taprobane   238
48: Home   241
   Epilogue   *246*

Timeline   247
Glossary   250
Acknowledgments   252
Preview: *The Centauri Surprise*   253
About the Author   259

THE ERIDANI CONVERGENCE

Previously . . .

Warning: Spoilers for the prior books.

In *The Chara Talisman*:

Archeologist Hannibal Carson finds the remains of a high-tech talisman in a primitive tomb on the planet Verdigris, in the Delta Pavonis system. A ruthless cult, the Velkaryans, believes it may be a clue to a lost cache of alien weapons. Homeworld Security enlists Carson, together with a starship pilot, Jacqueline "Jackie" Roberts, and Carson's timoan partner, Marten, to decipher the clue and find whatever it points to before the Velkaryans do.

On a planet orbiting the star Chara, thirty light years on the far side of terraformed space, they find a mysterious pyramid and its high-tech contents. After several run-ins with the Velkaryans, gaining an ally named Rico, they manage to return, but some of what they found was destroyed.

In *The Reticuli Deception*:

Captain Jackie Roberts uses the star patterns inscribed on several similar talismans to discover that they were drawn from a common point-of-view, a point somewhere near the Zeta Reticuli star systems. Carson recalls a legendary UFO encounter, the Betty Hill Incident, after which Ms. Hill drew a star map she claimed to have seen while aboard the alien craft. That map showed "trade routes" from Zeta Reticuli to our sun and other nearby stars. But the records of the map are second and third hand, virtually illegible.

Roberts, with Carson and Marten, takes her ship, *Sophie*, to Zeta Reticuli. Rico and another Homeworld Security man,

Brown, go to Earth to try to retrieve the original UFO reports. Everyone runs into trouble. En route to Zeta Reticuli, Roberts and company are initially refused landing on Verdigris, but land anyway. They find another pyramid, this one already broken into.

They continue on to Zeta Reticuli, where they have a close encounter of the third kind with a mysterious alien and another run-in with Velkaryans in the person of a man named Vaughan and his ship *Carcharodon*. The aliens temporarily isolate the Velkaryans, while our heroes return home empty-handed but for their knowledge of the encounter.

PART I: A SCATTER OF TIMELINES

Prologue

Epsilon Eridani star system

THE SMALL S-CLASS ship *Razgon* had just dropped off a group of geologists—two humans and three fellow timoans (the ship had been comfortably crowded)—on Spitzer in the Epsilon Eridani system. Captain Tevnar's next planned stop was a planet orbiting Zeta Tucanae, to pick up a team who would be due back at Kangara University in about six weeks. That gave her some margin in her schedule.

Zeta Tucanae was just beyond her single-hop range from Spitzer. The obvious place to refuel would be on Tanith in the 82 Eridani system, near the midway point. But there were other options. She checked the navigational database.

There. Kapteyn's Star, at eight-and-a-half light-years. A red dwarf, but this one was known to have planets. One, perhaps two, in the habitable zone. That didn't necessarily mean they were habitable of course, just that they were in the right temperature range for liquid water to exist. She read farther. No, not habitable. The outer one was frozen, and both were what was called "super-Earths", planets several times more massive than Earth. But the inner one was not as big; it was within her ship's limits. Sure, why not? Tevnar began to prep the ship for warp.

∞ ∞ ∞

Kapteyn's Star

A week after leaving Epsilon Eridani, Tevnar aerobraked the *Razgon* into a low orbit over Kapteyn's-II. The atmosphere was thick, but her instruments were up to the task of scanning for a body of open water and a large, flat area to set down on. Her database hadn't had many details about the planet, so she might well be the first to conduct such a scan. The data could be worth something. The scan could also take a while; there was a lot of planet to cover. She set the equipment to automatic and then headed to the galley to rustle up some grub. She could have done without the extra time in zero-gee, especially given the high gravity she'd be experiencing on the surface, but she didn't mind it as much as some other timoans did.

∞ ∞ ∞

It was a full day before the ship's systems alerted her to the presence of a small lake in the middle of a large, open plain—itself the dried bed of an earlier, much larger lake. That would do. It would be even better if the lake were freshwater. Did the lake have an outflow? She began to review her data scans of the area in detail.

It did have an outflow. The lake's size was constrained by the geography, not by evaporation. Perfect! Tevnar checked her position. The *Razgon* was on the far side of the planet from the lake, that simplified things. She went back to the cockpit and ran a course calculation, then modified the *Razgon*'s orbit to bring it over the lake as it came around the planet again. She'd make a final check first.

Two hours after that, Tevnar began her deorbit burn.

∞ ∞ ∞

As she brought the *Razgon* low over the old lake bed to a landing, she noticed something jutting out of the water near the shoreline ahead, almost on the beach. She was still too high to be sure, but it gave the impression of being artificial rather than natural, not the sort of thing you'd expect in the middle of a lake bed. Odd. She adjusted course to land near it. It was worth checking out.

Chapter I: Taxi!

Carson

Now: an autocab outside Sawyer City, Sawyers World

DR. HANNIBAL CARSON glanced out the window of the autocab. Just over seven weeks had passed since his meeting with Ketzshanass, a spacefaring alien of a species previously unknown to humans, in the Zeta Reticuli system. Now he had just learned of an encounter with a similar alien on *this* planet fifty years earlier. Lost in thought about the significance of what he had just heard, the absence of other traffic or buildings took a while to creep into his consciousness. The surroundings were unfamiliar. This wasn't the way back to the university.

"Cab, destination Drake University, Archeology Building."

"*Acknowledged,*" the cab responded, but made no indication it was about to change course.

"Cab, specify destination." *Stupid robot*, Carson thought, annoyed.

"*Acknowledged.*"

That wasn't right. Carson scanned the car's interior. Like other in-city autocabs, this had no manual controls for off-road use, nor even any display panel. Carson tapped a sequence on his omni to link it to the cab. That was a standard interface; it let a passenger interact with the cab using keypad and screen.

Nothing. As far as his omni was concerned, the cab didn't exist.

"Cab, stop here please," Carson said, raising his voice.

"*Acknowledged.*" The cab sped up.

What the hell? Am I being kidnapped by an autocab? Carson wondered, scarcely believing it. Could this have anything to do with the meeting he had just left?

Carson switched his omni to map mode; maybe he could figure out where the cab was taking him. His first glance at the map told him he couldn't. It showed him in the middle of Lake Victoria, a large lake thousands of kilometers from Sawyer City. *At least, I don't* think *it's the one in Africa*, Carson thought, his temper rising. Something was screwing with the signals from the positioning satellites. Hacked or not, the autocab shouldn't have had anything capable of such spoofing. Someone had made modifications. *What about the brakes?* Then Carson realized it wouldn't matter if the brakes had been tampered with, since they were under the cab computer's control anyway.

He tried the door. The cab's speed was higher than anyone in their right mind would jump from, but he was getting desperate. But the door was locked and the unlock button didn't do anything.

"Cab, slow down!"

"*Acknowledged,*" it responded, but made no change in speed. By now they were well away from the city—his meeting had been on the outskirts of town to begin with—hurtling down a narrow gravel road amid open fields.

Carson's gaze darted frantically around the interior of the cab. The door and window switches were inoperative. There was an interior light, for all the good that was. There were no obvious switches or indicators on the dashboard. Wait, the light . . . maybe?

He had a multi-purpose folding knife in his pocket. He pulled it out, opened it, and pried the plastic housing off the light. The fixture contained a switch and a small array of LEDs. He stabbed the blade into the ceiling at the edge of the light assembly and pried. The blade began to bend, but the light tore loose before it broke.

Carson ripped the wires from the back and scraped the insulation off, then twisted them all together. Sparks flew, and the wires heated up almost instantly, burning his fingers. The insulation began to melt and smoke. The whine of the car's motor faltered. Yes, it was working!

Then he heard a click as a circuit breaker tripped, and the car resumed speed. The wires stopped smoldering. *Damn.* Carson knew it had been a long shot. *Now what?*

Chapter 2: A Rude Awakening

Vaughan

Seven weeks ago: Starship Carcharodon, *near Zeta Reticuli*

KLAUS VAUGHAN WOKE up in the owner's seat, behind the captain's. *What the hell?* How had he dozed off in the middle of pursuing Hannibal Carson's ship? He had been anything but tired. The forward window showed black, with the occasional sparkle confirming that it wasn't switched off, but rather that they were in warp. *When did* that *happen?*

"Captain, give me a status report," he said.

There was no reply. The captain's head was slumped forward. Vaughan reached forward and shook his shoulder. "Captain Stinson!"

Stinson's head snapped up and he shook it. "Wha . . . ?" He stared at the screens for a moment. "What the *hell?* When did we go to warp?"

"I had hoped you could tell me that."

"Crap." Stinson's hands touched a sequence of controls, running status checks. "I'm going to drop us out of warp, to get a position check."

"Do it."

"All hands," the captain announced over the PA. "Prepare for zero-gee. Dropping out of warp in ten seconds."

Vaughan felt the familiar, half-imagined tingle of the warp bubble collapsing. Gravity went away. The forward viewscreen remained black, but now with a scattering of fixed stars. "Give me a rear view." he said. Someone switched the screen to an aft-pointing camera. A bright star was centered in the view, with another some distance from it.

"Position?" Vaughan demanded.

"Assuming those stars are Zeta 1 and Zeta 2 Reticuli—" Stinson checked an instrument "—and they are, then we're point-two-four light years from Zeta 1. On a path toward Earth, which we'd never reach with the fuel on board."

"What happened?"

"I'm still trying to figure that out," Stinson said as he continued his scan of the status screens. "What's the last thing you remember?"

Vaughan thought back. They had grabbed Carson from the ruins of an alien city, then soon after take-off there had been a power surge and an impact on the ship, like they'd been attacked. They had landed to check damage and Carson had managed to get loose, create a distraction, and escape. "Carson's ship came in and picked him up. There were shots fired but I don't think anyone got hit," Vaughan said. "We took off in pursuit, and then . . . I'm not sure. How long ago was that?"

"That's what I remember. Ship's clock says about six hours ago, my omni agrees."

Vaughan checked his own omniphone. He hadn't noted the time when the whole attack and Carson's escape had happened, but six hours ago seemed about right. "You say we're about a quarter of a light-year from Reticuli? That's four hours. What about the rest?"

"Could have been travel time to get somewhere clear enough to go to warp. As for why we don't remember . . . I don't know."

"There was a power surge earlier. Could that have done something to the warp drive? Maybe we had a weird side effect of going into warp?" *Inducing unconsciousness and amnesia? Really?*

"I'd think it would either work normally or not at all. And I wouldn't have lined us up on Sol. We'd need to stop somewhere closer to refuel."

"Anything in the logs?"

"No, that's the weird thing. The two hours prior to our going into warp are clean, like they've been erased."

That should have been impossible, but Vaughan was well aware that *Carcharodon* had a few modifications to allow such—strictly illegal—log modification. "Something we did?"

"No," Stinson said. "Our code would substitute something benign, not leave a gap."

"Okay. Run full diagnostics. We're not going anywhere until we figure out what happened. I'll question the rest of the crew."

"Got it."

∞ ∞ ∞

Nobody else remembered anything either. They had all awakened about the same time, although some of them had woken in response to the captain's warning about dropping out of warp. The last memories were something about another ship rescuing Carson, and the *Carcharodon* taking off in pursuit.

Vaughan racked his brain for an answer. A high-gee maneuver might have caused everyone to black out, but would have resulted in injuries or at least some bruises. And it didn't explain the missing log data, nor how they had gone into warp. What the hell had happened? Something tickled the edge of his memory. Something about a . . . no, it was gone again. Was it something about Carson's ship? It was, but not the ship itself. Then he had it. *The pyramid!* From orbit, they'd seen a flying pyramid glide over the landed ship and, apparently, take it aboard. Somehow Carson's crew had managed to retrieve it. But . . . a pyramid? Was he remembering that right?

"Captain, go back in the logs to before we picked up Carson. Let's take another look at that pyramid."

"Pyramid? I don't . . . oh, wait, there *was* a pyramid." Captain Stinson shook his head as though to clear it, then grabbed at a handhold. Vaughan noticed that, and recognized why—shaking one's head in zero-gee could cause momentary dizziness. Stinson touched a control, and one of the screens cut to an overhead view of a grassy area, like a park, in the middle of a ruined city. A delta-shaped ship, Sapphire class, sat in the middle of it. "There's Carson's ship. Let me fast forward."

The perspective shifted due to the *Carcharodon*'s earlier orbital motion while recording. There was a blur and the ship was gone, leaving a bare field.

"What? Slow that down."

Stinson backed up the video until the ship appeared again and re-ran the video more slowly. The image blurred on the left, the blur spread across the screen, then faded again to the right. The ship was gone.

Vaughan swore. "I remember that as being crystal clear before. A pyramid floated over, and took Carson's ship with it. Why is it a blur?"

"Do you suppose someone didn't want a record of that?" Stinson asked.

"Obviously, but who? And how did they change the recordings? For that matter, how did Carson get his ship back?"

"If that blur was a pyramid-shaped ship, then it I don't think it was crewed by humans. *Them?*"

"Freaking *aliens?* Shit." Not that aliens were unknown in T-space, but the mostly iron-age timoans of Taprobane, around Epsilon Indi, were the most advanced that humans had met so-far. There were a few stone age species and ruins, and there were the enigmatic tree squids of Kakuloa at Alpha Centauri B. Vaughan may have been a Velkaryan, but he wasn't committed to the dogma they peddled about the terraformed planets of T-space having been created by God just for humans. He agreed that humans deserved them, but he didn't have any particular belief in God. On the other hand, whoever *had* terraformed those planets, possibly including the one orbiting Zeta 1 Reticuli which they'd just left, had done it some 65 million years ago and were surely long gone.

The remaining possibility left Vaughan decidedly unsettled. Vaughan's organization, and independently the archaeologist Hannibal Carson, had discovered evidence of a technological spacefaring species which flourished about 15,000 years ago, one which had built pyramids—unrelated to those on Earth—on several different planets. At least two of the pyramids had housed samples of advanced technology. Carson had picked up on the coincidences between primitive alien architectures on those different planets and, from the reports Vaughan had heard, gone on to discover some high-tech artifacts of his own. Hence the Velkaryan interest in him.

But, so far as Vaughan knew, there had been no signs that those more-recent spacefaring aliens were still around. If they were, they'd had another fifteen millennia to advance their technology beyond a level that humans still hadn't quite reached. Never mind what that might do to Velkaryan dogma, the thought of what their current capabilities might be was, well, perhaps "unsettling" wasn't a strong enough word. If that's what they had encountered at Zeta Reticuli, then the Velkaryan council needed to know.

Going by what they'd done to the *Carcharodon*, the aliens didn't have any compunctions about interfering with human affairs. Not that Velkaryans had any when it came to alien affairs either, of course, but if aliens were involved there could be problems.

∞ ∞ ∞

"Shall I make course back to Zeta Reticuli?" the captain asked Vaughan.

Stinson's lack of enthusiasm for that idea was obvious in his voice, and Vaughan sympathized. "That's probably not a good idea," he said, "without knowing just what happened to us. Whoever—or whatever—wiped our records and knocked us out might be a little more forceful next time. No, I think we need to go back and report. We should also have some techs go over this ship with the proverbial fine-toothed comb to see what they find."

"So, back to Verdigris then? We can refuel at Ransom's Planet like we did on the way out. Zeta Tucanae—" the sun Ransom's Planet orbited "—is almost in line between here and Delta Pavonis."

Vaughan considered that. They had the FTL communicator at Delta Pavonis, a piece of ancient alien technology whose only mate—so far as Vaughan knew—was on a Velkaryan base in Neptune orbit around Sol. But even though it communicated faster than a ship could travel, it wasn't instant and its bandwidth was low. Discussion would take time, and this was something he should discuss with, or at least report to, his higher-ups. They'd be better able to analyze what might have been done to the ship with the facilities available on or near Earth, too.

"Can we make a direct run to the Sol system? Land at our base on Luna?"

"Negative," Stinson said. "Not in one hop. We'll need a refueling stop about half-way. Zeta Tucanae isn't close enough to Sol; we'll need to go another route or make another stop."

Vaughan wasn't sure he wanted to back that way anyway. They had come out here from Verdigris—in the Delta Pavonis system—via Ransom's Planet, which orbited Zeta Tucanae. Anyone there who had known they were headed to Zeta Reticuli would be curious about what they'd found. He'd just as soon keep people guessing about that. "Is there a way back to Verdigris, or to Earth, with only one stop which avoids Zeta Tucanae?" he asked.

"Most likely. Let me see." The captain turned to his console and worked with the navigation system for a few moments. "Ah, thought so. If you want to steer clear of civilization there are a couple of red dwarfs with bodies we can get ice from."

"I don't see a particular need to avoid people in general, just Ransom's Planet. What else have you got?"

"The most direct route would either be via Alpha Mensae, or P-Eridani. The latter at least has a small outpost. We could refuel, but they wouldn't have the facilities to do repairs or run enhanced diagnostics. I'd like to do that at our first opportunity. Tanith would be a better bet, although the whole trip would take longer. It's just within our range."

Vaughan knew Tanith, he'd been there before. It had a fair-sized settlement and a regular commercial run to Earth.

"That's perfect. We'll send a report back when we arrive. As soon as you're happy that the ship's systems are up to the trip, let's go."

"Already ahead of you. *Carcharodon* has been running diagnostics the whole time we were talking. There is some secondary damage, but nothing to prevent us going to warp."

Since they had been in warp when they woke up, that made sense. They could take care of further repairs on Tanith. "And?" Vaughan asked.

"And we're good to go." With that, he tapped a control on his panel and Vaughan felt the thrusters fire to rotate the ship, lining it up on Tanith's parent star, Eighty-Two Eridani.

"All hands," the captain announced over the PA, "secure for warp."

Chapter 3: Marten's Homecoming

Roberts

Ten days ago: Epsilon Indi system, planet Taprobane

CAPTAIN JACQUELINE "Jackie" Roberts guided her small starship into a low orbit over Taprobane and opened a circuit to spaceport control.

"Clarkeville Spaceport, this is Captain Roberts of the *Sophie*, a registered courier, requesting landing permission. We've been here before, and I have a timoan native aboard."

"*Roger*, Sophie. *Please squawk your information and identify your passenger.*"

Taprobane was a restricted world. Clarkeville, on the large island of Borealia, was the sole human settlement on the planet. It was primarily an academic facility, with a mixed human and timoan population. Most native timoans, on the mainland, were at an iron age cultural level and Earth's *Union de Terre* wanted to limit human contact with them.

"Squawking," Jackie replied, touching a control on her console. "My passenger is Doctor Marten, a professor of archeology at the university."

"*Thank you*, Sophie. *Identity confirmed, and we have you on radar. You are cleared to de-orbit on an approach trajectory. Nothing else inbound. Outgoing traffic left a half-hour ago; you're well clear. The port is wide open. Welcome back.*"

Outgoing ships would head out of the orbital plane to give them a clear path to warp, so well clear indeed. "Cleared on approach, no traffic. Thank you, Clarkeville."

She turned to Marten, who had strapped himself tightly into the copilot's seat. He gripped the armrests tightly. To say that he wasn't fond of zero-gee would be an understatement.

"Cheer up," Jackie said, "We'll be on the ground in a half-hour, and we'll have gravity back as soon as we hit atmosphere. Won't be long now."

"Thank you, Jackie. I'm looking forward to it."

She turned back to the console and maneuvered the ship for its entry burn.

Five minutes later, the burn complete and the spacecraft flipped over to take the entry belly first, the ship began to slow as the thin outer atmosphere began to glow gently with the speed of their passing. As the ship slowed, Jackie felt herself settling into the seat cushion. Beside her, Marten breathed a sigh of relief.

∞ ∞ ∞

Clarkeville Spaceport

Roberts secured her ship at a temporary parking area on the edge of the field. She didn't plan to stay more than a day. After helping Marten with his gear, and arranging to meet him later at the Kangara University campus for a meal, she gathered up a small bundle of packages and headed for the port office.

"Hi," she said to the human at the counter. Many of the jobs in Clarkeville were held by native timoans, but the Universal Postal Union, of which the Interstellar Courier Service was formally a part, was the domain of the *UdT*, and personnel rotated around. "I'm Roberts from the *Sophie*. Packages from Alpha Centauri." She held up the bundle. "Not much I'm afraid." On this trip, it would be the network data updates and Marten's passage —billed to Ducayne—that paid her expenses. Still, everything helped, and it was required to maintain her courier's permits.

"I'm surprised there's anything. We had a ship in just a couple of days ago. I'm afraid it headed back this morning, so there won't be anything for you unless you're staying a while."

"No problem. I plan to head to Tau Ceti, Skead, next. Anything for there?"

The man—the name-tag on his shirt read "Bill"—looked thoughtful. "Very likely. We haven't had a ship headed that way in a few weeks. I'll have to check."

"No rush," she assured him. "I'll be around for a day or so anyway."

"Fair enough. Your ship need any servicing? She's a Sapphire class, right? Weren't you here a few months back?"

"You've got a good memory. Better than mine; I don't remember meeting you." Which was odd, because she usually remembered spaceport folks; they were usually her kind of people.

"Oh, no worries, we didn't meet, I just remember your ship. My wife's name is Sofia."

"Ah, no wonder. Yes, a Sapphire. And thanks, but I just need the tanks topped off. She was overhauled recently." Roberts glanced at the omniphone wrapped around her wrist. "Anyway, I have other things I need to get to. I'll be back tomorrow."

"All right, Captain Roberts—"

"Call me Jackie, please," she said with a friendly smile.

"All right, Jackie. I'll see what we have for Tau Ceti. You enjoy your evening."

"Thanks, Bill. And give my regards to Sofia," Roberts said as she left the office.

It was true that all the *Sophie* needed was to have her fuel tanks filled, so she saw to that while considering her plans.

She'd told Bill the truth about heading to Tau Ceti next. Skead was her nominal home base—she lived aboard the Sophie but had friends and things in storage there—but it had been over a year since she had last been there. Frankly, she looked forward to something a bit less adventurous than her recent expeditions with Carson and Marten, but was acutely aware that the improvements Ducayne's organization had made to the *Sophie* put her in his debt. *Think of it as a long-term retainer*, she told herself. Unless and until she heard from him, she was free to conduct her charter and small freight business her way.

Chapter 4: Findings

Carson

Ten days ago: Sawyer City, Homeworld Security

HANNIBAL CARSON WATCHED Brown for a few moments before announcing his presence. Malcolm Brown was oblivious, intent on his work. "Excavating again?"

Brown looked up from his data-pad, his annoyed expression fading as he recognized his visitor. "Ah, Doctor Carson. You're here."

"Ducayne told me I would find you here," Carson said. "I hear you've been digging though the Blue Book files." Carson was certain that Brown wasn't his real last name, but Malcolm might be his first.

They were in one of the small conference rooms in a below-ground level of the Homeworld Security complex, or QD Shipping, or whatever Quentin Ducayne was calling it this month. He had called Carson in because Doctor Brown had asked. The room, like most of the others Carson had so far seen in this secret complex—which weren't very many—was nondescript, its most remarkable feature being the carpet, which was a hideous shade of chartreuse green.

"Digging is one word for it," said Brown with a disgusted look. "It's like excavating a cesspit, and I don't mean on an archeological dig, I mean a fresh one. But there are the occasional gems. I'm glad we got hold of the original pictures, the digitized microfilm copies were next to useless."

"So, the Betty Hill star map? What did the original show?"

Brown sighed and gestured dismissively. "Nothing significant that wasn't in some of the later copies we found. And on reviewing various accounts of how the map came to be drawn, I'm not sure how useful it would be anyway. She drew it two years after her alleged contact, albeit under hypnosis. It wouldn't take much in the way of position errors to totally throw off Marjorie Fish's later interpretation—something Fish herself admitted later, when more accurate astronomical data became available. On the other hand, Fish's still seems to make the most sense. There are other interpretations—one completely reverses the perspective and puts the main stars as Sol and 20 Leonis Minor, with the so-called trade routes going to another star in Leo Minor and two in Ursa Major. They're G-type stars, but some have a red dwarf companion, and all are outside of known T-Space."

"Well, we know the big Kesh ships aren't as range-limited as ours are," Carson said, "but supposedly they can't go FTL. How far are we talking?"

"Forty to fifty light years. So, not impossible, but extremely unlikely."

Carson agreed. Even if the Kesh were extremely long-lived, either through anti-aging drugs or naturally, forty or fifty years was a long trip. Relativistic time dilation didn't happen within an FTL warp field, it probably wouldn't in a sub-light warp either.

"You're probably right," he said. "Any conclusions from what you've read so far?"

Brown chuckled. "Yes. That there were a lot of imaginative and attention-seeking individuals around back then."

"Well, that hasn't changed much, I suppose."

"No, not really."

The thought that the mission to extract the Blue Book originals—and Rico's death—might have been wasted disturbed Carson. "Anything else?"

"Actually, yes. We have very solid evidence that an extra-terrestrial spacecraft visited Earth."

"That's in the Blue Book files?" Carson didn't remember anything like that. How could he have missed it?

"No. That's in the report that came in a week ago about the find off the coast of Belize, near Cay Caulker." Brown grinned broadly. "Got you!"

Carson shook his head, somewhat chagrined. He had heard a rumor about the find, but in his defense, didn't know any more details. "Okay, you did. Is that why you wanted to see me? And why do you say extra-terrestrial craft? I thought it could just as easily been a piece of old aircraft. Has an extra-terrestrial origin been announced?"

"Oh heck no. It's all hush hush." Brown tapped something on his data-pad, then turned it around and slid it across the table to Carson.

"Here," he said. "I think you'll find it interesting."

"What is it?" Hannibal picked up the pad and examined the image. It showed a piece of debris, possibly part of a control panel. He looked up at Brown. "From the Belize find?"

"Exactly. The pictures just came in. Zoom in on the markings below the panel in the left."

Carson did so. It was lettering, but not anything most people would be familiar with. A series of stylized, slightly wedge-shaped lines, almost as though the writing was all E's and F's and L's, but facing in different directions. "It's like what cuneiform might look like if it were printed rather than impressed into clay with a reed," he said. "Or perhaps a claw?" he added, thinking about the Kesh's hands.

"That's what I thought too."

"I've seen it before, recently. At least, I think I did."

Brown's gaze focused on Carson. "*What?* Where?"

∞ ∞ ∞

Homeworld Security, Quentin Ducayne's Office

Elsewhere in the Homeworld Security complex, a series of beeps alerted Quentin Ducayne to a sudden influx of messages to his in-box. The *Southern Sky* or one of her sister ships on the Sol-Alpha Centauri run, had just arrived in the system. Occasionally there'd be mail or a package on a ship from somewhere else, but even aside from the Earth-originating traffic, a lot of it went to Earth first. The emigration ships kept up a pretty steady cycle.

Ducayne finished pouring himself a cup of coffee and swung back to his terminal.

It was all encrypted, of course—that was routine. The more sensitive stuff was encrypted, buried in something innocuous-looking, then encrypted again. Anything *really* sensitive would be hand-delivered.

He skimmed the headers. Most of it was the usual updates from the *Union de Terre* Homeworld Security offices, reports from other field offices, and field agent reports. One of the latter had an URGENT flag on it. Oh?

It was from Jordan Burnside, also known as "John Smith", Ducayne's agent in the 82 Eridani system, on Tanith. Ducayne opened it.

Most of it was the same sort of routine report he got every week: local politics, significant business updates, potentially interesting ship goings and comings. It was one of the latter which caught his attention. The ship *Carcharodon*, suspected to be Velkaryan owned, along with known Velkaryan agent Klaus Vaughan and the rest of its crew, had made planetfall a just a few days earlier. *So that's where he got to*, Ducayne thought. He glanced at the timestamp on the report. As he had thought, it had been sent nearly three weeks earlier. That fit with the travel times from Tanith to Earth, and Earth to Sawyers World. But there was more.

Unrelated to the *Carcharodon*'s landing, someone had made contact with "Smith" about a possible alien artifact for sale. On some planets there would have been nothing unusual about that. Aside from the black market in legitimate alien artifacts, stone-age tools and trinkets, there was usually also a thriving market in fake artifacts for tourists or collectors dumb enough to buy them. What made this offer odd was that, for one, Smith's cover wouldn't lead anyone to think he would be interested in such things, but, more significantly, nobody had ever found any trace of any aliens at all on Tanith. If there were legitimate alien artifacts in the 82 Eridani system, somebody had brought them there. And Smith seemed to think these might be not only legitimate, but more advanced than the usual stone-age relics. He was sending details "under separate cover". Which meant hand-delivery, shortly after the *Southern Sky* landed. That should be soon.

There was something he should do in the meantime, though, and that was to talk to his local expert on advanced alien artifacts, Hannibal Carson. The timing was fortuitous, since there was a document whose classification had recently been lowered that he wanted to get Carson's reaction to.

Chapter 5: The Carcharodon Arrives

Vaughan

Five weeks ago: Starship Carcharodon

"MR. VAUGHAN, WE'LL be entering the 82 Eridani system in about six hours. I'll be dropping us out of warp in an hour for a position check," the captain said.

"Thank you. When we get to Tanith, we can do routine announcements and signals, but don't tell them where we came from, pick somewhere else."

"Can do." Stinson thought for a moment. "When we're out of warp I'll adjust our course so we arrive in-system looking like we come from Alpha Mensae. That way, when we contact Tanith, there won't be any questions if someone notices our position vector."

"That sounds good. Do it."

"How long do you want to stay there? We'll need a few days for repairs and resupply."

"At least that, obviously, but let's leave it open ended. While we're there I might as well look into our local operations." Vaughan was fairly sure that there were no senior Velkaryans on Tanith, although there was certainly a local organization and an affiliated church. They were probably due for a bit of a shake-up, and, as he thought about it, the system was in a strategic location relative to Earth, Verdigris, and the now-interesting Zeta Reticuli.

As he recalled, there were no native aliens on Tanith. While that was good, he wondered if it would make recruiting more difficult. Well, there were ways of stirring up sympathy.

∞ ∞ ∞

Half a ship's day later, the *Carcharodon* was deep in-system, nearing 82 Eridani IV—the planet Tanith—from north of the ecliptic. They picked up the usual data from the approach beacon and Captain Stinson adjusted their course and orbit appropriately before hailing the Harp City spaceport. He announced his presence and requested landing instructions.

"*Roger* Carcharodon, *this is Harp City. How long do you expect to be staying?*"

"At least a week or so, Harp. We had a run in with something and took some minor damage, I'd like to get the ship checked out. The owner's aboard, we may stay longer."

"*Understood,* Carcharodon. *Any injuries? Do you want to declare an emergency?*"

"Negative, Harp. Nothing like that, just minor."

"*Roger. Glad it wasn't anything more serious. We'll give you a parking area where a maintenance crew can get at the ship.*"

"Thank you."

"*Okay, you're cleared to land. No other traffic at the moment. Runway 05 is the active. Stay on this channel until landing, then contact ground when clear and we'll direct you to your spot.*"

"Roger, Harp, *Carcharodon* is cleared to land zero-five."

In atmosphere, the ship glided toward the runway like its marine namesake cruising for prey. Stinson brought it in over the threshold with the minimum use of the ventral thrusters, then increased power just as the ship neared the surface, letting ground effect help cushion the landing. He kept it in hover just above the runway, using reverse thrust to slow the ship down, until he turned off at the designated ramp.

"Harp Spaceport Ground, *Carcharodon* is clear of the active," he reported.

"*Roger* Carcharodon. *Would you like a tow in?*"

"Affirmative ground. A tow would be nice." Stinson could taxi the ship using thrusters, but it was simpler to let someone else worry about it. Of course, he'd keep an eye on them to make sure they were doing it right.

Chapter 6: The White Hart

Roberts

Ten days ago: Clarkeville Spaceport, Taprobane

WITH THE *SOPHIE'S* tanks topped off, Jackie Roberts was ready to head over to the Kangara University campus to meet Marten. She hadn't bothered to restock the kitchen or flush the life support holding tanks. The two of them on the short trip from Sawyers World hadn't reduced the supplies much, and she'd be alone on the trip to Skead. There was no sense in paying more port fees than she had to.

From the spaceport to town was about three kilometers. There was little public transportation in Clarkeville, just a few autocabs, so Roberts headed to her aft cargo bay to retrieve her motorbike, then changed her mind. Her next destination, Skead, was a large, dense planet. Its gravity was higher than Earth's, or any other planet she'd been on in the past year. No wonder she had felt out of shape on Zeta Reticuli III. She would walk into town; she could use the exercise. *Come to that*, she thought, *I should ramp up the ship's gravity on the way there*. The *Sophie*'s artificial gravity was a byproduct of the warp field. Within limits, it could be adjusted for just such acclimatization.

∞ ∞ ∞

By the time Jackie reached the edge of campus, she was feeling the exercise. She promised herself to do regular workouts on the way to Tau Ceti. Just ahead was the pub, the *Pragarth Maga*. A wooden sign hung from a bracket above the door, depicting a white deer-like creature; the name of the pub meant roughly "albino deer" in the local timoan dialect. The building appeared to be old stone and the sign was weather-beaten. Roberts knew that the whole town couldn't have been more than thirty years old. The medieval appearance was in tune with the iron-age native towns elsewhere on Borealia and on the nearby mainland. The timoan students selected to study here were well aware of the technology levels hidden behind the facade, but it helped ease their culture shock on arrival. At least, that was the theory. As Roberts opened the door and entered the pub, it was clear that the students, timoan and human alike, were equally comfortable with technology. She saw the same collection of omnis, computer pads, and smart-fabric clothing that she'd expect to see on any human campus on Earth or the settled worlds. There was also a lot of ornamental copper and iron jewelry, clothing that looked hand-spun, and leather belts and gear bags being worn by both timoans and humans, reflecting the locals' native culture.

There was a strong aroma of something savory cooking—timoans were as omnivorous as humans—overlaid by the smell of beer. Ceramic mugs of ale were on most of the occupied tables. Timoans had independently invented beer, or rather something beer-like considering the different heritage of the ingredients, and like any mammal, could—and did—get drunk on ethanol. Roberts decided she liked this place, but she'd have to watch her consumption, or she'd regret it later. Flying with a hangover was only slightly less stupid than flying drunk.

Marten was there ahead of her, sitting at a table with two other people, both probably students from their apparent youth and the deference they seemed to show him. Both female, one human and one timoan, although Roberts was less certain about the gender of the latter.

Marten stood as she came over to the table. "Jackie, good to see you. Ladies, this is Captain Jackie Roberts of the starship *Sophie*, which I just came in on. Jackie, this is Narina,"—the timoan female nodded—"and Suzanne,"—the human half-raised her hand. "They were in my Archeology 201 class last year."

"Narina, Suzanne," Jackie said, nodding to them, "nice to meet you." She sat down on one of the empty chairs at the table.

Marten said something to them in the local Taprobani dialect. Narina signaled agreement but Suzanne looked puzzled, perhaps she had only understood part of it. Narina said something to her, also in Taprobani. She looked a little disappointed and both students rose to leave.

"You don't have to leave on my account," Jackie said.

"Thanks, but that's not it," Suzanne said. "We have a class assignment we need to work on. Nice meeting you." With that, the two of them turned and walked toward the door. Narina, average height for a timoan but shorter than her human friend, stretched up and whispered something to Suzanne, who quickly glanced back at the table, then back at Narina. They both giggled.

Roberts looked at Marten. She had a suspicion about what that last was about, but she shrugged it off. "An assignment? Really? Or an assignation?"

"Not with my students," Marten protested. "Although I get the feeling they wouldn't object."

"I couldn't read Narina's body language, but you might be right about Suzanne. You behave yourself."

"No worries there. In fact, I used you as an excuse to get rid of them. Sometimes it's embarrassing. I sort of understand Suzanne's reaction—to her I'm exotic, although there are plenty of male timoan students. Not sure about Narina though."

"Does she know your background?"

"Not from me, but I suppose it's somewhat public knowledge. Timoan who stowed away on one of the first visiting starships as a kit, partially raised by humans, and as much or more time off-planet as almost any other timoan. I think I see what you're getting at. I must seem like some kind of bold adventurer."

Roberts grinned. "They haven't seen you in zero gee."

"Hey!"

"But other than that, I've seen you take care of yourself. I'm not complaining."

"So," she said, changing the subject, "last meal together for a while. And speaking of, I am kind of hungry. What's good?"

∞ ∞ ∞

What was good turned out to be food not too unlike traditional English pub grub. In Jackie's case, it was a bowl of a meaty stew with local root vegetables, washed down with a mug of the pub's own brew.

"Where are you headed next, Jackie?" Marten asked.

"I'll go where the cargo takes me, if the port here has anything," she said. "But Bill at the cargo office is checking for anything for Skead, at Tau Ceti. Home, as much as any planet is. What are your plans?"

"I have courses to teach, so I won't be going off-planet for a while. I'm still working through the collection of artifacts that Carson and I gathered at Zeta Tucanae over a year ago. There's a remote chance I'll get back there again for a follow up during mid-semester break, if I can work it out with the department."

"That's about two weeks each way from here. How long a break do you get?"

"Not that long, which is why I'd have to work it out. Some of my classes would need to be covered for a few weeks, especially if I want to do more than just turn around and come back when I get there. But I can do a lot of the other work during the trip. Journals to read, papers to write, that sort of thing. More likely, though, I'll be here until end of semester."

"Well, if you need a ship and a pilot . . . ."

"You'd be at the top of my list, Jackie. But Kangara has an S-class of its own, and there's usually a charter available at the port. There aren't a lot of timoan-owned ships—"

"I'm surprised there are any," she said, and grinned.

"Not everyone reacts to zero-gee the same way I do, and there's no prohibition on us owning ships, although I suppose the Velkaryans would like to change that. Anyway, university rules require preference given to them if available. That might have been one just leaving when we came in."

"No problem. I understand."

The relationship between timoans and humans was a strange one. While contact with most mainland timoans was deliberately limited, the planet had been discovered early in the history of human exploration. Epsilon Indi was only a dozen light years from Sol, so there had been plenty of "cultural contamination" before the *UdT* had started imposing rules about contact with sentient extra-terrestrials. Not that those rules were easy to enforce.

The Clarkeville settlement on Borealia, an isolated landmass about the size of Great Britain or New Zealand some forty kilometers from the mainland at its closest, was both an experiment and a compromise. Timoans had the opportunity to interact with humans and learn from them, and humans could observe an alien species up close and learn from it. Any "contamination" was confined to the island. Timoans were free to travel to the mainland, but the nature of timoan society made it hard to reintegrate. They could take their knowledge but not the hardware. The native culture could still progress at an accelerated rate with that knowledge, but when you had to make the tools to make the tools to make the tools, the rate was easier for the locals to assimilate. Or to reject, if they felt so inclined.

Dinner over, Roberts and Marten said their goodbyes and went their separate ways. The sun, Epsilon Indi, was just sinking below the western horizon as Jackie reached the spaceport. She checked the *Sophie*'s communications console for any messages, not expecting any unless the port master had come up with a cargo for her. It turned out that he had. Mostly small packages, from his message. It must have been collecting for a while.

She acknowledged his message and then set the Sophie's perimeter alarm and secured the ship for the night. Local time was still relatively early evening, but her personal schedule was off. She hit the fresher for a quick shower and then retired to her bunk. She would lift for Tau Ceti in the morning, as soon as she got her cargo loaded.

Chapter 7: Cuneiform

Carson

Ten days ago: Homeworld Security conference room

BROWN PEERED INTENTLY at Carson. "You've seen glyphs like these before? Where? The pyramid?"

Carson shook his head. "No. During our meeting with Ketzshanass. I caught a glimpse of his communicator screen while we were talking. It wasn't long enough for me to get a good look, but I had the same impression of cuneiform that I get from this." He looked up at Brown. "Sumerian was never my strong suit. If it *is* cuneiform, any idea what it says?"

Brown shook his head. "Not mine either, but we have translation programs. If indeed it is translatable. What would the Sumerian be for 'airspeed' or 'frequency', for example?"

"That's a good question. And, of course, the language might be completely different, but using similar symbols." He flipped through the images on the pad. Most of them were relatively unremarkable pieces of metal, some with attached conduit or wiring. Only a few had markings that might be writing.

"Come to think of it," Carson said, "neither Jackie nor Marten mentioned seeing anything in the way of signs on the halls or doors of the Kesh ship. You'd think there'd at least be deck numbers or something." Carson himself hadn't seen the interior of the Kesh pyramid ship, he'd been aboard the Velkaryan ship at the time. It was Jackie Roberts and Marten, Carson's timoan archeologist colleague, who had been taken aboard the Kesh

ship. They'd discussed what they'd seen on the trip back from
Zeta Reticuli.

"How many decks did they see?"

"I think just the one, now that you mention it. The trip to
Jackie's ship was in some kind of elevator. But the ship was huge
enough to have plenty of decks."

"So, maybe they color code them."

Carson couldn't see an obvious flaw in that, but it didn't feel
right. He held up the data-pad. "Is this all they found?"

"So far. The Belize government has declared the site off-limits to everyone, and there's a British marine archeology team ne-
gotiating for access. Guatemala is of course laying claim to the
find, but nobody takes that seriously."

Guatemala had been claiming Belize as Guatemalan territory
off and on just about forever, although mostly that just made
things difficult for archaeologists wanting to work Mayan ruins
on both sides of the border. Guatemalan border guards were
again being picky if your passport showed you'd been in Belize.

"Okay. Well, let's get whatever we can, and get as much of
this text or whatever it is to analyze. If it is Kesh, I wonder how
much the language has changed in the last thousand years."

"Perhaps not much if they're still using cuneiform. Was there
any sign of that in the Chara pyramid?"

"No, at least not that I noticed. The language there was more
pictographic, intended to be easily understood. Besides, the pyramid predates the Kesh by a few thousand years."

"Well, that's what they'd like you to believe, anyway."

Carson shook his head. "You're as paranoid as Ducayne."

"Occupational hazard, I'm afraid."

Chapter 8: Report Received

Vaughan

Two weeks ago: Church of Divine Stellar Providence HQ, Earth

EXECUTIVE PROJECTS DIRECTOR Lancaster Hubble sat at the head of the polished stone conference table, idly examining one the spiral fossils embedded in the Marston Magna marble, as he pondered the report they had just received from the *Carcharodon* and their man Klaus Vaughan. There had been surprises. The damned complications were getting as convoluted as that ammonite shell.

"Help me be clear on this, Blomberg" he said. "The message was sent from, Tanith, was it?"

"Yes, in the 82 Eridani system," Samuel Blomberg, his deputy director, said.

Hubble knew where Tanith was. He let it slide. "Then he sent it, what, a bit over two weeks ago?"

"That's right. It just came in on the migration ship *Mayflower*." That ship did a regular Earth-Tanith run, roughly once a month.

"So, the *Carcharodon* must have departed Zeta Reticuli how long before that?"

"Two weeks for that too, at least." Blomberg said. "Add a couple of days to synch up with the *Mayflower*'s schedule."

"What about our friend Hannibal Carson? If he left Reticuli at the same time, when would he have got back to Sawyers World?"

"About now, give or take a few days."

That wasn't as bad as Hubble had feared. Vaughan's report had mentioned city ruins at Zeta 1 Reticuli, something technological. If Sawyer had been back for several weeks, Quentin Ducayne's people would have an expedition already on the way there. "Assume that Homeworld Security also knows about the city remains at Zeta Reticuli. Probably in a lot more detail than we do." Hubble wanted that information. The city, perhaps the entire system, could be a source of useful technology. "Maybe we should arrange a talk with Carson."

"Why would he want to talk to us?" Blomberg asked.

"I didn't say we would invite him to tea," Hubble said, putting an edge of sarcasm into his voice.

"Oh. Of course. Maybe we can use Roberts as leverage."

That was a possibility, Hubble thought. Carson had made enough trips with Jackie Roberts that there was probably more than a business connection. "If she's still on-planet. Charter captains don't hang around."

"We'll look into it."

"Good," Hubble said. That was one thing settled, for now. "Now, about Vaughan. He wants to hang around on Tanith for a while and, as he put it, 'reinvigorate the local office'. Something about increasing recruiting and getting more of our people into local politics. That could be an advantage, but it would be useful to have him back in New Toronto too. And we could communicate better with him there."

"What about this artifact he mentioned?"

That was another complication. Shortly after arriving on Tanith, Vaughan had heard of an alien artifact being offered up for sale on the local black market. Not just old stone pots or a sculpture, but something that sounded high-tech. If it really was such an artifact, the Velkaryans were interested. But as far as anyone knew, Tanith had never had natives. Hubble was skeptical.

"A little sketchy on the details," he said. "Vaughan can retrieve it if he really thinks it's interesting, but it could just be some tomb raider running a scam. More trouble for them if so, but Vaughan's probably not his target."

"Or it could be a legitimate find. Tanith hasn't been well-explored. Or . . . ."

"Or what?"

"Suppose somebody brought the artifact from the Zeta Reticuli system?"

Hubble shook his head dismissively. "Vaughan considered that and discounted it. The timing would also be a wild coincidence."

"Fair enough. But given the city there, expanding our influence in the 82 Eridani system could be a strategic advantage."

"It also sounds like a lot of effort, but go on."

Blomberg explained. "Delta Pavonis is well placed; it's equidistant from Sol and Zeta Reticuli, but it's off-axis."

"Meaning what?"

"It's not in-line between here and there. There's about a thirty-degree dog-leg."

"And 82 Eridani is better positioned?" Hubble asked.

"It's also roughly equidistant and dog-legged, but in the other direction. Delta Pavonis and 82 Eridani nicely straddle the line between Sol and Zeta Reticuli, although they're some distance apart."

"Then you think it's worth investing some strategic assets on Tanith, or in the system?"

"I do," Blomberg said, nodding once. "It's terraformed, has a lot of in-system resources, and no indigenous alien population. It's been settled long enough to have a manufacturing base. Not like Sawyers World or Verdigris, but it's getting there."

"You're starting to interest me. No natives is a plus."

"It's also a designated emigration destination. If it looks good, we can slip some of our folks into the pipeline. Less obvious than using our own ships."

Hubble nodded. "I like the way you're thinking on this. Very well, while Vaughan is checking into that artifact, he can also pursue that. Have him continue to work with our office there, and I want to see a report on possible changes to Operation Jade Ribbon because of this."

"I'll get right on that." Blomberg scribbled something on his data pad.

"How long to get those orders to him? Two weeks?"

"And a few days. The *Mayflower* is usually a day in turnaround, and it just landed this morning."

Hubble considered this. There was another option. "And if we use the Communicator and send it via Delta Pavonis?"

"That's also two weeks; Verdigris is almost as far from Tanith as we are, but with less scheduled traffic between them."

"All right. A couple of days won't make much difference."

"What about the damage the *Carcharodon* took?"

"What about it?" Hubble asked.

"Well, Vaughan's report suggests a beam weapon. Certainly, Roberts' ship isn't mounting anything like that. The aliens?"

"Odd that they would shoot the *Carcharodon*, then let it go unharmed."

"That's what I was thinking." Blomberg hesitated, then said, "Another Eridani incident, do you suppose?"

"Eridani? Explain."

"The original Chinese expedition, fifty years ago. There was a rumor that one of their ships was attacked by something with a beam weapon."

"A rumor denied by the Chinese." Hubble, like most people who even knew or still cared about it, assumed it had been a cover story to save face after an accident, a cover story quickly dropped because it was potentially even worse than the truth. "There have also been rumors of little green men, aliens mutilating cattle, and ghosts. That's not much to go on."

"I suppose you're right."

"Have Vaughan take samples of the damaged material, if he hasn't already had everything repaired by the time he gets the message. Maybe our labs can find something interesting."

"I'll do that," said Blomberg, making a note on his pad.

"Good. Are we done with Vaughan's report?"

"I think so."

"All right then. Next order of business, Operation Piranha. The Venezuelan election . . ."

Chapter 9: Old Records

Carson

Four days ago: Homeworld Security, Ducayne's Office

QUENTIN DUCAYNE HANDED a data-pad to Hannibal Carson, with a document open on its screen, it looked like an official report of some kind. "Read this, tell me what you think."

"What is it?" Carson asked, taking the pad. "And why not just send it to me?"

"It's classified. I didn't even know about it until recently. Just read it."

Carson scanned the text.

"Unconfirmed observation report," it began. "Elizabeth Sawyer, then Captain of the *USS Anderson* in charge of the Planet Able landing team—"

"Elizabeth Sawyer?" Carson looked up at Ducayne in surprise. "*The* Captain Sawyer?"

"Do you know of another Sawyer who led the *Anderson* team and who this planet is named after?"

"No. So, this is what, fifty standard years old?"

"Which is why it came to my attention. Its classification was just lowered. Keep reading."

"—reported sighting an unknown and unidentified, but apparently intelligent, biped creature about one kilometer from the *Anderson* landing site. She was alone at the time, and had gone out to check and replace a non-functioning observation camera. There were no recordings of the sighting because of the camera's offline state. Sawyer reported that an attempt to observe and record using her omniphone was frustrated by the temporary failure of said omniphone. She refrained from reporting this at the time due to lack of corroborating evidence. This report was passed on to Commodore Drake, then Sawyer's superior officer, as a classified intelligence briefing upon his follow-up landing in the *Endeavour*. In Captain Sawyer's own words:

"I had just replaced the camera and was waiting for my engineer, Maclaren, to verify connectivity. While waiting I noticed movement just beyond a low ridge to the south. There had been terror-bird sightings but none this close to camp. I moved cautiously to the peak of the ridge.

"About fifty meters beyond it a figure was standing, on two legs. I knew that none of the other crew were in the vicinity. I considered the possibility that it was a descendent of the toolmakers, since we had already discovered old obsidian spear-points. It was grayish brown in color, but details were hard to make out at the distance involved. It did not seem fur covered. It turned toward me, as though it had heard me, and a frill or crest rose on its head. The crest resembled feathers, like a cockatoo's, but it was hard to tell. The forelimbs were arms rather than wings. It held something in its hands.

"I ducked down behind the ridge and configured my omniphone for periscope mode, then looked again. I could make out more detail of the feathered crest, and the skin was rough, or scaled. It had no beak. At that point the creature looked directly at me and then back at the device in its hands, whereupon my omni screen went blank. My assumption is that it was being jammed, because it recovered full functionality a few minutes later.

"When I raised my head above the ridge to look again, the creature, the alien, was no longer in sight. As there were no obvious points of concealment, my conjecture is that it had some sort of advanced camouflage or stealth capability.

"Later, when Maclaren examined the camera I had retrieved, she found nothing wrong with it. Subsequently, we had other signs of possible disturbance of scientific instruments at remote locations, although they were neither damaged nor did they record any anomalies. Video surveillance of those sites experience data dropouts during the time the equipment was disturbed.

"In the three-plus Earth years between those occurrences and the arrival of the *Endeavour*, there were no further sightings. I did not discuss this sighting with the rest of the crew until we spotted the *Endeavour* and her sister ships in orbit. I discussed it then because the V-Class ships were unfamiliar to us, and with our communications inoperative, we didn't know who or what they might be."

The report went on about Sawyer being regarded as a reliable observer, no official action required, and so on. Not unlike the old Project Blue Book reports Carson and Brown had spent considerable time wading through. A close encounter of the third kind, as they used to call it. Except this one rung true. Carson himself had met aliens, or rather, a single alien, who seemed to match what Sawyer had seen. He let out a low whistle, then looked up at Ducayne again.

"That figure she saw. That might well be a Kesh."

Ducayne nodded. "Yes, that's what I thought, but I haven't seen one. You have. Interesting."

"That means the Kesh were keeping an eye on Camp Anderson, at least at first. I wonder if they did anything to help them survive."

"And if so, why?" Ducayne shook his head. "I would really like to know what the Kesh are playing at. At least they don't seem hostile, but I can't take that for granted. That goes against my job."

"To say nothing of your personality," Carson said, and grinned. "You are a professional paranoid."

Ducayne shrugged. "I've never denied it."

"So, does that change your decision about keeping the Kesh secret?" So far that had been easy. The one Kesh who Carson—along with his timoan colleague Marten and human pilot Jackie Roberts—had met had been in the Zeta Reticuli system, forty-four light-years away, although their pyramid-like ships had been spotted at Chara and Epsilon Eridani. And if old space-hand rumors were to be believed, elsewhere too.

"Not in the least. This report is still classified, and while we've met low-tech aliens, as far as most of humanity knows humans are still the most advanced species in T-Space since the Terraformers themselves, who are long gone. The last thing we want to do is give the Velkaryan xenophobes any more ammunition. Did you hear about what's happening in Venezuela?"

"I don't follow Earth politics."

"Maybe you should. Sure, most of the planet is self-centered, but Earth is still the most powerful planet in T-Space by orders of magnitude. Anyway, the Velkaryans have a political party running in the Venezuela elections. It's doing alarmingly well." He glanced up at an array of displays on his wall, each displaying a map of a different inhabited world, and below the map, the planet's current standard calendar date and time.

The maps were each shaded to depict the current day-night cycle on that planet. Carson knew that each could be switched to show the time in the past or future representing the date a ship would have left there to reach here now, or would arrive there if leaving from here now. Physics might prevent Ducayne from running off-world operations in anything like real time, but he made sure that was the *only* thing preventing him. Of course, no information about where Ducayne's agents might be was currently being displayed.

"In fact," Ducayne continued, "I think the election is going on today." He shrugged. "Not my department, anyway. We'll hear soon enough."

Carson handed back the data-pad. "Any other contact reports by the *Anderson* crew, or since then? Better yet, any pictures or sketches?"

"Not that I'm aware of. There are some other reports whose classification was recently dropped. You might be better off talking to Sawyer herself."

"I doubt that will ever happen."

"Why not? She has a place in town, although she likes her privacy as much as the other original landers. I might be able to set it up."

Carson peered at Ducayne. He was serious, of course. Sawyer must be what, in her late eighties or early nineties now? What would he say to get her to listen to him? He had an idea.

"Do you have an artist? Like a sketch artist for drawing things a witness has seen?"

"We're not a police agency, but we've got software like that, yes."

"Which I'm probably not familiar with. I can sketch artifacts and ruins, but I've never been good at drawing people. Do you have someone I could work with? I'd like to get a sketch of Ketzshanass and see if it looks familiar to Sawyer."

"That's a good idea. We should have had a sketch like that made for the files anyway." Ducayne thought for a moment, then looked something up on his computer console. "Yes, perfect," he said to himself, then looked at Carson. "Do you know a Doctor Bob Williams at the university?"

The name sounded familiar. "I think so. Paleontologist?"

"That's right. Talented artist too, and discreet. I'll set it up. Don't tell him the circumstances, just describe your Kesh to him. He doesn't need to know the rest."

"You have a paleontologist on call? Why?"

"And you don't need to know *that*," Ducayne said. "But it's for his artistic talent, too."

The answer frustrated but didn't surprise Carson. And he knew better than to try to ask Williams either. "Okay."

"Anyway," Ducayne said, "thanks for checking into the Kesh involvement. I'll let you know when I get the meetings with Williams and with Sawyer set up, or if there's anything else."

Carson recognized the dismissal, and rose to leave. As he reached the door, Ducayne spoke again.

"Carson, I might have something else I want your opinion on. You'll be around, won't you?"

"I don't have any travel plans, if that's what you mean," Carson said, wondering what Ducayne might be referring to. "Is this about the Belize find?"

"Probably not. Thank you, that's all."

As Carson closed the door behind him, the phrasing nagged at him. *Probably* not? What did that mean? He hoped he'd have a need to know.

Chapter 10: Planet Skead

Roberts

A few hours ago: Skead Spaceport, Tau Ceti III-1

JACKIE ROBERTS BANKED the *Sophie* onto final approach at 200 meters, bleeding off airspeed and aiming for a point a third of the way down the long runway. She checked the panel: gear down, thrusters at idle. As she crossed the runway threshold, she pulled back gently into pre-flare and began powering up the vertical thrusters. *Hold it off, hold it off . . . now!*

Roberts eased the *Sophie*'s nose up, goosed the thrusters, and let forward motion bleed off, gracefully settling the *Sophie* down onto the runway surface, continuing her roll-out to turn off onto the adjacent paved apron, and stopped.

She touched a control to change her comm frequency, and said "Skead Ground, *Sophie* is clear the runway, requesting taxi clearance to pad three-seven." They'd already have her ship's details from her data squawk when she entered atmosphere.

"Sophie *this is Ground. Nicely done, Jackie, and welcome home. Cleared at your discretion, report arrival.*"

She grinned to herself. That had sounded like George in the tower.

"Copy cleared to three-seven. And thanks, it's good to be back."

It *was* good to be back, despite the higher gravity. She'd been away from Tau Ceti for nearly a year. Not that she had family here or even a place to live—she generally stayed aboard the *So-*

phie to save costs—but it had been her base of operations for several years now. She had friends here, and a few worldly goods in storage that were impractical to keep aboard a small starship.

Halfway through her shutdown checklist, the *Sophie*'s data cargo computer system beeped and flashed a message saying that it had finished synchronizing its data load with the planetary network. A few moments later, it chimed again to let Jackie know there were personal messages waiting for her on the local net. Since the *Sophie*'s last sync was just over a week ago at Taprobane, and a week before that at Sawyers World, this was probably something recent, either local or directly from Sol or Alpha Centauri. She'd check it later; a few minutes wouldn't make a difference.

She finished safing the engines and generally securing the *Sophie* from space. The mail would keep a while longer; she liked to make it a point of making sure her ship was taken care of before anything else. She checked her manifest. There was nothing urgent in the physical cargo she was carrying, which was mostly just small packages. She put a call through to the port cargo office to have someone come and offload it. Now it was time for some dirty work. She headed back to the main hatch.

Connecting up the water and air purge lines to the ground fittings in her parking area went quickly. Next was the larger sludge hose. That was the dirty part. She flipped the cover plate off the drain fitting and attached one end of the hose to it. Dragging the hose with her, she crouched down under the *Sophie*'s hull and opened the hatch covering the connector to the life-support waste management system, and secured the hose. An indicator lit up green, the seal was good. She'd just started the pump when a flatbed dolly pulled up next to the ship.

"Roberts of the *Sophie*?" a young man in orange spaceport coveralls asked.

"That's me," she said, coming out from under the hull. "You the cargo office?" He looked like he was barely out of his teens. That didn't necessarily mean much given the current state of biomedicine, but there was an eager, somewhat naive wide-eyed air about his expression. He was stockily built, which suggested he may have spent many of his earlier years here on Skead or, less likely, some other high gravity world.

"Affirm. David Tefera. Pleased to meet you." He held out a hand.

Roberts peeled off her gloves to shake his hand. "Jackie Roberts. Have you been working here long? I think you're new since I was last here."

"Yes ma'am. Just a couple of months. Looking to get a chance on a ship sometime."

Ah, to be so young and eager again. Of course, Jackie had been on and off starships as long as she could remember—she'd been born on one, although on-planet, not in space—so it wasn't quite the adventure to her that it seemed to young David here. But . . . .

"Never been on a ship? Are you native?" The Tau Ceti colony was about thirty years old, it was possible.

He nodded. "Yes'm. My folks were part of the second wave. Coffee farmers. We have a plantation up on Mount Sharon."

Ah, that would explain the farm-boy air, too. I should have let *him* hook up the sludge hose. No, that would be taking advantage.

"I'm looking forward to Tau Cetan coffee again. Anyway, let's get my cargo unloaded."

"Yes ma'am".

"And lay off the 'ma'am'. Call me Jackie, or if it's official, Captain Roberts. Only crew calls me 'ma'am', and I don't have crew at the moment."

He looked up at that. Hopeful? "Er, yes ma—, er, Jackie. Just being polite."

"Nothing wrong with that. But let's get this done." She touched a sequence on her wrist omni, and the *Sophie* opened the aft hatch nearest the cargo compartment.

∞ ∞ ∞

In an hour, they had a just under a ton of packages and containers piled up on the flatbed, all duly transferred from her manifest to David's data-pad. She checked her list. "That's it. Not much this time."

"Yeah, we had a ship in from Alpha Centauri a few days ago, and I guess Epsilon Indi doesn't ship much out." The kid had been paying attention. "Hopefully you'll have more cargo for your next destination. You going back to Alpha Cen or

Taprobane? Or . . . ?" His voice trailed off and he looked at her expectantly.

Jackie grinned. "In my business it's more like me going where the cargo wants to than vice versa. It depends what's available."

"Ah, sure. Well, I should get this load back to the warehouse." He turned and put a foot up on the flatbed, hesitated, then turned back.

"Yes?"

"Uh, if you happen to need someone to help with cargo, or anything else on your next trip . . . , well, I'm available."

She'd been right. This kid wanted off-planet. "Thanks, David. I'm generally not doing crew these days, my margins are too slim, but I'll keep that in mind." No way would she ship out with a space newbie. Carson's timoan friend Marten was bad enough, with his innate aversion to free-fall, but she didn't want that on top of some kid's first time away from home. But there was no reason to tell him all that.

"Oh, you wouldn't have to—" he started to say, then broke off. "Uh, sure, thanks. Oh, one other thing?"

"Yes?"

"If you're looking for some on-spec cargo, my family has some of the best coffee on the planet, and we'll do small lots."

"Really? That's good to know." Roberts preferred just to do the shipping and let someone else worry about the buying and selling, but as portable, high-value and easy-to-sell cargoes went, Tau Cetan coffee ranked pretty highly. Just so long as her next port was away from the established markets; she couldn't compete with the high-volume dealers. "Send the details to my ship. If it makes sense for my next haul, I give them a call."

"Sure thing," he beamed. "Okay then. See you around the port?"

"I'll be around." She held out her hand. "Good to meet you, David."

"And you." He shook her hand, remounted the flatbed, and drove off toward the warehouse end of the port building.

She watched him go. His family name, Tefera, *did* sound familiar when it came to the local coffee trade, although it wasn't something she'd paid much attention to the specifics of. She wondered why David was hanging around the spaceport if he was part of that. She shrugged, then turned back to the Sophie. The sludge system was done, so she gloved up again; this was potentially the messiest part. After disconnecting and stowing the hose she headed back inside to check the level on the water tanks.

The blinking message light caught her attention. Right, she'd had mail. She touched a control to display the list. It wasn't a question of who knew she was here, the message would have bounced around the various planetary networks until it eventually caught up with the *Sophie*, but she generally didn't get much. A job, maybe? She looked at the message, and the sender name.

"Quiche Desjardins? Who or what is Quiche Desjardins? Am I getting *spam*?" Unlikely. Her filters were excellent, and the penalties for sending junk messages, especially interstellar junk messages, were draconian. She considered just deleting it unread, then the initials clicked. Quiche Desjardins. QD. *Quentin Ducayne.*

Oh sludge. It probably was a job. And it was probably one she wasn't going to like.

Chapter II: Stirring the Pot

Vaughan

A week ago: Tanith

KLAUS VAUGHAN AND the rest of the *Carcharodon* crew had been on-planet for nearly four weeks now. Vaughan himself was staying in a guest room at the local Church of Divine Stellar Providence. It was hardly luxurious, even in comparison with his cabin on the Carcharodon, but he saw enough of *that* while in space. He sat at the small table drinking coffee and scanning the news feed on his data pad. There wasn't much there to hold his attention. At least he was making some progress with recruiting.

It turned out that although Tanith had no native aliens, there were several farmsteads settled by timoans. The politics of that disgusted Vaughan, something about encouraging cross-cultural fertilization and good relations with the more influential clan matriarchs on Taprobane. The theory was that the timoans, being not too far from the iron age heritage and developing on a terraformed planet, might be well-suited to helping tame a new planet which had limited resources. Vaughan felt it was nonsense: if humans built more ships they could just import the necessary technology. Some of the settled planets were already close to being able to build ships of their own. *Probably more than Homeworld Security and the* Union de Terre *realize,* thought Vaughan, although Verdigris wasn't completely autonomous yet.

There was little interaction in Harp City with timoans, they were mostly clustered several hundred kilometers southwest, but the locals knew of them. A little rumor mongering and muckraking about how the timoans would eventually cut into living space for humans helped. Hell, it might even be true.

The human colonies on Tanith, of which Harp City was by far the biggest, were still too small and too loosely organized for serious organized crime. There were a few gangs, but small and more inclined to petty crimes and hooliganism than anything that took much organization. With few regulations against most human vices, there weren't the niches that organized crime tended to flourish in. It was a frontier world; it was easy enough to pack up and move away from trouble.

But there was still a level of bureaucracy and law enforcement that some folks would pay to avoid, either in money or favors. Vaughan was quite used to working that angle. His team had already hooked into the trading system to get an edge when unconsigned cargo came in. He'd also gained influence with the local spaceport board, and had been encouraging them to raise fees to pay for improvements. The local port could stand some upgrades but that wasn't the point. It would ultimately raise the cost of imports, and *that*, and the resentment it would cause, Vaughan could leverage in several ways.

The one thing he hadn't made any progress on was that artifact he'd heard rumors of shortly after they'd arrived. Supposedly it was something high tech, found off-planet, although it wasn't clear if it was from elsewhere in the 82 Eridani system or somewhere else. Maybe there'd been nothing to it.

Vaughan raised his coffee mug to his lips, then grimaced. It was cold. As he put the mug down again, there was a knock at the door.

"Yes?"

"Boss, it's me, Mignon."

"Enter." As the man did so, Vaughan asked, "What is it?"

"It's about that Homeworld Security guy, John Smith."

They didn't have proof that Smith, or whatever his real name was, was a Homeworld Security agent, but Vaughan strongly suspected it. The Velkaryan office in the local Church had hacked into a number of public cameras around the city, and as a matter of routine ran the feeds through facial recognition against their database of known or suspected Homeworld Security personnel. They'd hit a match on John Smith. It was a loose one—the

Velkaryans weren't going for forensic-level accuracy—but enough to warrant keeping an eye on Smith.

"What about him?" Vaughan asked.

"Garcia says that a cluster analysis on his network traffic, what we could pick up, shows a lot of connections with an account linked to where we heard about that artifact you're interested in."

Garcia was their local signals analyst and general systems hacker. If his analysis was correct, and Vaughan had no reason to doubt it, it meant that Smith was interested in this mysterious artifact too. Interesting. "When was the latest message in that cluster?"

Mignon checked his omniphone. "Day before yesterday. They go back about four weeks. I guess he's getting the runaround too."

"You'd think that somebody who wanted to sell something would respond a little faster," Vaughan said. "But maybe there *is* something to it. Have a closer watch kept on Smith, and notify me if there are any more messages between him and whoever this is." They couldn't crack the encryption on the messages themselves, of course, but sooner or later one of them would be about setting up the exchange. *Any* message exchanged would be a trigger to watch Smith even more closely.

Chapter 12: Ducayne's Message

Roberts

A few hours ago: Tau Ceti III-1

JACKIE OPENED DUCAYNE'S message—it was his, she'd verified the signature key—and skimmed it.

"*Captain Roberts,*" it read, "*if this message catches up with you at Tau Ceti, Epsilon Eridani, or that general vicinity within three weeks of the send date, I have a courier job for you.*" There were still eight days left in the window; he must have sent it a week after she left Sawyers World for Taprobane.

"*I need a package picked up from 82 Eridani and delivered here as soon as possible. It should be a straightforward pickup and delivery; the package should be considerably less than a cubic meter in volume and less than 50kg mass. Contact information—*" was just a name and care-of the Tanith cargo office.

That shouldn't be too difficult. Jackie wondered what the rush was. That he wanted to engage a courier wasn't that surprising. Eighty-Two Eridani's habitable world, Tanith, was lightly inhabited and the system didn't see much traffic from Sawyers World, despite being only two weeks away from there. There were scheduled emigration runs from Earth, but Ducayne would want a private delivery.

She didn't for a moment consider refusing the job. She owed Ducayne for repairs and enhancements to the *Sophie*, and a readiness to perform special jobs was part of that deal. Until now, though, they'd generally involved ferrying Hannibal Carson to places where he usually managed to find trouble, or trouble found him. A pick up and delivery might turn out to be simple after all. It was, though, a little odd that the package hadn't just accompanied the message that had informed Ducayne of it in the first place.

Maybe the package hadn't been ready or available to ship when Ducayne first heard of it. Or, she realized, the message could have been sent by torpedo, a small self-guided warp ship powered by antimatter and with no room for any cargo but the data stored in its memory. Either way, she realized, this probably *wasn't* going to be simple.

Jackie had been to 82 Eridani before, back when she was an executive officer, before she acquired the *Sophie*. Tanith, the terraformed planet, had a town and some small settlements. A G8 star with three "super-Earths," rocky planets ranging from two to four times Earth's diameter, bigger even than Skead, that were in relatively tight orbits, with the outermost being almost as close to its sun as Mercury to Sol. Tanith, a near Earth-sized world, was farther out in the habitable zone, where it had managed to ignore perturbations from the inner planets for at least sixty-five million years. Beyond that there was a Saturn-sized gas giant, a Neptune-like ice giant, and a number of dwarf planets. Oh yes, and a dust disk that meant a safe approach would be well above or below the ecliptic.

There was something else about it that she'd learned recently, but couldn't remember quite what. Something to do with the spaceport? Never mind, anything important would be in the database.

"*As soon as possible*," Ducayne's message had read. So much for catching up with old acquaintances. But she was damned if she was leaving before having a meal that didn't come from her ship's autochef.

She checked the local web. Her favorite restaurant—Sherwood's Chophouse, locals pronounced it *Shophouse*—was still thriving, so she made a reservation for one. Her plans to depart at first light conflicted with having company; she'd be pressured to make an evening of it, catch up on old times, that sort of thing. It was simpler just to enjoy dinner by herself and then get back to the *Sophie* for pre-departure prep.

She drafted a reply to Ducayne, letting him know she'd got the message and had taken the job, estimating arrival at 82 Eridani some nine days from now. Then she contacted the port cargo office—fortunately the over-eager David Tefera wasn't the one answering the comm—and notified them of a light cargo opportunity going to 82 Eridani in the morning. Ducayne hadn't said anything about her deadheading there, and if she could pick some credit with a little freight, so much the better. Either way, she'd be taking a network data dump. The mail must go through.

Chapter 13: Sawyer

Carson

A few hours ago: Anderson Office Park, outskirts of Sawyer City

ELIZABETH SAWYER'S OFFICE was in a small suite in a rather generic-looking building, part of a small office park on what was still the outskirts of Sawyer City. Judging from the construction, though, the city would soon expand past it. A half-kilometer away a large construction fabber was busily extruding the walls of yet another building.

The autocab stopped outside the main entrance to the building and opened its door. Carson got out, double checked the address, and entered the lobby. "Hannibal Carson visiting Sawyer Enterprises," he announced to the air.

"*Confirmed*," announced a pleasant female-sounding voice, almost certainly robotic. "*Third floor.*" An elevator door slid open. He entered, and noted that the third floor had already been selected. *Points for efficiency*, he thought as the door closed and the elevator rose.

Hannibal Carson hadn't felt this nervous about meeting someone since his first date back in high school. He knew it was silly; the worst that could happen was that Sawyer or her office staff, if any, could just tell him to go away; but Captain Elizabeth Sawyer was a legendary figure. The planet was *named* for her, after all. She had been second-in-command of the first expedition to the Alpha Centauri system, one of a handful of people to have been on the first landings on *two* terraformed planets, and the leader of the expedition which first landed on this one. Among her other accomplishments.

The elevator stopped and the opened. There was a single office door of the foyer, with a sign bearing a simple SE logo. He straightened his clothes, ran a hand through his hair, took a breath and opened the office door.

Unlike the building's lobby, Sawyer Enterprise's office had a human receptionist, a very fit-looking blond man who could have been, given modern antagathic drugs, anywhere from his early-thirties to mid-fifties. He had an air of confidence which suggested more the latter, and idly Carson wondered if "bodyguard" was included in his job description. He looked vaguely familiar, but Carson couldn't place him.

The man looked up from his desk as Carson entered. "Can I help you?"

"I'm Doctor Hannibal Carson. I have an appointment."

The man looked him up and down, like a sergeant inspecting a grunt, then touched a comm-panel on his desk. "He's here."

"*Thanks, Poul. Show him in.*"

Poul? Carson wondered. "Are you—"

"This way, please," Poul said, cutting him off, and steered him toward the inner doorway which had opened in the wall behind the desk.

A woman, gray-haired and tall, surprisingly fit for someone ninety and looking more like sixty, rose to meet him, extending her hand. "Doctor Carson, I take it?"

"Yes Ma'am, uh, Captain."

"I retired from that a long time ago. You can call me Elizabeth, or Doctor Sawyer if you prefer." She sat back down in her chair, wincing slightly as she did so.

"Elizabeth . . . ." the blond man began.

"Hush Poul, I'm fine. Run along now."

The man frowned at Carson, but turned and left.

Carson couldn't help himself. "Was that . . . ?"

"Poul Tyrell? Yes. You'll have to excuse him; he's very protective of me. Pain in the ass sometimes, to tell the truth. He insisted on being here today."

No wonder he'd looked familiar. Poul Tyrell had been born on this planet, back in the days of the *Anderson* expedition. His story was part of the legend. Carson realized that Sawyer was looking at him expectantly. "Sorry, I . . ." Carson gathered himself together. "Doctor Sawyer, first, thank you for your time. I'm honored to—"

"Thanks son, but stow it. Several people persuaded me I should see you, and that I was the only one who could answer some important questions, but they were kind of cagey about just what. So, what does an archeologist want with me? Surely not permission to excavate the *Anderson*, right? It's not even buried."

"What? No, nothing like that. Here," he said, pulling out his data-pad and bringing up the sketch Williams had done of Ketzshanass. It was a pretty good likeness. "I understand you may have once seen something like this." He turned the pad and placed it on Sawyer's desk, facing her.

She paled slightly, then looked at him intently. "What is this, and why would you think that?"

"This is a sketch of an alien I encountered some parsecs from here. It's a sketch because my camera wouldn't record. And I read a recently declassified report that you had a similar experience shortly after you first landed."

"Declassified?"

"Well, classification lowered."

"They probably thought I'd be dead by now. Bureaucrats."

He wasn't sure how to respond to that. "It's still secret," he said. "So, is this what you saw?"

Sawyer sat back in her chair and put her hands together, steepling her fingers. "That was a long time ago. I never saw it up close. But yes, it could have been the same species. Who are they?"

"Unfortunately, they're not ready to make contact, so the one I met wasn't prepared to go into detail. He did imply that they have been observing us for a while. Can you tell me anything else about that siting, or any others?"

"It should all have been in the report. I never saw it again, in fact it disappeared almost as I watched. I asked Naomi later about stealth or camouflage technology. Other than data dropouts on our recording devices—like your camera I imagine —there was nothing."

"Okay." Carson was reminded of something. "Camouflage, you said?"

"Well, here one minute, gone the next, with no obvious places to hide. Why?"

"Back on . . . well, the first time I saw their ship, it seemed to disappear soon after. Stealth or camouflage could explain that."

"Their ship? What was it like?"

"That was the crazy thing. It looked like a flying pyramid." He probably shouldn't have said that, but there wasn't much anyone could do with that information. Just another UFO report.

"A pyramid? Have you talked to Finley?"

Finley? The name clicked. He was also on the original *Anderson* team. "Do you mean Peter Finley, the geologist? No, why?"

"Yes, him. What do you know about Pete's Peak, or whatever they're calling it these days?

Carson wondered where that question had come from.

"Near your original landing site?" Carson said. "Not much. An old volcanic neck, isn't it?"

"That's what our reports said, yes. It hasn't been explored since, as far as I know."

"And you would likely know."

Sawyer and the other original crew weren't officially part of the Sawyers World government, but from what Carson had heard, very little escaped them. "It's off-limits, isn't it? Part of the range of the Finley's leopard, or something."

"It is, yes."

"Then why the question? You don't think it's a volcanic neck? You're a geologist, you would know."

"I would. There's a lot that the write-up on that peak carefully doesn't say. When we first saw it, Pete said it reminded him of pyramids in the Yucatan jungle, poking up above the tree tops."

"*What?*"

"It's dirt and vegetation covered, and I can't imagine that it's a spaceship, but from the air it had a squarish outline. But then sometimes so do volcanic remains, especially if there are radiating dikes."

Carson took a minute to digest this. He'd seen similar tree-covered pyramids himself, once, back on Earth. He'd never paid much attention to Pete's Peak; extinct volcanoes weren't his passion. He knew there had been intelligent natives here on Sawyers World at one point, since ancient paleolithic sites had been found. But they were far from the *Anderson* site, except for a few, even older, scattered stone knives and spear-points. It had probably been a hunting area, tens or hundreds of thousands of years ago. The pyramid-building Spacefarers, from what Carson had deduced about them, had preferred to build near early agricultural societies. He had to admit, though, that his hypothesis was based on extremely limited evidence.

"So, you think it might be a pyramid? That there's a connection?"

"I have no idea. I never went near it after our first flyover. But Pete and Naomi climbed it. He's the one you should ask, especially if you've seen one of those, too."

Carson thought her tone suggested she knew more than she was letting on. "Just how much do you know about what I've seen?"

"Officially? Just what you've told me. But we have our sources." She smiled at him.

Carson could imagine. The common saying that the Families owned half the planet was of course a complete exaggeration. It wasn't even technically correct to call them the Founding Families. Most of the team members of the *Anderson* expedition, who had spent nearly four Earth-years voluntarily marooned on this planet until the return expedition, had indeed formed families and even, as in the case of Maclaren Arms, thriving companies. But the founders of Sawyer City had been part of the second wave of colonization. The Original Eight had parlayed their valuable experience settling the planet into considerable holdings, but none of them had particularly aspired to political or economic power beyond that necessary to be left the hell alone when they wanted to be.

And therein was the problem. From what Carson knew—although he rarely followed even local politics, except where it interacted with his university or possible expedition funding—Peter Finley *liked* to be left the hell alone.

"You think I should talk to Doctor Finley."

"Didn't I just say that? But you'll have to set up the meeting yourself. I'll mention it to him, but you go through your own channels, and leave my name out of it."

"I . . . all right. I'll do that." Carson rose to leave. "Thank you so much for your time."

"Not at all. It's nice to have some confirmation that I did see something. Sometimes I wondered. Oh, before you go . . . ."

"Yes?" Carson said, turning back to her.

"The alien you met. What do they call themselves?"

"Ketzshanass. The individual was named Ketzshanass. He said to refer to them as Kesh." He paused as a realization struck him, then added, "I've been assuming that refers to their home-world rather than a species name, but I could be wrong. In fact, given how little he was willing to reveal about their homeworld, it could have been made up on the spot and they call themselves something else entirely."

"Oh? One name is as good as another, I suppose. Thank you, Doctor Carson."

∞ ∞ ∞

As Carson left the office, he signaled for an autocab to take him back to campus. It pulled up just as he exited the building. Its promptness surprised Carson; the building was toward the edge of town, and he wouldn't have expected much demand. The mysteries of autocab optimization were something Carson occasionally wondered about, but never for long enough to actually look into.

He climbed into the cab. "Drake University," he told it.

"*Acknowledged*," the cab responded, and pulled away from the office building.

Chapter 14: Dinner

Roberts

Now: Aboard the Sophie

WITH SOME FREE time before dinner, Jackie Roberts sat cross-legged on the bunk in her cabin, working with the celestial navigation program on her tablet. Eighty-Two Eridani was a pretty easy straight run from Tau Ceti, just under nine days in warp, but it had been long enough since the last time she'd been there that a refresher was in order.

She set the display's origin at Tau Ceti and centered the image on 82 Eridani. There was a bright yellow star just a few degrees away from it, the sort of thing that could get you messed up if you were sloppy about lining up on your target before engaging warp. She knew that star. It was actually a loose binary. Zeta Reticuli. She, Carson and Marten had been there just two months ago. Jackie wondered if there was more to this pick-up job than Ducayne had told her. *It's Ducayne. Of course there is*, she thought.

She continued to review the 82 Eridani data. The habitable planet was Tanith. The nearest other star was a brown dwarf at 1.3 parsecs, well off her course and not particularly interesting. There was the usual sprinkling of red dwarfs but nothing close enough to worry about. At almost twelve light years, 82 Eridani was just beyond her there-and-back range without refueling, but that wouldn't be an issue; she'd refuel at Tanith. Then she remembered the "and back" wouldn't be back *here*. Ducayne wanted the package delivered to him at Sawyers World, Alpha Centauri. On her pad, she moved the origin to 82 Eridani and set the display to look back at Alpha Centauri. 19.17 light years. Close enough to her full range that she would want to stop somewhere to top up the fuel tanks.

She scanned the route. There really wasn't much without being way off track. The Epsilon Eridani system was roughly equidistant from Alpha Centauri and 82 Eridani, the three stars making a shallow triangle, but the detour was an additional six light years, or four-and-a-half days. Hmm, that would be nearly the same for return via Tau Ceti. She checked the numbers. Yes, hypothetically returning via Tau Ceti would take all of six hours longer than via Epsilon Eridani, but with Eridani's thick dust disk and dual asteroid belts, in-system maneuvering would more than exceed that. Maybe she could stop back here on the return leg after all.

On the other hand, with stopover and refueling time, taking either indirect route would add five or more days to the trip back, and it wasn't strictly necessary. She wondered just how urgent Ducayne's pickup was. He'd had the *Sophie* equipped with a few extras. In addition to a message torpedo, she had a range booster. A kilogram of anti-matter and the conversion equipment to let it power her warp modules added several light years to her range. But that was only for emergencies.

Okay, the direct route it would be. If she found herself dangerously low on fuel a light year or two short of Alpha Centauri, that would constitute enough of an emergency to use the antimatter.

That was another subsystem she'd need to run checks on. Antimatter storage was reliable—it had to be—but she had the irrational feeling that antimatter would slowly evaporate in storage if it wasn't used. Actually, she realized, it *wasn't* such an irrational feeling. The containment was *designed* to let the antimatter "evaporate" slowly, to power the container itself. A kilogram could power it for thousands of years. It wouldn't run out that way in her lifetime.

She was contemplating that when her omni's alarm tweedled at her. It was time to clean up and change for dinner.

Chapter 15: Going for a Ride

Carson

Now: An autocab, near Sawyer City

AS THE AUTOCAB headed back toward campus, Hannibal Carson reviewed what little Sawyer had told him about the Kesh contact—he was sure that's what it had been—and about Finley's peak. Could it be a pyramid? Had there been one under their noses all this time?

Nothing Sawyer had said proved it to be a pyramid, but neither was anything he recalled about it inconsistent with it being a pyramid either. He didn't remember much. He'd have to read the reports before talking to Finley. That it was completely covered in soil and vegetation was odd, but not impossible. The Verdigris pyramid had been partially buried, and the Mayan pyramids of the Yucatan were vegetation-covered before they'd been excavated, although the stepped-nature of those pyramids made that easier.

Carson glanced out the window of the cab. The surroundings were unfamiliar; this wasn't the way he had come.

"Cab, destination Drake University, Archeology Building."

The cab acknowledged the command, but continued on-course.

"Cab, specify destination."

"*Acknowledged,*" was all the cab said.

Great, thought Carson. *The cab's software has a glitch.* There were no manual controls; this was a city cab, not an off-road vehicle.

But there would be an interface to connect via an omniphone. Carson tapped an icon on his.

There was no response. His omni didn't register the presence of the cab. *What the hell?*

Carson raised his voice. "Cab. Stop here please."

"*Acknowledged.*" The cab increased speed.

That word was beginning to annoy Carson. He flashed on Edgar Allen Poe's raven, forever quothing "nevermore". He'd have laughed if the situation weren't so serious.

He had no idea where the cab was taking him. The map on his omni was useless; somehow the cab must be interfering with the positioning system, which shouldn't be possible. He had to get out, even though the cab was moving faster than any sane person would try to jump from.

He tried the door. It was locked, and the release did nothing.

"Cab, slow down!" He might as well try that again while he thought of something.

It said "*acknowledged,*" but otherwise failed to respond. By now the cab was in open countryside, rolling down a narrow gravel road at speed.

Carson looked at the cab's interior light. Maybe a short circuit would drain the battery, or reset the computer? He pulled out his folding knife and attacked the lamp fixture. The wires sparked violently when he shorted them, and grew hot enough to burn his fingers, but he held on as the whine of the motor dropped in pitch. It was slowing down!

Then a circuit breaker tripped with a *click* and the cab sped up again, the wires cooling. *Damn it, now what?*

Knife in hand, Carson looked around the interior of the cab. He was more angry than scared. He stabbed at the back of the rear seat and slashed at it. Maybe he could open a way into the trunk. He'd figure out what to do then when he got there.

The synthetic fabric and padding yielded under his onslaught, and he tore great chunks of it away, revealing the metal frame of the seat back. The diagonal cross-members of the frame had big triangular gaps between them, but it would be a squeeze.

He squeezed. With his head through the gap, he pushed and pulled himself forward, but couldn't get his shoulders through.

He backed up and pushed one arm through first, then his head and other shoulder. No good, he got stuck part way. He tried to back out, but the awkward position of his limbs made that nearly impossible. He squirmed and wriggled, finally pulling himself loose, tearing his shirt and some skin in the process.

He tried the doors again. Maybe the locks had been on the same circuit as the light. He tugged and pushed at the handle and lock switch, but to no effect. The inside of the door, like the rest of the cab, was lined with a fabric like that of the seat cover. Maybe?

He grabbed his knife up from where he'd left it on the floor of the cab and slashed at the door covering near the switch. It cut easily, but there was metal behind it. Of course. The switch had to mount into something. He kept slashing at the door until he found a gap between the frame pieces, and ripped the fabric away.

Yes! The lock and latch mechanisms, and their wires, were exposed. Carson hacked the wires apart. There was no time for finesse. He didn't want to still be in the cab when it arrived wherever it was taking him, and that might be any minute now.

Carson pried at the mechanism until it released, and the door . . . stayed closed. Now what? The force of the slipstream was holding it closed, of course. Carson pushed hard and it opened a few centimeters, the wind and road noise coming in with a roar.

Why the bloody hell isn't this cab designed to come to a stop if someone opens the door? Carson wondered, but realized that could have been overridden too. He looked through the gap at the rough surface of the road rushing by, with the grass verge just beyond. *This is going to hurt.*

He jammed a piece of torn seat cover into the edge of the door to keep it from latching shut. Then he cut two long strips of the fabric, which he managed to wrap around his hands. He was not dressed for this—it had been a social call, not a field trip—but the wrappings should help save his skin.

Carson curled up in the seat beside the unlatched door, the roar of the wind and crunch of the gravel loud through the gap between door and frame. He curled his hands over his head, his fists balled and gripping the insides of the seat-cover wrappings, put his back against the door, then drew his knees up, planted his feet against the edge of the seat supports where he had cut away the cover, and took a deep breath. He gave quick silent thanks that this wasn't a *flying* autocab, then as hard as he could, pushed himself out.

Chapter 16: Dessert

Roberts

Sherwood's Chophouse, Skead City

DINNER HAD BEEN wonderful. Jackie had ordered the elk medallions, which weren't really elk but a native Skead animal that resembled it, in a tanberry sauce with roast potatoes. It had been delicious. She was just taking a sip of her dessert coffee, a hot sweet drink piled high with whipped cream, when a familiar voice came from behind her.

"Is that Jackie Roberts? It *is* you! How long have you been back on Skead? And how's the *Sophie*?" The voice belonged to Andrei Sarsfield, who'd been her co-pilot for the better part of a year. There was another man with him.

"Andrei, what a surprise! It's good to see you. *Sophie* is doing fine, in fact I'm lifting in the morning." Better get that out up front, to justify leaving early if she needed to. "Join me, please," she said, gesturing at the empty seats at her table.

The waiter looked momentarily nonplussed, but accommodated them.

"What about you?" she asked Andrei as they sat. "Still with Nakamura?"

"Nope. Ben here," Sarsfield gestured to his companion, "and I went partners in a C-class, the *Cerulean Cloud*. I missed the freedom we had with the *Sophie*."

"Don't you miss the regular paycheck? I thought that was one reason you left *Sophie* to join Nakamura."

"It was, but I got bored doing the same run all the time. Speaking of, where are you headed?"

There was no reason not to tell him, anyone who really wanted to know could get the information from the cargo office. "Eighty-Two Eridani. Know of any cargo headed in that direction?" Even though technically they were competitors, it sometimes made sense to subcontract a load to another ship, particularly on a long run with unknown chances of a return load.

"*Tanith?* What takes you out that way?"

There was a hint of, what, concern? incredulity? in Andrei's voice. "Why? Is something going on there I should know about?" And if so, why wasn't it on the net?

"Nothing really. It's just coincidence. Ben and I were out there seven, maybe eight weeks ago. Nothing more than the usual frontier world hassles. Some talk of imposing landing fees, that kind of nonsense."

"Landing fees? They need us more than we need them, surely?" Except for the purpose-built spaceliners intended for high-traffic routes like the Earth-Alpha Centauri run, most small starships could land on almost any flat stretch of ground, and a few could also land on water. Which wasn't to say that there weren't amenities in a developed spaceport worth paying for—sewage connections for one, and a cargo office for another—but on many planets the local spaceport was just a cleared field. The inhabitants, whether temporary or permanent settlers, generally needed the goods and data brought by small time charter and freight operators more than those operators needed any particular location's business.

"It's just talk. Anyway, we operators would roll it into the price of the service," Ben put in.

"And at the margin, folks wouldn't ship or travel as much, which still hurts us in the long run," Jackie said. "The independent freighters and traders compete a little harder, cutting our margins even more, and we'll tend to avoid places like Tanith. Either way the colonies grow a little more slowly, or even shrink. It wouldn't be the first time."

"Jackie was born off-Earth," Andrei said in an aside to Ben. "She's seen it happen."

"Really?" Ben said. He looked at her. "Then you are as young as you look. Hard to tell these days."

Jackie wasn't sure how to take that. Yes, past adolescence, physical appearance didn't correlate much with age anymore, but she knew she was young for a pilot. Never mind that she was literally born on a starship. "The Sawyer colony is over fifty years old," she said.

"And I don't recall any of the original settlers being named Roberts," Ben said. "But no offense was intended, I'm sorry if it sounded that way." He didn't look particularly sorry, but Jackie let it pass.

Andrei turned back to her. "How is Renee, by the way?"

"Mom? She's fine, the last I heard. It's been a while, she's on another expedition." It had been on a multi-year, extended expedition that Jackie had been born, not that she had any personal memory of that. But her mother was a field astrophysicist, and Jackie had grown up in and around starships.

"Ah. Anyway," Sarsfield continued, "Kakuloa's problem wasn't exorbitant landing fees; the economy collapsed when the pharmaceutical companies on Earth learned to duplicate the biologicals Kakuloa was exporting."

Jackie shook her head, smiled, and raised her hand in a gesture that was part surrender, part halting further discussion. "We've had that argument before, Andrei, let's not get into it again. Not my fight. Besides, I really can't stay. I have a ship to prep for departure in the morning." She pushed her chair back from the table.

Andrei looked as though he were about to protest, but Ben looked relieved. Andrei caught that too. "Sure. Ben and I need to order dinner anyway. Keep in touch, we'll have to catch up next time our paths cross."

Jackie caught Ben's scowl at that. Jealousy? He didn't have anything to worry about. Jackie's only interest in Andrei was that he'd been a great co-pilot, and as far as she knew, the feeling was mutual.

"Sure," she said, then had a sudden thought. "Oh, by the way . . . ."

"Yes?"

"Just curious, when you were at Tanith did you happen to pick up anything bound for Sawyers World?"

Andrei raised his brows. "Not that I recall, certainly that wasn't our first stop after leaving there. Ben?"

Jackie saw Ben's scowl but couldn't decide if it was the same one continued or a new one at the question.

"That was a while back. Without going back through the manifest I'd have to say no. Why?" There was a suspicious tone to Ben's question, but considering most ship owner-operators considered manifests as trade secrets—everyone had their own favored customers and routes—that wasn't surprising.

"No particular reason. I'm picking up a small load bound for Sawyers and wondered what the odds were that there might be other cargo to be had." Put that way, her question seemed legitimate enough and her answer seemed to satisfy Ben.

"Sorry, can't help you there. Good luck, though." The latter lacked any genuine enthusiasm.

Oh well. "Thanks. Um, one other question, and please don't take offense. I wouldn't mention it but since Andrei and I go back a way, I wouldn't want to step on any toes."

"What's on your mind, Jackie?" Andrei asked.

"A contact at the port recommended a local grower for some on-spec, small lot coffee loads. If I don't have another cargo lined up for Tanith, I'm thinking of pursuing that. That wouldn't undercut you, would it?"

"I thought you didn't like being the middleman, just the delivery person?"

Jackie shrugged. "As a rule, yes. But my pick-up contract doesn't say I have to dead-head, so why not?"

"Go for it, Jackie," Andrei said. "We do take coffee when we're headed out that way, but I don't think you'll hurt our business. A lot of coffee drinkers on Tanith."

"Andrei!" Ben sounded annoyed.

"Relax, Ben," Andrei said to him. "She didn't have to bring it up in the first place. And you're a little too paranoid." Andrei turned back to Jackie. "Sorry. Ben's last captain played business really tight to the firewall. I think it rubbed off." He turned back to Ben and glared at him.

"No, forgive me," Roberts said. "I don't want to cause a fuss."

"My fault," Ben said. "Andrei is right, I do get a little paranoid about business sometimes. But you're a friend of his, I should mind my manners."

Jackie wondered at this sudden solicitousness. She wouldn't have challenged anyone, let alone a friend of Andrei's, over something so trivial, nor was she conspicuously armed at the moment, but Ben didn't know her. On the other hand, space could be a lonely, dangerous place. Business aside, small ship owner-operators tended to stick together. Ben seemed sincere.

"Your manners were never an issue," she said. "Perhaps mine were. Can we forget it?"

Ben nodded. Andrei looked back and forth between him and Jackie and, wearing a wide-eyed expression of innocence, asked "Forget what?"

"Nothing," Ben said.

"What he said." Roberts looked at her omni. "And I've delayed your dinner long enough, gentlemen. You can keep this table if you like, but I need to get back to the Sophie." She rose and took a step back. "It was good to meet you, Ben. Next time, Andrei. Enjoy your dinner." With that she turned and left the restaurant.

∞ ∞ ∞

Riding in the autocab on the way back to the spaceport, Jackie pondered the conversation again. She didn't see how it could be anything but coincidence that they'd met at the restaurant, or that the *Cerulean Cloud* had recently visited 82 Eridani. They'd surely done a couple of other trips since then, and back before Andrei left the *Sophie* they'd eaten at Sherwood's together before. A cut above spaceport fare but still reasonable.

Still, there had been something about their reaction when she'd mentioned her destination. *Was* there something going on there that she should know about? If Quentin Ducayne was involved, then the answer was almost certainly, emphatically, *yes*. And equally certainly, she wouldn't find out *what* until she got there.

And as annoying as Hannibal Carson could sometimes be, Jackie found herself wishing that he were coming along on this trip. *Stop that!* she told herself. *He's just as likely to get you* into *trouble as out of it.* That was certainly true so far. But despite the fact that, as she'd once told him, spaceflight is *supposed* to be boring, the trips with him had been *fun* . . . once you got past the sheer terror of almost getting killed or being abducted by spacefaring aliens.

The thought sobered her. *Be careful what you wish for,* she told herself, *you might get it.*

Chapter 17: Homeworld Security

Carson

Homeworld Security HQ, Sawyers World

"YOU LOOK LIKE hell," Ducayne said.

"I feel like road-kill." Carson said. He lay in an infirmary bed at Homeworld Security headquarters, thoroughly bandaged, with an IV tube in his arm.

"I'm not surprised. Your right leg has the worst case of road rash I've ever seen—fortunately just skin, you didn't lose any muscle—bruised ribs, a broken finger, and assorted other scrapes and contusions. And a concussion, they tell me. Poul Tyrell said it gave him flashbacks to a giranno stampede.

"Tyrell! This was his doing!"

"No, actually, I don't think it was. He was horrified. He was the one who got to you first, and had a copter with an autodoc there in minutes. It flew you here."

"How?"

"How did he find you? Smart omniphone you've got there. Between the gee-loads and the physiological changes it sensed in you—good thing you had it on your wrist and not in a pocket—it figured something was seriously wrong and started calling for help."

"Uh, yeah. Useful on field trips, if there's anyone nearby to help."

"So, what happened?"

"What did Tyrell say?"

"He found you by the side of the road, looking like you'd been thrown from a car, although there was no car around. That was maybe ten or fifteen minutes after you left the office. He didn't go himself, it was one of his drones that followed your beacon."

"Oh. Handy."

"The founders like their toys. So, what do you remember?"

"Damned autocab tried to kidnap me. I managed to get out."

"What? The same cab that picked you up from Sawyer's?"

Carson nodded.

"No wonder you thought it was Tyrell. Okay, we'll track that cab down, although I imagine Tyrell or Sawyer already has someone working on that."

"If not him, who did this?"

"The most obvious guess is the Velkaryans; you've managed to upset them a couple of times now. But the timing of the attack is suspicious. Did you tell anyone you were going to visit Sawyer?"

"No. But if they're watching me, or hacked into the autocab dispatch system . . . ."

"Then they'd know. And the most logical reason for you to visit her—or for her to agree to a visit—would be what? Nothing they could know about."

"Her report?"

"I guess there could be other sources, second hand. But maybe the timing was just coincidence, and they want you for something else."

"What?"

"You tell me. If Vaughan has reported back, they know something about Zeta Reticuli. They certainly know you were on Verdigris, and probably that you checked out the pyramid."

"Oh, right. Sorry, not thinking clearly. By the way, Sawyer said I should talk to Peter Finley about Pete's Peak. It might actually be a pyramid."

"Really? That's interesting. I'll pass along a warning to the local government about potential poachers on the wildlife preserve, and some more details to Finley. *Is* it a pyramid?"

"I haven't looked into it. I'd want to talk to Finley, he's the one who found and climbed it. Sawyer seemed to think that he thought so."

Ducayne nodded. "I'll want a full debriefing on your discussion, as best you remember, of course. But not right now. Make a few notes while it's fresh in your mind and we can go over it later."

He looked thoughtful for a minute, then added "I don't have anything else for you right now. There are some possibilities in the works. If the Velkaryans are after you, maybe we should get you off-planet. I'll let you know when I have something. Contact me if anything comes up on your end."

"Fair enough."

Ducayne rose and left.

Chapter 18: Departure

Roberts

Starship Sophie, *Skead Spaceport*

JACKIE SET *SOPHIE*'S computer to do one more diagnostics check while she did her walk-around. In theory, there wasn't much that she could find on a walk-around that the computer wouldn't also detect, but that assumed all the sensors were working correctly and assumptions could lead to problems. She idly wondered how many aircraft pilots had run into trouble because they'd believed the fuel gauges without eyeballing the tanks.

This would be a long trip, nine days to 82 Eridani and then fourteen more back to Sawyers World, with only short stops between. The night before she had considered making a trip out to her storage facility to swap out some of her personal effects on the *Sophie* with what was in storage—in particular, she'd considered grabbing the leather-bound volumes of Patrick O'Brian's Aubrey-Maturin sea-faring series which her father had given her, and from where she'd got her ship's name. She'd finally decided it wasn't worth the time; those books and tens of thousands of others were in *Sophie*'s memory anyway.

David Tefera had showed up early that morning, riding a flatbed with several crates of his family's coffee, Mount Sharon Premiere Roast.

"I, uh, I checked with the office and saw you didn't have a cargo, and were headed for Tanith. Um, Eighty-Two Eridani."

They both knew where Tanith was. There was a nervous edge to David's chatter.

"So I figured I'd bring a consignment by, just in case. Save you some time. Since you're a courier too, we trust you. I checked with my folks."

"Uh . . . ." Roberts had decided to pass on the coffee cargo primarily because Ducayne was in a hurry and she didn't want to take the extra time out of today before lifting. But there was David being helpful again. He was certainly a go-getter, she had to give him that. "Wow. All right, help me get it aboard and stowed. You have the documentation for this? Is it raw or roasted?" Aside from the usual contracts and invoices, organic cargo like coffee was subject to quarantine regulations, to reduce the chance of organisms from one planet contaminating another. *As if that ship hadn't sailed sixty-five million years ago*, she thought, but recognized that evolution since then had produced some surprising differences between the terraformed planets, as well as the similarities.

"The coffee's roasted. We do it ourselves to ensure consistent quality."

"Okay, good." That should let her skip the quarantine process and she could go straight to finding a broker.

"So," she said, making conversation as they finished stowing the cargo, "do you do much business in small lots like this?"

"My dad says he likes to help out the small independent ship operators, so actually, yes, we do. Did a bigger shipment out to Tanith a month or two back, but I'm sure you'll find a buyer for these."

"A month or two? That wouldn't have been the *Cerulean Cloud*, would it?"

David looked thoughtful. "Might have been, yes, the name sounds right. A C-class. You know it?"

"Old shipmate of mine is one of the partners. I ran into him last night."

"Ah, okay. Yeah, they're headed out soon with another load. To Verdigris, I think."

"Verdigris? Don't they grow their own coffee there?"

David shook his head. "I don't think so. Growing conditions are weird on that planet. Or maybe the local stuff just isn't as good as ours."

"There is that," Roberts agreed as they finished stowing the last of the crates.

Roberts sealed the cargo hatch, and David reluctantly departed. Had he hoped to ride along with the crates?

She made her way around the *Sophie's* hull, checking that access port covers were secure, that exhaust ports were clear, and finally under the hull to check that nothing had decided to nest in the landing gear wells, and to disconnect the shore-side umbilicals. It all looked good.

Back aboard, she secured the hatch then strapped in to the command chair. The diagnostics looked good. She initiated the pre-launch sequence and got on the comm.

"Skead Ground, this is the *Sophie* at pad three-seven requesting clearance to the active for departure to space."

"*Roger* Sophie, *cleared to Runway two-three, hold short and contact Departure on one-one-eight.*"

"Twenty-three and hold, departure on one-one-eight. Roger and thank you."

Sophie's landing gear was configured for wheels down; with the weight of full tanks and a long trip ahead, Roberts didn't want to waste fuel on hover taxi or vertical takeoff, not in this gravity. Skead Spaceport had nice runways, she might as well take advantage of them. She released the wheel brakes, eased in the horizontal thrusters and began taxiing to the active runway.

Holding short at the threshold of runway twenty-three, she brought up the vertical thrusters until they took half the weight off the Sophie's landing gear, enough to verify they were functioning properly, then eased them back.

"Skead Tower, this is the *Sophie* holding at two-three requesting permission to takeoff for space."

"*Roger* Sophie, *cleared at your discretion for straight out departure, call clear of the zone.*" Unlike some of the busier planets, there was no air or space traffic control as such, as soon as she cleared 5000 meters from the field she was on her own.

"Thank you, straight out and call when clear."

Jackie let the *Sophie* roll forward onto the runway, turning to line up with it. She held it in place with the toe brakes while she ran up the throttle enough to ensure response—the brakes wouldn't hold *Sophie's* full thrust—then released the brakes and pushed the throttle to 20%—0.8 gees—as the *Sophie* rolled down the runway. As the thrust built it felt to Jackie like the *Sophie* was tilting back at a sharp angle. The airspeed built quickly, and she rotated the ship to lift off halfway down the field. Within a minute she was at 5000 meters altitude and nearly ten kilometers from the spaceport. She signaled control that she was clear of the zone and pitched the *Sophie* into a higher angle, increasing to 80% thrust as she did so. She'd be too high for any useful aerodynamic lift in a few moments more. The acceleration pushed her back in her seat until it felt like the *Sophie* was pointed straight up. The sky above her darkened rapidly.

This was what it was all about, the rush of adrenaline as her ship leapt for space and for freedom. Jackie wasn't headed for an orbit, she was on a ballistic path that took her nearly straight up. She'd kill the engines shortly after clearing atmosphere and the Sophie would coast up another few hundred kilometers, plenty of time to get her lined up on 82 Eridani and engage the warp drive.

The ship's computer helpfully announced, "Ten seconds to MECO, mark", and displayed a countdown in one corner of the screen. Jackie grinned. This wasn't a rendezvous; the timing wasn't so critical that it would matter if the main engines cut off a little early or late. She reached to cut the throttle just as the timer hit zero.

The thrusters went suddenly quiet and there came a feeling of falling. In fact the *Sophie was* falling, pulled back by Skead's gravitational field at nearly 14.3 meters per second every second—but at ten percent of escape velocity, the *Sophie* was already rising so fast it would take a good several minutes before she stopped moving away from the planet and began falling toward it. She'd be in warp before that. Roberts was already orienting the ship toward their destination, the RCS thrusters firing in a series of short bursts. Zero gee didn't bother her at all, she rather enjoyed it.

She had planned her takeoff well enough that within two minutes she had 82 Eridani lined up in the Sophie's guide-scope and had run the spectrum check to confirm that the point of light the ship was aiming at was indeed the G2-type star she wanted to go to and not some other random star, close in angle but parsecs off in distance. With passengers she might have entered orbit and taken a bit more time to let them enjoy the view, but this was a

bit of a game for her. Besides, by not accelerating to orbital velocity she'd save fuel, and of course Ducayne was in a hurry for
his package.

Satisfied that everything was secure for warp and the ship was
pointed in the right direction, she hit the "engage warp" button.
The windows went black and gravity—in this case a subtle and
deliberate bias in the warp field—came back. Jackie sat at the
controls for another minute, enough time to get well clear of the
Tau Ceti system, then unbuckled and headed back to the galley to
fix herself breakfast. With any luck the next nine days would be
of the "space travel is boring" class, although there were plenty of
minor routine maintenance tasks to keep her from getting *too*
bored.

Chapter 19: Ducayne Has News

Carson

Homeworld Security HQ, Sawyers World

HANNIBAL CARSON HAD been out of the infirmary for a day when Ducayne called him into his office. He was standing, glaring at the displays on his wall, when Carson entered.

"You've heard the news from Earth?" Ducayne growled the words out. The last time Hannibal Carson had seen that look on his face, Ducayne had just lost an agent.

"Is this about the Belize find?"

"No, I wanted to talk to you and Brown about something else." Ducayne glanced at the time. "Where is he? Anyway, the news I meant is about the elections in Venezuela. The Velkaryan party won. They've given extra-terrestrials ten days to leave the country or be put in internment camps."

Carson considered that. It fit the Velkaryans' agenda; they were xenophobic, felt that the long-ago terraformed planets were rightfully the property of mankind, and he knew from his own experience that they occasionally adopted Nazi tactics. But . . . "I didn't know there were any aliens in Venezuela. There can't be that many on Earth at all, surely?"

"That's not exactly the point, but yes, there are a few. Just because none of them have native high-tech cultures doesn't mean they can't adapt quickly to ours. You of all people should know that."

"No, of course." Marten, Carson's principal colleague on expeditions, was a timoan. "I just didn't think there'd been much influx to Earth. But that's not what you wanted to talk about."

"No. The Velkaryan hold on Venezuela gives them an air of legitimacy they didn't have before, not to mention access to resources we'd rather they didn't have."

"Their Church of Divine Stellar Providence already gave them a fair bit of legitimacy in some circles. What kind of resources?"

"More access to the inner workings of the *Union de Terre* for one, although they've had moles or sympathizers in there for a while."

"And Homeworld Security reports to the *UdT*."

Ducayne grinned. The expression was almost as scary as his growl, but it seemed to calm him down. "Nothing quite that straightforward, and certainly not for my little piece of it."

"Are the Velkaryans setting themselves up for a theocracy?"

Ducayne turned from his map display and sat down, gesturing for Carson to do the same. "Unlikely. They've always been more political than religious. Oh, sure, there's a big overlap with the CDSP, and probably many of the rank and file believe their myths. We see it as more of a recruiting tool. The *UdT* puts a lot of restrictions on theocracies."

"True, but would they fall under the Technology Rule? They were founded after the first landings."

"It's not quite that simple," Ducayne said.

The so-called Technology Rule was part of the fundamental charter of the *Union de Terre*, in no small part a reaction to the events that had triggered the nuclear Unholy War nearly a century earlier.

Theocracies, and indeed any large religious organization, were, even before the war and certainly after, seen by many as a repulsive token of humanity's primitive past. Conversely, the modern Catholic Church, for one, had been held up as a counter-example, but a nuclear weapon—presumed to have been Islamic but in the post-war confusion that couldn't be proven—had taken out much of Rome and Vatican City with it.

The rule allowed theocratically-governed countries to join the *UdT*, but only under strict limitations on the technology they were allowed access to. It made the restrictions that the Treaty of Versailles imposed on post-World War I Germany look like a mere time-out. Humanitarian technologies for medicine and education were allowed, but others like communications were limited and restricted to unencrypted channels. Weapons technology was strictly limited to what was current at the time the religion was founded. The latter was later amended to "available to the founder" when it had been pointed out that Scientology, for one, was post-nuclear. Not that anyone had seriously suggested they might want nukes, of course, but the point was made that L. Ron Hubbard himself had had no access to them.

Unlike with Germany during the rise of the Nazi party, however, the restrictions were strictly enforced. Although the world had suffered greatly during the "limited" nuclear war, the most powerful nations hadn't suffered as much, and were in better shape than Europe and America had been during the Great Depression. This time, there were no concessions. *UdT* "peace enforcers" could make surprise inspections at any time on a suspected weapons facility in the banned countries. This wasn't just a few guys with suits and briefcases showing up and asking to look at a site, this was an airborne drop of well-trained and well-armed troops who would secure the area and make sure the inspectors had full access to anything they wished.

Resistance would be—and had been—met with draconian counter-force. History—two wars in which nuclear weapons had been used—had demonstrated the less pleasant alternative. Eventually, people got the idea.

"You're right up to a point," Ducayne said. "The Velkaryans and the CDSP would be allowed starships and a lot of other high-tech gear under the Technology Rule. However, there are other rules in place governing weapons-grade fissionables and certain other technologies. Warp generators have a series of fail-safe interlocks to prevent them from being activated in atmosphere or even on the ground in a vacuum chamber, for example. Not impossible to bypass, but not easy."

"Good to know." Carson himself had witnessed what happened when even a small warp field—they had guessed that was how the device worked—was activated in atmosphere. Like a nuclear hand grenade, he remembered.

"Yeah. The thing is, because those rules aren't part of the Technology Rule agreement, the peace enforcers can't do surprise armed inspections. Criminal laws apply, so with probable cause we—well, the police authorities—can get search warrants, but that's not the same."

"So," Carson said, "the Velkaryans could be building weapons in secret."

"It's no secret that they're making weapons. There's a small-arms company owned by known Velkaryans, for example." Ducayne shook his head. "There's nothing illegal about that. It's just the mass-destruction type stuff they're banned from, like everyone else.

"The question is," he continued, "what are they planning to do with it? That weapons company, for example. They sell most of their product. It's a legitimate business, it makes money. But they don't sell it all. They have warehouses loaded with the stuff. That's not illegal either; any manufacturing business does that. The local regulatory agencies—in the countries that worry about it—will even do spot checks to make sure the inventory is in the warehouse like they say it is. But so long as they're not selling it to prohibited countries, or local criminals, nobody really much cares. As far as the Velkaryans are concerned, the latter is too small a market for them to risk, and the former would open them up to Union enforcement.

"Of course, there are places that aren't so fussy. Some of the colonies, for example. Or now Venezuela." Ducayne made a sour look at that last.

This was mostly new to Carson. He was dimly aware of some of it, from general reading and his short time in the reserves, but it wasn't something he thought much about. "Then they could be arming for . . . something. But there's no real evidence that they are?"

"My job is to worry about capabilities more than probabilities. If someone isn't capable of something, they aren't going to do it. If they do have the capability, then we start worrying about intentions. And the Velkaryans have the capability."

"And we already know their intentions are, well, not good." Carson had had enough personal experience with that.

"Now you're getting it."

"I'm not sure I want to."

Just then Malcolm Brown rapped at the door frame, the office door being still open. "Sorry I'm late, something came up. You wanted to see me?"

"Yes, come on in." Carson rose to leave, but Ducayne stopped him. "Stay, you should hear this too."

"Hear what?" Brown asked.

"Confirmation from Earth. They checked all the reports; local and state police, hospitals, federal authorities, the lot. Rico's body was never found."

"What?" Brown said. "Does that mean he's still alive?"

"No confirmation of that either. We don't think the Velkaryans took him. They'd certainly have no reason to take his body unless they thought he was still alive, but they had some cleanup of their own to do. If he is in their hands, it might not be going well for him."

"You don't think he'd just change sides?" Carson asked. "He switched to ours pretty readily when we were his only way off of Chara III."

"And then he went above and beyond to help you get away from the Velkaryans at Lalande 21185, didn't he? I don't think he likes the Velkaryans. We did some digging into his background."

It was true. Rico might have been a criminal, but he was intelligent and from what Carson had seen, had no love for Velkaryans. He'd blown up their ship at Lalande 21185. "You're right, I shouldn't have said that. But they could have retrieved his body on the off-chance he was still alive, then dumped it somewhere if he wasn't."

Brown wore a sour expression. Rico had been, apparently, killed in a shoot-out at the Denver Spaceport. Brown and Rico had gone to Earth to obtain—steal, as it turned out—the photographs from the original Blue Book files, because the available digitized microfilm copies were unreadable. The Velkaryans also wanted them, and Rico's shoot-out had bought Brown time to get away with the files. "What are we doing about it?" he asked.

"There isn't a lot that we can do," said Ducayne. "Keeping our eyes and ears open for any sign of him, as well as signs of any information that the Velkaryans, or anyone else, might have now that they didn't before, and could have come from Rico. All we know is that by the time the authorities responded to the shoot-out, everyone was gone. Sorry I don't have anything more positive."

"No," Brown said. "That's something, anyway. He would have made a good field agent; he was very resourceful."

He was that, Carson mused.

Chapter 20: Operation Jade Ribbon

Vaughan

Velkaryan HQ, Earth

PROJECTS DIRECTOR Lancaster Hubble finished congratulating the others at the conference table on the success of Operation Piranha. The Velkaryan party had, by massive campaigning as well as bullying, bribing and downright hacking, won the government elections in Venezuela, their most significant win yet. But there would be more to come, both on Earth and off.

"So again," Hubble said, "let me extend the High Command's congratulations to those of you involved with Piranha. But that brings me to the next item. Because of that success, Command wants to accelerate the schedule for Jade Ribbon, and that presents us with a problem."

Operation Jade Ribbon was named for an extremely venomous flying snake native to Verdigris. The operation covered both increasing Velkaryan hold over the planet's regional government, and stepping up the output of their starship factory in New Toronto. If Velkaryan-held planets were ultimately going to declare independence from Earth government, they had to be self-sufficient. If those starships were armed, so much the better. But there were problems with production. While they had a few completed ships, dozens more were on the ground at New Toronto awaiting critical parts. That was bad.

Missed deliveries aside, having them in one place like that increased the risk of discovery. They were usually screened by the floating skyweed over the city, but that wasn't perfect cover. A picture from an overflying spacecraft would be evidence that Homeworld Security, or some similar agency, could take to the *Union de Terre*. The next step could be *UdT* forces dropping and forcing inspections or sanctions, with little even their new Venezuelan presence on the council could do about it. Hubble and the others knew that would come eventually, but they wanted to be prepared for it. They weren't yet. The former Operations Director on Verdigris had, along with his deputy and several technicians, suffered an unfortunate accident during a weapons test. The physical damage had been repaired quickly enough, that wasn't the issue. But the current acting-director just wasn't up to the job.

After some discussion around the table, the consensus was that the New Toronto operation needed some more-forceful oversight. Klaus Vaughan, who had worked for the old Operations Director before being ordered to follow Carson to Zeta Reticuli, was the ideal candidate. Except that he was useful where he was, on Tanith at 82 Eridani, nineteen light-years from Verdigris. And four weeks away, by the time orders reached him.

∞ ∞ ∞

"Do we have anyone else who has been on the ground there and is as good?" Hubble asked.

"Max Lafont is doing a good job for us on Kakuloa. He could be there in under three weeks, if we want to move him."

"He hasn't been to Verdigris in over a year, he's not up on the current situation." Blomberg objected.

"What about someone from here? Lippert has been working Jade Ribbon from this side for a while," Collani, at the far end of the table, said.

"Not him, I need him here. A week or two shouldn't make that much difference. Vaughan it is. Agreed?"

There were murmurs of agreement and nods of assent from around the table.

"Okay, let's tell Vaughan to get his ass back to New Toronto. I assume *Mayflower* is halfway to Tanith by now, so send a message to Verdigris, tell them to courier the orders."

"You're right about the *Mayflower*," Blomberg said, "but her sister ship *Speedwell* is in port and departs tomorrow. A message sent that way will get there close to the same time one via Verdigris does."

"That would mean we don't have to dispatch a ship from there, and would attract less attention," Collani said.

"All right. That still gives him two more weeks to continue organizing at Tanith. Good." Hubble turned to Blomberg. "Send the orders. Give him a couple of days to wrap things up and turn operations over to the local office, but tell him to get to New Toronto asap. We'll have orders waiting for him when he arrives."

"Yes, sir."

"Oh, and include an update of the situation here and on Verdigris. Give him a chance to catch up on the trip."

"Got it," Blomberg said, scribbling away on his data pad.

"And step up training. We need more people capable of taking over large operations on short notice."

Chapter 21: Approaching Tanith

Roberts

Starship Sophie, *deep space near 82 Eridani*

AS PROGRAMMED, the *Sophie* dropped out of warp high above the ecliptic plane of 82 Eridani, avoiding the debris disk, and took high-resolution images to let Roberts ascertain her position in the system.

The three inner, hot super-Earths were easy to pick out from both their optical and infra-red brightness. These all orbited within what would be the orbit of Mercury in the Sol system, rocky worlds nearly three times the mass of Earth, inhospitable to life. *More like super-Venuses than super-Earths,* thought Roberts.

The outer gas giant was also easily spotted, although it was more of a ringless Saturn than a Jupiter. Where was Tanith?

There, a small azure dot in the habitable zone, 118 million kilometers from the yellow star. Although dimmer than Sol, making it as bright as her own Tau Ceti, the difference wasn't noticeable to the eye. There should be an automated beacon in this system, but it wasn't detectable this far out. The *Cerulean Cloud*'s recent visit notwithstanding, this place was still far enough out that it didn't get a lot of traffic.

She checked the database and had the computer cross check the images she'd just taken, then set a course for deeper into the system. Two minutes in warp ought to do it.

∞ ∞ ∞

The *Sophie* picked up the beacon's transmission when she was a bit over a million kilometers from the planet, twice the distance of Tanith's single moon, Anaid. The transmission gave the usual information—which frequencies were monitored, typical approach vectors, specifics of planetary mass, rotation and atmosphere (as if those wouldn't be in every ship's database) and so on. That all assumed a ship was interested in landing at the main settlement, the only one with any kind of spaceport. In practice there was little to prevent her from landing almost anywhere on the planet, local terrain permitting.

Roberts had no reason to avoid the spaceport, and several good reasons to land there. Aside from the package pick-up for Ducayne, she had mail to deliver. The "mail" was mostly electronic, and most of *that* was data dumps to synchronize Tanith's planetary internet with the interstellar net. When she left she'd be taking any local updates with her; interstellar courier fees helped keep her in business, and there were occasionally other perks as well. In Tanith's case, a significant reduction in landing fees. The beacon had told her about those, too. Ben had warned her back on Skead, but she'd been skeptical. There was plenty of empty space on the planet, so the fees were avoidable unless one had good reason to visit Harp City. The fee hike didn't make much sense to her.

There was one other item of information about the spaceport: it was closed for the night. *What?*

Roberts checked the planetary map on another of her control screens. Yes, Harp City was on the dark side of the planet right now; local time was almost two hours until midnight. She had no problem landing in the dark on a prepared field, but there was a local noise ordinance in effect. Apparently, the locals didn't like being woken up by the sound of spacecraft taking off or landing. *Then why put the spaceport so close to town?* Jackie rolled her eyes. On the other hand, the port would save on personnel costs if it didn't have to be staffed around the clock. Any inbound ships would have already been in space for a week or more. If another few hours made a difference, they could declare an emergency. She had plenty of life support reserves; she could wait until morning.

Chapter 22: A New Artifact

Carson

Homeworld Security, Sawyers World

IT WAS THE day after Ducayne's news about Rico's body, or lack thereof, and about the Velkaryans in Venezuela, when he called Carson and Brown into his office again.

"Doctors," Ducayne said as Carson and Brown entered the office, and gestured to the visitor chairs. "Coffee?"

"Certainly. I never turn down your coffee, you get the good stuff. Black please," Brown said.

"Rank does have its privileges."

Brown nodded. "Indeed. You're being solicitous," he said. "What horrible thing are you about to spring on us?"

"You know me too well, Malcolm. I'll get to that in a moment. Carson?"

Carson thought Malcolm might be right about Ducayne's intentions. "No coffee, thanks. But now I am intrigued."

Ducayne handed Brown a cup from the small autochef, then took another and seated himself. He took a sip, paused for a moment, then said, "I see you've been running queries regarding various kinds of cuneiform, the symbols on the Belize wreckage, and any reported markings on vehicles described in the Blue Book files."

"Sure," said Brown, "I told you we were investigating that."

"You did. What you didn't know is that there's another source of alien script, and the search looked at that, too. It found a match."

"What?" Carson sat forward in his chair. This was new. "What script? What did it match?" He hesitated, and then "And why didn't it report it to us, or at least Brown?"

Ducayne held up a hand. "I'll get to that. As to the last, it's because the other item was for my eyes only for now."

"Oh?"

"I had my reasons. Here's the story:

"Two weeks ago I got a message from my agent on Tanith. Apparently, an artifact had been found in the system, high tech but old. I got a description and some images. My agent didn't have the actual artifact in hand at the time."

"Tanith? 82 Eridani?" Carson was confused. "There's never been signs of an intelligent species there. Why would Spacefarers, or the Kesh, be interested?"

"I didn't say Spacefarers, but the place *is* halfway between Sol and Zeta Reticuli. It's on the Betty Hill star map, for whatever that's worth."

Carson scoffed at that. It didn't seem to be worth much, from what Brown had told him. "Where is the artifact now, and what was the context of the finding?"

"As far as I know, still at 82 Eridani. My agent expected to be able to retrieve it shortly and I arranged for a ship to get out there to pick it up. Most likely the *Sophie* if Captain Roberts stuck to her flight plan." Ducayne nodded in Carson's direction. "There are also backup options if not. I haven't heard back yet, but could any day now."

"And the language?" Brown asked.

"Matched the fragments on the Belize wreckage, and also matched—to the same degree of confidence that the description was accurate—the symbol on your Socorro 'close encounter of the second kind.'"

Brown raised his eyebrows. "I'm surprised you know the phrase, you must have been reading my reports."

"I don't ask you to write those just for make-work," Ducayne said.

"Then the Eridani script has curved as well as straight lines?" Carson asked. "Can we see the images?"

"Yes, and yes." Ducayne touched a control to bring up an image on the small wall screen beside his desk.

The screen showed an apparatus of some kind—nothing in the image gave it scale—which could have been a piece of avionics gear, or lab equipment, or even a musical instrument so far as Carson could tell. From the picture, it looked metallic and cylindrical. There was no reference for scale, although if what looked like a display panel and control pads were human-sized, the thing would be maybe a half-meter in diameter. The writing on it looked like labels for controls or read-outs, so more probably a piece of equipment, and not the alien equivalent of a tuba. The marks had a strong stylized-cuneiform feel, similar to those he'd seen on Ketzshanass's communicator back at Zeta Reticuli. Some of the glyphs also included short curved segments, almost like accent marks in some European languages. He could see why the search had picked up the connections.

Carson studied the image. "It certainly looks like industrial or better level technology, not terrestrial. The symbols and general style are nothing like the disintegrator we found back on Chara III, so it probably wasn't something the Spacefarers left."

"The style is similar to what we've seen of the Belize wreckage. If there are markings that match, it would have to be Kesh, wouldn't it?" Brown said. "The Spacefarers were ten-thousand years earlier."

"Right. There's a chance that the Spacefarer written language was different from what we found in the Chara pyramid. They might have designed that to be more pictographic, to be easier for other species to learn once they got in, given that those pyramids seemed to be intended as teaching tools." Carson had another thought, though. "That's even assuming the Belize wreckage *is* Kesh."

"Let's stick with the simplest hypotheses for now," Ducayne interrupted, "although in my business that's hardly ever the case. But it fits better with the Kesh, or perhaps one of the Kesh civil war factions, than anyone else, including your yet unidentified Spacefarers."

Carson bristled a little at that. This whole thing had started because he'd been trying to show some spacefaring connection between several early civilizations on different planets. Outside of a few people in Homeworld Security and perhaps the Velkaryans, everyone believed the last spacefaring species to have been the

Terraformers, back at the time of the dinosaur extinction on Earth. On the other hand, Ducayne was correct; though they now had sufficient evidence that there *were* Spacefarers ten-thousand years before the Kesh, they had yet to find anything to indicate who or what they were, or exactly *why* they built their pyramidal "teaching museums".

"Fair enough. Supposing it is Kesh, and contemporary with the Belize wreck, I don't suppose you have any idea what the damn thing is?"

"No. But I have reason to believe the Velkaryans have heard of it, and are interested. That's another reason for getting to it first. Which brings me to the horrible thing that Malcolm guessed at. I want you to go out to 82 Eridani to see what else is there, and to help bring the artifact back if my agent ran into problems."

Brown set his coffee cup down. "But I'm not a field agent."

"You did fine on Earth. But I meant Carson, not you. He needs to get off-planet for a while, both for his own safety and to throw the Velkaryans off. You're certainly free to go along if you think it worthwhile."

"Uh, no, no. I'm sure Hannibal can handle it."

Carson grinned, the byplay had amused him. But he had questions. "Things are already in motion. By the time I get there, there's a good chance that Jackie or whomever has already picked up the package and is on her way back." He leaned forward in his chair. "Or is there actually more to this? Could Jackie be headed into trouble?"

Ducayne picked up his coffee cup in both hands, then set it down again. "Fair enough. Frankly I'm not certain. If all goes well, the package will be on its way back when you get there and Jackie or one of my other couriers won't have had any trouble, in which case I'd still like you to see if there's anything else of interest in that system."

"And if it doesn't go well?"

"Then I'd want you on the spot as quickly as possible to help turn the situation around. Do what you seem to do best at, retrieve the artifacts and foil the Velkaryans."

"You make me sound like some kind of action hero. It may have worked out that way on Chara, but it was different on Zeta

Reticuli. Roberts saved *my* ass there. And I'm still mending from my little autocab ride."

"I think you and the Kesh both had something to do with what happened at Reticuli, but the fact remains that you're the best person I have available for the job. You'll need a couple of days to prep, and I'll need a bit of time to work out the best way to get *you* to 82 Eridani, too. You can ride in a traumapod for some of the trip, we have some accelerated healing protocols. Will you be wanting to bring your timoan partner?"

"Marten's teaching, as far as I know. It's mid-semester back on Taprobane. It'd be nice to have him along, but I don't think so."

"Very well. That simplifies things." Ducayne stood up, and the others did likewise. "Go get things taken care of," he said to Carson. "Get back with me tomorrow."

"What about me?" Brown asked.

"Help Carson get ready if he needs it—" Carson signaled in the negative "—otherwise see what you can make of the Belize and Tanith artifacts. I'll send you what I have on the latter."

∞ ∞ ∞

Next day

"I've got a ship lined up for you," Ducayne told Carson. "It's a charter out of Sawyer Spaceport. Departs tomorrow, it'll take two weeks to get there."

"Two weeks?" Carson sighed. "Unavoidable, of course. I just wish there was a faster way to travel."

Ducayne eyed him speculatively. "Really?"

"Well, sure. Nothing against space travel but as Jackie always says, 'it's *supposed* to be boring.' I just wish it were faster."

"Be careful what you wish for, friend, you might get it."

Carson examined Ducayne's expression. He was serious. Homeworld Security did have a few tricks up its sleeves, but there was usually a cost. "All right, I'll bite. What do you have?"

"Something like an oversized message torpedo, big enough to hold a traumapod. We load you up, the pod keeps you in medical stasis for duration—which minimizes life support requirements and keeps you from going crazy in the confined space, like a hibernation pod on an emigration ship, and it finishes your healing process—and the torpedo makes the trip in eight days instead of fourteen. To you it will seem like no time at all."

"You're joki . . . No, you don't joke. How does this torpedo get off planet, and better yet, how does it land?"

"The first part's easy, we just lift it to space on a regular ship, same as with regular message torpedoes. It makes its way to the destination planet and the pod awakens you before entry so you're ready to make a rapid egress. Then it enters like an old time ballistic reentry craft and ejects you at a safe parachute altitude. There's a few milligrams of anti-matter left as a self-destruct charge; we don't want this technology generally known. If anyone happens to be watching, it looks like a large meteorite impact."

"And it blows up while I'm nearby dangling from a parachute? I'm not even going to ask what could go wrong, I can already think of a list as long as my arm." Carson thought for a moment. He could see the uses for this in Ducayne's line of business, something akin to the way some agencies on Earth would deploy divers out of submarine torpedo tubes to make covert entry into another country.

"I take it you've used this kind of system before?" Carson added.

Ducayne grinned and nodded, although what he said aloud was "I can neither confirm nor deny, *et cetera, et cetera.*"

Carson still wasn't convinced, and Ducayne obviously read the doubt on his face.

"Look, Carson, I need you on Tanith. Sooner would be better than later but you're a good man and I wouldn't even have suggested it if the odds weren't in your favor. I'd rather you get there late than never."

"Parachute landing, you say. But I'll be completely healed by then, in the pod?"

Ducayne nodded. "Yes."

"I guess I won't be bringing much in the way of gear with me. Can this thing put me somewhere on the planet with reasonable precision? Like, within walking distance of civilization?"

"Heck yes. ICBM precision. The main body will go another hundred kilometers or so before detonating, no worry on that score. Worst case you should be able to contact Roberts on your omni, and we'll give you a backup radio, and she can pick you up."

Carson considered the prospect. What could possibly go wrong? Well, there was mis-jump, meteoroid impact, bad reentry, life-support failure . . . , but those were things that could, potentially, happen on any ship. Travelling this way? He supposed the thing could try to kidnap him like that damned autocab, but if the Velkaryans could hijack Homeworld Security gear he had bigger things to worry about. The pod could get stuck, the parachute could fail, he could make a bad landing, or he could land in the middle of a swamp or ocean . . . . It was all fun and games until somebody drowns or gets burnt to a crisp on entry.

"It sounds like a damn-fool way to travel," Carson finally said "especially for an archeologist, but I've done my share of damn-fool things in my time. Sure, let's go for it."

"Great. In that case, you leave tonight."

Chapter 23: Harp City

Roberts

Harp City Spaceport, next day

ROBERTS CONTACTED the port cargo office as soon as she'd cleared the runway and rolled to the parking area.

"Good morning. I have four crates of Mount Sharon Premium Roast coffee from Tau Ceti as consignment cargo, if you want to send an inspector aboard before offloading," Roberts said over the radio. The cargo office also did duty as the customs office, the immigration office, and the quarantine office. Customs and quarantine tended to get upset if you started offloading before getting their approval.

"Tau Cetan coffee? Did you say roasted?"

"Affirmative. Mount Sharon Premium Roast, from the Tefera farm."

There was a pause, probably while the officer checked the manifest she had transmitted earlier.

"Got it, Sophie. Nope, you're good to unload. We'll send someone out with a pallet and a freight lifter."

"Much appreciated, thank you."

A short while later, with the cargo unloaded and the usual paperwork dealt with, Roberts posted the data to the local broker net. To her surprise, she got a bite immediately, and at a fair price. Someone must have software watching for just such an opportunity. That worked for her. She completed the transaction and then made her way in person to the outgoing cargo office, pleased to have a few extra credits in her local account.

∞ ∞ ∞

"'Smith?' No, we have no package from a Smith. Nothing much at all outgoing anywhere, as a matter of fact. The usual data updates, but nothing for Tau Ceti or Alpha Centauri. We had a ship here a few weeks back, maybe it went with them, or via Earth on the regular run. Although, I don't recall anything from anyone named Smith."

Roberts was in the cargo office at the Harp City spaceport, wondering what had happened to the package she was supposed to pick up. "Well, I suppose Smith is an easy name to forget. But what ship? If it was the *Cerulean Cloud*, I ran into their skipper on Skead, an old friend of mine. He didn't say anything about that."

"Now I'm not saying anything about your friend as such, but you freight runners do tend to keep your business secrets. Not that there's anything wrong with that." The cargo master seemed strangely eager to please without actually being helpful.

As if sensing that thought, he added: "Could it have gone via Earth? Last Solar run was two weeks ago."

She didn't think that likely, but wasn't going to argue the point yet. "I suppose that's possible. Okay, never mind Smith. Any cargo going back in that direction? Alpha Centauri? Or Sol? I'd hate to have made this trip for nothing."

"You can still bill whoever requisitioned you, right? Who did you say it was?"

"I didn't." *Business secrets indeed*, thought Roberts. "Anyway, I'm not leaving right away, I'll be here for a few days. Maybe something will turn up."

"Your choice. Cargo for Sol is pretty much reserved for the *Speedwell* or the *Mayflower*."

Jackie guessed from the names that these were regular immigration ships. If one had left two weeks ago, the other would be due in within the next few days.

"By the way," he continued, "you do know about the docking fee, right? I don't mean the landing fee, more like a parking fee."

"What? For a few square meters of ground? I'm not using any spaceport facilities." Not that there was much to use. "You're not exactly cramped for space here."

"Now, don't bite my head off, I don't make the rules. Some folks on the spaceport board thought it would be a good way to raise money, pay to improve the facilities. Not my idea."

Not that the facilities couldn't stand some improvement. "Yeah, I get it." Roberts fought to hold in her temper. Pissing off the port cargo master was a good way to guarantee she wouldn't get any cargo at all, although if she could find this mysterious Smith and whatever he had to ship to Ducayne, that wouldn't be a problem. *Damn you, Ducayne.*

"Okay, thanks for your time. I guess I'll head into town for a bit. What is there to see?"

"Oh, now, I'm no expert on that. It's not like we have a tourist board or a traveller's aid society. But there's an information kiosk in the main spaceport building lobby, you could check there."

It was all Jackie could do not to roll her eyes. Instead she smiled politely and said "Thank you, I'll do that."

As she turned to leave the cargo master's office, he said "No problem. Glad to be of service."

She wondered if he had any grasp of the level of irony in that statement.

∞ ∞ ∞

As she walked back to the *Sophie*, Jackie pondered her next move. She had to make contact with "Smith", somehow, or put herself in a position where he could contact her. He would know there was a new ship in port; it wasn't as if this place saw a lot of traffic. There were a handful of ships parked on the ramp across the field, longer term parking than where she'd put the *Sophie*. Ships belonging to locals, no doubt. She hadn't paid much attention to them on the way in. They were part of the background; every spaceport had a few. But something looked familiar about one of those ships.

Half of them were S-class ships, perhaps the most common class and inexpensive enough that some owners could afford to let them sit idle—not that she herself could. Two were Sapphires, although Jackie's practiced eye could pick out a few differences from her own *Sophie*. But that larger one, the Y-class, wasn't decked out the way she would expect a cargo ship to be. Nor would a cargo ship be likely to be in long term storage unless it needed maintenance or repair work; it didn't make money if it wasn't flying cargo. But this one looked like it was fitted more as an upscale charter, or even a personal yacht. It had more than the usual number of windows, and personnel hatches instead of cargo doors. Why did it look so familiar? And then she remembered, and froze. It was the *Carcharodon*, the Velkaryan ship they'd had a run-in with back at Zeta Reticuli. What was it doing *here*?

She mulled that over as she got over her surprise and continued back to her ship. Yes, 82 Eridani was on a path back from there if they'd needed to refuel, but that was weeks ago, why was it still here? Had it been more seriously damaged than she thought? It had taken a hit from an alien energy beam, but it had flown again after that, pursuing the *Sophie* until the Kesh intervened. What had the Kesh done? Had the *Carcharodon* been here ever since? Or somewhere else? Maybe it was on its way back . . . but then why the long-term parking?

Suddenly Jackie was very glad that her *Sophie* looked like any other Sapphire model, with its functional hull colors and utilitarian styling. Then she remembered that she'd broadcast her identity to all and sundry when she'd requested landing clearance, and her gut tightened. *Damn!*

She considered her options. Would they hold a grudge? Yeah, Velkaryans. Sure they would. She didn't have anything they wanted right now, but they wouldn't know that, and might want some level of revenge for Zeta Reticuli. Did this tie into Ducayne's interest in something here? Silly question, of course it must.

Jackie tapped a sequence into her omni, checking that the *Sophie*'s security systems were still operative and that nothing unusual had happened while she was at the cargo office. She felt a lot more paranoid now than ten minutes ago. All clear. With a sigh of relief, she keyed another sequence and the hatch slid open. She entered the control cabin and slumped into her command chair. Now what?

If the *Carcharodon* crew were staying in town rather than at the spaceport, they might not yet know she was here. They had no reason to expect her. She had some time. She turned and looked around the *Sophie*'s cabin. She had spent all but a few days of the last month here. *Screw this*, she decided. She was going into town for some real food. The *Carcharodon* crew didn't know what she looked like, she could hit the main hotel or whatever passed for it without attracting unusual attention. And maybe Smith was staying there too. She just had to figure out how to attract his attention.

∞ ∞ ∞

Roberts considered her options. She had local credit from her commission on the cargo, plus the courier fees earned from the net data updates and email from Tau Ceti. The increased landing fees had taken a bigger chunk than usual out of that, but she had some. She could afford to eat at the hotel a few times, but perhaps not to stay there. She had off-world credit secured by her blockchain keys, but many places discounted that because of the processing delays.

The problem was to figure out a way to get her contact's attention. All she knew was a name, Smith, which wouldn't be his real name but might at least be what he was going by locally. He wouldn't know her from Eve, but at least being a recently-arrived off-worlder should attract his attention, assuming he was expecting a contact. He had to be, the natural reaction to the messages he'd sent Ducayne would be to send someone back to follow up.

Ducayne, that was it. What was the name he'd used on that message, *Quiche Desjardins*? Two could play that game. She went back to her cabin, sat cross-legged on her bunk, and grabbed a computer pad. Time to see just what the ship's fabber was capable of in the clothing department. But first she needed an image of a playing card. It had to be big, it had to be flashy, and it had to be the Queen of Diamonds.

∞ ∞ ∞

Several hours later, after some adjustments and settings which Jackie hadn't used before, the fabber put the final touches on a dark green synth-leather ship jacket, the back panel emblazoned with the image of the Queen of Diamonds, and on the front, over her left breast, a calligraphic letter **Q** outlined by a diamond, picked out in rhinestones. It wasn't embroidered, but for all Jackie could tell it might well have been. It fit perfectly, of course, and she had already swapped her baggy but comfortable ship coveralls for a flight suit that fit more snugly, and looked a little dressier. Not her captain's dress uniform, which wasn't the image she needed to convey. Dressed up, but approachable, maybe a little tough. She thought for a moment, then strapped on a sidearm. Not *too* approachable.

She checked her omni. It was time to go for dinner. She headed back to the aft compartment. Taking an autocab into town was an option but not one she chose. It would cost credits and project the wrong image. She had her motorbike; small, easily stowed, and designed for streets or rugged terrain. Just the thing for short excursions planet-side, and perfect for tonight.

Jackie lowered the aft cargo ramp and wheeled the bike down it. She straddled it, donned her helmet, then watched as, at command sequence from her omni, the Sophie retracted the ramp and sealed the aft door. Her omni's nav system had already synched to the bike's dash display. With a whine from the bike's motor, she steered around her ship and headed for the starport gate, then into town.

∞ ∞ ∞

The Wheatley was no Hotel Interplanetary, but it wasn't horrible. Harp City was growing, but it was too distant to attract upscale tourists from Earth. That was just as well; she was looking for somewhere more relaxed, but a step up from a bar. If Ducayne's man was smart—and if he was Ducayne's man, he would be—he might think to check the hotels after a ship landed. Besides, she really did want some good food.

There were a few other patrons in the restaurant, and Jackie noticed a few heads turn her way as she entered. So far, so good. As long as Vaughan's crew wasn't here. She didn't think they would recognize her, she'd been a hundred meters away and shooting at them back on Zeta Reticuli, so they'd kept their heads down. On the other hand, someone might remember her green hair. Oh well.

A waiter took her order and she sat back with a glass of wine, idly glancing about at the other diners. There was a young man, sitting alone, who kept eying her. He seemed to be gathering the nerve to talk to her. Sure enough, after a minute he stood up and walked over.

"Uh, hi. You by yourself? I am too. Would you like some company?"

Somehow this did not seem like her contact. He seemed a bit young and unsure of himself, although that could be part of the cover.

"Actually, I'm waiting for somebody." She casually moved her hand to her thigh, near where her pistol was holstered. That shouldn't intimidate anyone working for Ducayne.

"Oh, uh, oh." He took a step back.

"But thanks for asking," she said, softening the rejection. This wasn't John Smith.

"Well, enjoy your dinner."

"Thanks." She looked around once more. Nobody else seemed to be paying attention. She hadn't really expected it to be that easy.

The waiter arrived with her dinner, placing the plate in front of her and warning that it was hot. Then from his apron pocket he withdrew a folded slip of paper. "Uh, excuse me ma'am, but there was a gentleman here who was leaving shortly after you came in. He asked me to pass this to you." He handed her the note.

She took it and opened it. "Diamond Lady," it began, "Sorry, but I have an appointment to keep. Same time tomorrow?" It was signed with the initials "J.S." John Smith? Had she just missed him? The "Diamond Lady" at least seemed to acknowledge her signal.

"Everything all right, ma'am?"

"Yes, fine, thank you. Can I get a refill on the wine?"

"Of course." The waiter departed, leaving Roberts in thought. She hadn't noticed anyone passing a note to the waiter, or leaving as she came in, but that didn't prove anything. She could have just missed it, especially if "J.S." hadn't wanted to call attention to himself.

Tomorrow night it would have to be.

Chapter 24: Carson's Other Ride

Carson

Aboard the system boat Aspis

"OKAY, DOCTOR CARSON, if you'll come with me back to the cargo bay we'll get you set."

They were aboard the *Aspis*, a ship designed for shuttle flights between Sawyers World, around Alpha Centauri A, and Kakuloa, orbiting Alpha Centauri B. Most of the trip time was on regular thrusters, to and from the planets' surfaces. The warp jump between the two stars took twenty seconds, so what on a deep-space starship might be fuel tankage had been built out as cargo space. This particular ship's cargo bay could be depressurized and had a large bay door to allow message torpedoes—or other small spacecraft—to be deployed or retrieved.

Hannibal Carson looked over the passenger torpedo. At five meters long, *it* took up a good portion of the cargo bay's length, but it was less than two meters wide at its widest. A long, slender cone with a rounded base, not unlike those old ICBM warheads whose precision Ducayne had compared it to. This, of course, was considerably bigger than those had been, and with two kilograms of antimatter fuel, had the potential to pack a bigger punch than even the largest ICBM.

And he was going to *ride* in the damn thing!

"All right, sir, if you just float over here we'll get you secured into the pod."

They were in orbit, and so weightless, and over his regular clothes Carson wore a lightweight pressure suit. He wore a helmet with its visor open; if needed, it would close automatically, and the bailout bottle strapped to his thigh would provide air.

The pod itself was nestled in the middle of the oversized torpedo, whose aft section was currently unlatched and pivoted back on hinges. The pod, what Carson could see of it, was a custom design, similar to a civilian hibernation pod or a traumapod, but without all the latter's surgical gear. Its door was also open, with the patient table or bed extended on its slide rails.

The technician guided Carson into the pod, and began securing him to the padded table surface loosely with straps. "These are just to keep you from floating around in there, they'll yield if you pull hard enough. There's an emergency switch beside your right hand; you shouldn't need it." He slid the bed halfway into the pod.

Carson felt gently along the right edge of the bed. It was more of a pull handle than a switch. "Got it."

"Okay. Now, let me hook this up." He pushed Carson in a little farther then grasped a cable attached to the instrumented cuff around Carson's upper left arm, and reached in to plug it into a socket inside the pod housing. "Not strictly necessary, the pod can read your signs without it and can insert an IV if needed. Again, it shouldn't be needed; the drug, hiberzine, is delivered through the air supply. When you wake up, a feeding tube will be positioned within reach of your mouth, it'll supply a nutrient and sugar rich fluid to help wake you up and give you energy for the entry phase. It *will* IV you if you don't drink from it within a few minutes after the pod thinks you should be awake."

"Okay, so wake up, take a drink."

"You've got it. You'll be in zero gee; the plan is to wake you up a couple of hours from the planet so you have time to come fully awake and assess the situation."

"Assess the situation? Is there anything I can do if something's wrong?"

The tech grinned. "Well that depends on what's wrong, but you can abort the entry sequence, establish an orbit, and send a radio signal. That might prove helpful. Although you might want to eject before a rescue ship comes close, the torpedo will still want to self-destruct if approached by an unknown."

Lovely, Carson thought. "Is the *Sophie* an unknown?"

"Roberts' ship? Let me check." The tech did something on his omniphone. "No worries, the *Sophie* has a Homeworld Security transponder; the torpedo will recognize it."

"Okay. If something does go wrong let's hope she's the one who rescues me." Something about that last phrase gave Carson pause. He and Roberts seemed to be doing a lot of rescuing each other lately. They really should find a better way to get together.

"So, assuming things go well—and they should—you'll stay in the traumapod for the peak heating of entry, then the pod will eject and stabilize on a drogue 'chute while the rest of the torpedo goes on farther to play meteorite. It will airburst while you're still in the pod, between that and the distance you'll be fine. Then at a couple of thousand meters the pod will pop you out. If it doesn't—" The tech reached in to activate a small screen above Carson's face "—this screen will show your altitude. If you still haven't ejected by 1500 meters, pull the emergency handle by your right hand."

"Got it." Carson had been briefed on this already, but he didn't object to the refresher.

"It's a smart chute. It will seem a bit fast at first but nearer the ground it will open further, and glide you down nice and gentle. Just to be safe, keep your legs together and roll with the impact. May look a bit silly if you're coming in slow, but better than a broken leg if you're not."

"Actually, I have jumped once before, but that was years ago."

"Oh? Sport or military?"

"Military, a training exercise."

"Well, good. This will be similar, but don't get overconfident."

"What's the rest of the traumapod doing all this while?"

"It will have hit the ground before you do. It'll be pretty broken up. If you're near enough to civilization you think it might be found, go ahead and cover up the pieces, but there's nothing unusual about it that would survive the impact. Hiding it is more so nobody gets to wondering if someone came down in it. Hide your chute too, although it'll disintegrate in a few days."

"Uh, it's okay now, though, right?"

"No worries. Built in sensors assure me that it is, and the re-action doesn't start until it's opened. Now, if you're all set, let me finish sealing you up. You should be asleep within a minute."

Carson took a deep breath and let it out. "Okay. Oh, quick question . . . ever done this yourself?"

The tech grinned. "No, but I once had to bail out of a ship using something similar."

"Ah, okay."

"If it makes you feel better—" the tech lowered his voice "—I probably shouldn't tell you this, but I *have* done this side of the process before, and I did see the, ah, passenger again a couple of months later, so he survived."

That did make him feel better, a little. "Okay, thanks. Button me up."

The tech touched a switch and the bed slid rest of the way into the pod. Carson heard sounds of the hatch being secured. The pod's interior light began to dim, and before it was all the way out, Carson was asleep and sliding into a medical coma.

Chapter 25: The Whereabouts of Smith

Vaughan

Vaughan's HQ, Harp City Church of Divine Stellar Providence

"SMITH DIDN'T GO anywhere interesting tonight, boss. He might have known we were tailing him."

"What happened?"

"He went to the restaurant at the hotel, the Wheatley, ate a meal. Checked his omni a few times like he was looking at the time, not any messages. At least, he didn't send any. He kept an eye on who came and went. Then he got up and left."

"Anyone come in or leave about the time he left? Maybe he was following somebody."

"Nobody left. A gal came in just before. Jumpsuit, leather jacket, big sparkly design on it. Eye-catching. Haven't seen her around before. She might have come in on that Sapphire that landed this morning."

"Huh. Did she pay any attention to Smith?"

"Nope. Walked in, got seated at a table, ordered wine. Young guy came up to her, but it looked like she gave him the brush off. Smith was already on his way out, so we didn't stay."

"Where did he go from there?"

"He wandered toward the warehouse district. Stayed on foot rather than calling a cab, so we couldn't track him that way. Walked around for about an hour. Either he was looking for something but wasn't sure of the address, or he knew he was being tailed."

"So, you were sloppy, and he saw you."

"No, boss. We gave him plenty of space, traded off following him."

"In the warehouse district. At night." Vaughan shook his head. "Don't you suppose he found it a little odd to have so many people wandering around there at that time? There's not much night life in that part of town."

"Aw, geez. What were we supposed to do?"

"Next time, see if you can plant a tracker on him. If he's wandering around there, odds are the item is in a crate waiting for shipment."

"Okay, we hack into the databases and see what's recently manifested for outbound. How hard can that be?"

"Hard enough." Vaughan knew it was possible, especially if the computer security was as lax as it often was. A few hours of computer time to brute-force some keys or snoop network traffic could do it. But there was no single system covering all the warehouses, they were owned or operated by several different small companies. It would days or weeks to try each of them, and if they had good security, perhaps without success at all. "If we can narrow it down to one company or one warehouse, the odds are better."

"Is it really that big a deal? We have other things to be doing here."

Vaughan's temper flared. "I know exactly what it is we need to be doing. And we're doing them. But I also want to know why the Homeworld Security agent-in-residence is sniffing around warehouses and making arrangements for something to be shipped out."

The thought had occurred to Vaughan that the whole thing was a charade on Homeworld Security's part to smoke out or confuse Velkaryan operations here. The rumors of an alien artifact were a little too convenient in light of what he had heard about Chara III, and what they had seen in the Zeta 1 Reticuli system. But he couldn't be certain of that, and if it was a high-tech alien artifact, the Velkaryans had to have it.

Chapter 26: Rendezvous

Roberts

Hotel Wheatley restaurant, next night

ROBERTS RETURNED TO the restaurant at the Hotel Wheatley the next evening. She had spent the day on routine ship maintenance, making sure it was fueled up and ready for space on short notice, before changing into the outfit she'd worn the previous evening.

Again, she looked around on entering the restaurant. There were a few solo diners, but nobody she recognized from the previous evening. But then, if Smith had left just as she arrived, she might not have seen him at all.

She noticed a couple of heads turn to look at her as she entered and was shown to a table, but then she wasn't exactly inconspicuous. One man had glanced up briefly then return to whatever he was looking at on his omni. As she sat, she saw him look up again, not at her, but around at the rest of the room. As though he might be looking to see who might be watching her. Her waiter, the same one who had slipped her the note the previous evening, caught her eye and then tilted his head in the direction of the seated man, who was back to looking at his omni. Jackie raised an eyebrow questioningly. The waiter nodded slightly. She nodded back. He took her drink order and left.

The waiter returned with her drink, and as he left her table, the man who'd been looking at his omni stood up and took a couple of steps in her direction, calling out "Hey there, Diamond

Lady. Sorry, I didn't see you come in. I don't know where my head was at."

Well, that was one approach. The note had also addressed her as "Diamond Lady," a clear reference to the Queen of Diamonds emblazoned on the back of her jacket. She looked back at him, not quite in acknowledgment but open to further contact. He came over.

"Hello, John," she said to him, then in a quieter voice: "It is John, isn't it?" Worst case, if this wasn't her contact, he might think she meant something else. She'd deal with that if she had to.

"For you, my queen, I'd be a Jack, but the last name is Smith. Sorry about last night, I really did have an appointment."

Bingo. Maybe. "Have a seat. If you're not who I'm waiting for, at least you'll keep the others at bay."

As he sat, he looked pointedly at her sidearm and nodded. "You realize, of course, this hotel has a peace-bond transmitter."

"High class. I suppose you know how easy it is to hack an override?"

Smith grinned. "So, are you a card player, Miss . . . ?"

"Call me Sophie," Roberts said.

"Sophie. That's a mighty fine Queen of Diamonds on your jacket. Do you play?"

"Not much. Solitaire gets old quickly."

"Solitaire? That's not much of a game for a lady like you."

"Which is why I don't play it. What about you?" She paused, then: "Poker?"

A brief frown crossed his face at that last word, as if he wasn't sure he'd heard her right. Jackie smiled inwardly and raised an eyebrow at him.

Smith's frown had gone, his face neutral. He grinned, then said: "Hardly. I knew a guy back on Sawyers World though, great poker player. Queer duck, he was."

"Oh? Sounds like someone I met once. I imagine he'd be a good poker player, he was *quite* devious."

Smith gave a short nod, then leaned in and lowered his voice. "Okay, so QD sent you?"

"Ducayne, yes. I'm a courier, my ship is the *Sophie*."

"Ah, and for now Jack works fine for me, but the name is actually Burnside, Jordan Burnside. And you're Captain . . . ?"

"Roberts, Jacqueline Roberts. And yes, I go by Jackie," she added at his raised eyebrow. "And I do want dinner. What's your schedule?" She didn't want to have to just take the package and fly, but surely a few hours wouldn't make a difference.

"More flexible than I'd like. We can chat while you eat, I was hanging here hoping to make contact."

"With me? Have you been coming here every night?"

"Not quite. I guessed Ducayne would send someone and I guesstimated the time frame, but there's another contact I need to make." "By the way, that Queen of Diamonds was inspired. I had no clue who to expect, but Quentin likes his little jokes."

His use of Quentin reassured Jackie; she hadn't mentioned that name. "Is this in relation to the pickup I'm here for?"

"Yes. I expected to have the package in hand before now, but, ah, complications arose."

"Do you have an ETA?"

"That's one of the complications."

Just then her meal arrived. Burnside ordered a coffee. He'd already eaten, and didn't want to stay much longer.

"I have a couple of other places to check for my other contact. Are you staying here at the hotel?"

"No, aboard my ship at the spaceport."

"Would you mind if I came by later? To talk, that is. The situation here merits discussion but I'd rather it was somewhere more private."

Roberts thought about it briefly. She wasn't worried about Burnside, as a charter pilot her ship had systems which could quickly deal with unruly passengers—or potential hijackers—and in a hurry if needed. But if someone was tailing him . . . well, she'd probably burned that bridge already. "Okay. It's the *Sophie*, a Sapphire. Shouldn't be too hard to find."

"No. All right then, I'll be by late this evening. If you don't hear from me by tomorrow—" he paused, considering "—did Ducayne give you any other instructions?"

"No. I guess he didn't think there'd be problem, or he thought I could handle it if there was."

"He's probably right, but if you don't hear from me by to-morrow noon, check his message for a hidden attachment."

"Check for . . . ? There was nothing else."

"You might be surprised. Could be timed to reveal itself after you arrived here. Or there's nothing. Anyway, I'll contact you by then."

As far as Jackie knew, there was no way to hide, or time-delay, an attachment using standard messaging software. However, 'standard' was a term that rarely applied within Ducayne's organization. "Got it. Noon tomorrow. I don't suppose there's any way to reach you?"

"Sorry, no, best not. I'll be in touch, probably tonight." With that he finished his coffee and stood up. "All right, Diamond Lady, until later then." He put a hand on her shoulder and leaned forward, whispering "let's make this look good" in her ear before kissing her cheek like an old friend.

She paused but a fraction of a second before rising slightly from her chair and kissing his cheek in return. "Later, Jack."

As he turned and left, she sat back down and picked up her fork. She held it a while, paying no attention to her food, trying to decide how she felt about the whole situation. It was certainly a change from the usual—hopefully—boredom of interstellar space. *I wonder what Carson is up to?* she wondered. Then: *And where did* that *come from?*

Chapter 27: Approaching Convergence

Carson

Deep space, approaching 82 Eridani

CARSON SNAPPED AWAKE. The interior of the pod was dimly lit, and he was still weightless. *It didn't work!*

Then he noticed the feeding tube on the little mechanical arm in front of his face, and how weak and hungry he felt. The screen in front of him lit up, with text on it. It took him a moment to focus on the words, and meanwhile a soft voice came from a speaker somewhere in the pod. "You have reached your destination. Please drink some nutrient."

Reaching the feeding tube was relatively easy, he didn't have to lift the weight of his head against gravity. He took a sip. The fluid had a slight flavor of salty orange, and sweet, with a hint of savory aftertaste. It would never be a popular soft drink, but it did the job. He took a deeper swig. *Might not be bad with a little vodka and ice*, Carson thought. Another swig. Either the beverage or something the pod was putting in his breathing air worked quickly, he was already feeling stronger and more alert. The stuff would make a pretty good hangover cure, too.

Okay, let's see what's up. "Status report," he said. The pod's computer would be linked with the ship's—or rather torpedo's— computer, and both would take basic voice commands.

"We are in the outer reaches of the 82 Eridani system. We have dropped out of warp for position fixes. All systems are nominal."

'Nominal'. That was a relief. "Thank you. How long to Tanith?"

"I am still obtaining a precise position and velocity fix. Impossible to state at this time."

"Approximation to the hour is fine." *Stupid computer.*

"Approximately six hours to entry."

Six hours in this tube? "Why waken me so early?"

"A minimum of four hours normal sleep is recommended after waking from hibernation before activity."

"You woke me up to tell me to go to sleep?"

"That is correct."

Irony was lost on this computer. But Carson had to admit he did feel strangely tired, considering he had been asleep—well, technically in a coma—for the past week. "All right, wake me in four hours."

"Affirmative."

One of the valuable skills Carson had learned in the army was how to go to sleep quickly. Part of that, at least for Carson, was to have a wake-up plan. There *was* something he would need to do.

"Computer, can you establish a stealth radio link with Captain Roberts and/or the *Sophie?*"

"By stealth radio link, do you mean one not using normal radio channels?"

"Yes."

"We are out of range for such contact, even if Captain Roberts and/or the *Sophie* are equipped with the correct equipment."

Of course we are. "But if the *Sophie* has it and we're within range?"

"Yes."

"Fine, that's all." Carson wondered if it was just him, or if this ship's computer was particularly obtuse. Whatever. He closed his eyes and dropped off to sleep for the next few hours.

Chapter 28: An Unexpected Caller

Roberts

Aboard the Sophie

PING-PING. JACKIE ROBERTS lay asleep in her small cabin aboard ship. *Ping-ping.* She always slept more soundly when on-planet, without the constant low whirr of life-support fans and power system pumps. *Ping-ping!* The insistent chime of the comm system finally broke into her consciousness. *Ping-ping!* PING-PI— Roberts slapped a hand down on the comm button.

"This is the *Sophie*. Who is hailing?" As she came wider awake, she realized the signal was coming in over the suit-to-ship channel. What the . . . ?

"Sophie, *this is Jordan Burnside. I'll be there in two minutes. Permission to come aboard?*"

"Uh, what? Ah, roger that. Affirmative." She could ask questions when he got here. It occurred to her that Burnside might be using the suit channel to avoid eavesdroppers. It was unlikely anyone would be listening on those frequencies here planet-side, and by default the comms would be encrypted to a specific ship's ID. How had Burnside gotten hold of that? *Ducayne.*

She rolled out of her bunk and pulled on her ship-suit. Another change planet-side; in space she'd sleep in it, often as not. Shaking her head to help clear it—she should have avoided the wine at dinner—she called out "Sophie! Coffee!" It was a sign of how tired she was; she almost never used the *Sophie*'s voice interface. She'd heard too many stories of solo captains who started developing weird relationships with their vehicles because it was the only verbal interaction they had for days or weeks at a time. She didn't need that. Sure, she loved her ship, but not *that* way. In the end it was just a machine.

As she reached the galley to get her coffee, the perimeter warning sounded and then came a thumping at the main hatch. *One of these days I should put in a doorbell*, she thought, and clicked the selector on the galley screen to view the hatch camera image. It was Burnside. She keyed the control to open the outer hatch, then shut it again as he entered, leaving him locked in the airlock.

There was another thump, this time on the inner hatch, then Burnside found the intercom button and his voice came. *"Captain Roberts? It's Burnside, I'm alone. Can I come in?"*

Jackie had walked forward to the hatch and palmed it open. "Welcome aboard. Not quite the timing I was expecting, it's what, three AM?"

"Sorry about that. Hazard of the job. Is that coffee? I'd love some."

"All right, come on back to the galley," she said, gesturing the way. "So, this couldn't wait until morning?"

"Wanted to make sure I got here before noon."

"The days aren't *that* short here." She handed him coffee. "Have a seat, I think I need some explanations."

Burnside winced as he sat down. Under the galley lights he seemed a bit pale. "Sure, what—" he gasped and held a hand to his side "—what did you want to know?"

"Are you all right?" She looked him over. His dark shirt made it hard to tell, but his hand was red where he'd pressed it against himself. "Are you bleeding?"

"Probably. It's nothing." The last was through gritted teeth.

Jackie got up and went over to him. "I'll be the judge of that. Let me see." She pulled his hand away. The shirt was wet. Red fluid dripped from it onto the deck. Blood.

She began to lift his shirt up.

"No, really—"

She slapped his hand away. "You're on my ship, you'll do as your told." She continued to pull up the shirt, but it was stuck to the wound. "Did you put quick-clot on it?"

"Uh, yeah."

"You're not supposed to do that through clothing."

"I was in a hurry."

"Let's get you to the traumapod. What happened?"

"I don't need a 'pod. A bandage and I'll be fine. Maybe a staple or some wound glue."

"The pod can do that for you. Clean the wound, too."

She looked at it as best she could while helping him to the med-bay. There was a several-centimeter gash in the shirt, not noticed at first because the clotting agent holding it to his skin. The blood loss didn't look serious, it didn't look like the abdominal wall had been punctured.

"Were you shot, or is that a knife wound?"

"Would you believe I scraped it climbing over the spaceport fence?"

"No." She thumbed a switch on the traumapod and the bed slid out. "Lie down."

"I can't stay."

"Let it check you out. If it's only a scratch the pod will clean it up and bandage it better than I could. If your abdomen did get punctured, you need to be in there, stat. That's an order."

"I'm not crew."

"One more word and I'll have the anti-hijack system knock you out. That's a lot less comfortable than the traumapod anesthetic."

"All right. Leave me conscious. I need to fill you in."

"Done. Now lie down."

As he did so, Jackie touched a sequence on the pod's control panel. The bed retracted most of the way, stopping short to leave Burnside's head exposed.

There was a brief whirring as the pods internal scanners checked Burnside out, then mechanical noises as its internal robot arms began to cut the shirt away and debride the wound. Burnside grimaced.

"Want a local?" Jackie asked.

"Uh, sure. Be easier to talk."

She touched the control panel again and a brief hiss sounded from within the pod. "Better?"

"Yeah, thanks."

"Okay, now, tell me what's going on. Start with whether I should expect anyone else to be hammering on my airlock."

"I don't think so. Nobody was chasing me, if that's what you mean. Nobody should know I was headed here."

"Good. So, what happened?"

"I made contact," Burnside said, then grinned wryly.

"With someone who didn't want to be contacted?" Jackie nodded toward where the traumapod was busy cleaning Burnside's wound.

"There was someone else who didn't want me to make contact. I don't think he wanted competition."

"Competition for what, exactly?"

"The package you're supposed to pick up."

"Which is . . . ?"

"Alien technology."

"Why am I not surprised?" Everything she'd been involved with since meeting Ducayne seemed to have something to do with alien technology. Before that, even, considering how they'd first met.

"Roberts. The *Sophie*. You were on Chara III, weren't you? With the archeologist?"

"Hannibal Carson, yes. You heard about that?"

"It was in a briefing. Come to think of it, weren't you also in the Zeta Reticuli system?"

Roberts felt herself come to full alert; the hair on the back of her neck rose, and she felt her stomach tighten. How had news of that reached here ahead of her? *Carcharodon?* She did some quick mental math. She had made a side trip, and Ducayne had message torpedoes. Okay, it was plausible without Burnside having a connection to the Velkaryans. She relaxed a bit. "What does that have to do with the package I'm picking up? It didn't come from there, did it? We were warned off."

"I don't know where it came from. But I remember mention of an anomaly in the signals from the warning beacons. Was there?"

Jackie thought back. She'd broadcast a hail when the *Sophie* entered the Reticuli system. They then detected two anomalous signals, one when their broadcast would have reached halfway to the terraformed planet in the system, and the second from the planet itself, too soon for her broadcast to have reached it. If whatever had triggered the first signal had sent a message torpedo at warp to the planet, that would account for it, but there had been no evidence of something entering warp then.

"Yeah, you could call it that. You must have had a pretty in-depth briefing."

"It was. Secretive as Ducayne is, if he thinks an agent has a need to know, he makes sure they know as much as possible. Or at least as much as the opposition is likely to. This anomaly, would FTL radio explain it?"

"FTL radio is an oxymoron, radio is a kind of light. But yes, an FTL signal of some kind would explain it. We thought it might be a message torpedo with too weak a warp signature for the *Sophie*'s instruments to detect."

"We think it might be an FTL communicator. Maybe gravity waves, or something. But it would explain a few other things."

"An FTL communi . . . ." Jackie's voice trailed off as she considered the implications. It wouldn't be gravity waves, at least not through normal space. But the energy from warp drives mostly bled off through extra dimensions; could there be a connection? That could change everything about interstellar travel—and the courier business—as she knew it. "And that's what this package is?"

"We have no idea, but the very possibility makes it worth in-vestigating. It would also explain why the Velkaryans are inter-ested. We have some hints they already have a pair of them."

"A pair?"

"Obviously just one doesn't do much good, and if it's alien technology we may not be able to figure out how it works, let alone reproduce it. If that's even what it is."

"But one might let you eavesdrop on Velkaryan communica-tions, if they do have a pair."

"Depends on the technology, but yes, maybe. Whatever it is, if it's alien and it's high tech, we want it."

"Yet another cosmic Maguffin."

"I was thinking more of the Polish Enigma machine."

"The what now?"

"Mid twentieth century, just before World War II. The Nazis had an encryption machine called the Enigma. Poland had a copy of one. The story goes that Polish cryptanalysts got it to England before the war broke out, and helped the English crack the Enigma code."

"You seem to know quite a bit about it."

"Call it professional interest."

An indicator light on the traumapod changed color, accompanied by a soft *ding*. It had finished suturing Burnside's wound.

"Looks like you're done, Jordan." Jackie touched the panel and the traumapod bed slid out. "Can you sit up?"

Burnside swung his legs around then sat up, wincing a bit as he did so. "Still a bit sore, but yeah. Thank you."

"Looks like you could use a new shirt."

The man was well muscled, Jackie noted. If he had a desk job, he also worked out. There were several scars on his torso and arms; one might have been an old bullet wound.

She realized she was staring. "I think I have spares. Wait one."

She stepped over to a storage drawer, rifled through it briefly, and pulled out a package containing a dark blue tee-shirt. She handed it to him. "That should fit."

"You're well equipped." He glanced at her chest. Jackie snorted. She was hardly flat, but she took it as meaning the spare shirt.

"I used to have a co-pilot, and you're about his size. Uniform came with the job, but there are no logos on the undershirt."

"I'm just thankful the color isn't pink or bright yellow."

Roberts grinned. "Dark colors hide the dirt, and for what it's worth, the *Sophie* is named after a warship."

"Hey, no offense meant."

"None taken. So, about this gizmo. Where did it come from and who has it?"

"Not certain on the former, possibly this system, but I don't think anywhere on Tanith. One of the outer moons, perhaps. I heard a rumor of it just before a Velkaryan ship showed up, so I assumed there was a connection."

"Velkaryan ship? You mean the *Carcharodon*?"

"You know it?"

"Had a run-in with it at Zeta Reticuli. I wondered why it was here. But you said *before* it arrived?"

"Yes."

"I don't see how they could have known about it then. Carson said they took some hull damage, nothing major, but if they've been here more than a week or two, the timing doesn't fit with them coming here from anywhere but Zeta Reticuli, at least not from anywhere inward and then back out here. When did they arrive?"

"They've been here for, oh, six or seven weeks now," Burnside said. "But the port arrival board showed them coming from Alpha Mensae."

"Same general direction, and they could have lied." She thought about it. Between her own indirect return to Sawyers World from Zeta Reticuli, and then dropping Marten back at Taprobane before heading on to Tau Ceti, plus the time getting here from there, the *Sophie* had left Zeta Reticuli nearly eight weeks ago now. Two weeks' travel time from Zeta Reticuli to here was about right, if they pushed their range limit and came direct. "They must have come straight from Zeta Reticuli and they've been here ever since. That's interesting. Why, I wonder?"

"A few days to fix the damage you said they had. If they heard about the artifact in the meantime, they might want to get hold of it themselves, and are getting the same run around I am." He frowned. "Communication with the seller has all been by email, and they've kept putting off the meeting . . . until a few days ago."

"There's also been agitation lately about the few timoan settlers on Tanith," Burnside continued. "The Velkaryans may well be behind that. Then there are subtle things like the landing fee hike."

"So much for a simple cargo pick-up job," said Roberts with a sigh. "What now?"

"Tell me what you know about the *Carcharodon*."

"Not much, I'm afraid. Carson could tell you more, they had him aboard for a while, so most of what I know I got from him." She proceeded to fill Burnside in on the details, what she knew of them, of Carson's capture by the Velkaryans, the *Carcharodon*'s run in with an automated defense system, and his escape and her rescue of him.

"The guy in charge was named Vaughan," Roberts continued, "but he wasn't the captain. There were at least three others aboard, the captain and two crew that Carson saw, there may have been others. You've seen the *Carcharodon*, you know it's a Y-class ship, so room for as many as a half-dozen more. Port landing records should have passenger and crew details, if you can access them."

"Vaughan, you say?"

"That's what Carson told me, why?"

"A man with that name has been involved in local politics lately, the last four or five weeks as a matter of fact. I wondered if he was the same person as a known Velkaryan. If he came on the *Carcharodon*, that would confirm it."

"Why do Velkaryans care about local politics? Are there natives on Tanith?"

"None sentient, if that's what you mean. But there are a few timoan settlers on Tanith, and lately someone has been trying to stir up fear and resentment about them. As far as Tanith-origin though, I haven't heard of any archeological evidence of that, although that's not my field. Your boyfriend would know."

"My boyfr- what? What makes you think Carson is my boyfriend?"

"Oh, sorry. It's just that . . . never mind. My mistake."

The part of Roberts that wasn't seething with indignation allowed as how he might have a point. She and Carson had had a fling once, and despite the fact that he occasionally infuriated her, and had got her kidnapped by tomb raiders at least twice, there was something about him. An even more remote part of her realized that as an agent, Burnside would be fine-tuned to nuances of vocal tone and body language. Had she revealed something she that even she wasn't aware of? *Nonsense.* Although she had put "archeological" and "boyfriend" together a little too quickly.

"The relationship is strictly professional. And for the record I make it a point to never date crew, spaceport staff or passengers, and since you might become the latter, don't even think about it."

"Uh, right. No ma'am." He paused a moment, then, grinning, asked "And just who does that leave?"

"Drop it," Jackie said flatly.

"Dropped. You were asking about the Velkaryans. Aside from the whole religious 'God terraformed the planets for humans' angle, there's a strong political component to them too. In fact, I'm not sure which came first, the religion or the politics. There's no question they want political power, and disagree strongly with some of Earth's policies with regard to aliens and settling T-space. It's only natural for them to try to influence off-Earth governments in their favor, and that gets easier the closer to the frontier. Tanith would be a strategic asset to them, especially so close to Zeta Reticuli, if that turns out to be significant."

"Oh, it's significant. Carson convinced me of that, and from what I saw I agree. I'm pretty sure Ducayne does too. In fact, he ordered us to stay away from it."

"Really? Was that before or after you went there?"

Jackie hesitated, remembering. "Well, both, actually."

"Ha! Don't sweat it. If I know Ducayne, the first warning wasn't serious, it was so he could disavow you if things went horribly wrong. If he really hadn't wanted you to go, there are ways he could have prevented it."

"That's about what we thought. And the second warning?"

"Do you *want* to go back there?"

"Gods no. I came close to losing my ship, encountered some scary technology, and we were warned off by the Kesh."

"The Kesh?"

"I thought you were briefed on the Reticuli mission."

"Apparently there were some details it was felt I didn't need to know."

"Then I'm not going to be the one to fill you in, unless a need to know does come up."

"Fair enough. I can make some guesses, but—"

"Which I could neither confirm nor deny."

He grinned. "Nor would I expect you to. Anyway, whatever guesses I could come up with that you'll neither confirm nor deny, I think that's yet another reason for not wanting the Velkaryans anywhere near the place. I'd just as soon not be involved in an interstellar war, whether that's with the Velkaryans or who or whatever the Kesh are, and especially not on this side of T-Space."

"Never mind the Kesh," Jackie said, regretting that she'd ever mentioned them. She'd been surprised that Burnside hadn't been briefed, but maybe that information hadn't made it here from Sawyers World yet. "Do you think war with the Velkaryans is likely? They strike me as little more than a bunch of thugs with some xenophobic ideas."

"Remember how the Unholy War got started? Or the Nazi War in Europe before that?"

Jackie realized he was right. The Nazis had been xenophobic thugs with some strange quasi-religious ideas who'd gained control of an industrial economy. The Unholy War had been started by religious fanatic xenophobic thugs who had lucked into immense energy wealth and nuclear weapons. The Velkaryans were xenophobic thugs with strange religious ideas who were actively pursuing advanced alien technology and, as Burnside said, political influence. She shuddered. "Why can't the craxies take their crazy and go find some other corner of the galaxy?"

It was a rhetorical question, but Burnside answered it anyway. "And what happens a century or five centuries from now when our spheres of influence meet? Or they offend some species with the power of the Terraformers who don't make subtle distinctions over what particular kind of crazy the humans they meet represent, and decide to just eliminate us all?"

Remembering what the alien Ketzshanass had said about the degkhidesh, the mysterious "enemy of the Kesh", Jackie shuddered again. "And this is really what Ducayne's outfit is all about, isn't it." It wasn't really a question.

"You could say that, yes."

Jackie suspected that there was more to it, given Burnside's response, but he wasn't going to tell her anything else any more than she was going to tell him about the Kesh, or the degkhidesh. Need to know. *When, exactly, did I become a spook?* she wondered. Speaking of which . . . . "This contact of yours, and the package. Did you pick it up? I'm guessing not since you didn't bring it with you."

"No, and it would be too awkward to have brought with me anyway. Probably masses about 50 kilos. Crate was about a half cubic meter."

"Light for the size."

"Yes, but still awkward. Anyway, I need to schedule a pickup. We didn't get a chance to discuss that, and now my contact is probably scared off."

"Any chance the Velkaryans, or whoever, will get to it first?"

"I don't think they made my contact, but even if they managed to trace her she's got no reason to return to it. She can just tell me where it is."

"Her? Your contact is female?"

"Yes, so?"

There wasn't a huge number of ship owner/operators, and less than half of them female. Jackie knew, or knew of, many of them. "I just wondered if it might be someone I know." Of course she didn't have to be a pilot, she might just be a dealer or broker, even a prospector who made a lucky find. "Probably not, though."

"I'd be surprised," Jordan said. "Anyway, I need to make contact again and get the pickup details."

"Why is she doing this? You're sure she won't just sell it to the Velkaryans instead?"

"It's not that kind of deal, and she has no particular love of xenophobes."

"Sounds like you don't want my help for any of that. Fine, just get the package or tell me when and where to pick it up. Is there anything I can be doing in the meantime?"

"Try not to attract attention to yourself."

Jackie snickered at that. "You mean like wearing a flashy Queen of Diamonds jacket?"

"Well, the color matches your hair, but yeah, exactly not like that. Just go about whatever business you would do. Look for small cargo to carry, mail packets, whatever. No passengers though." Jackie rolled her eyes at that, she wasn't that stupid. "And be ready for a quick getaway."

"Time-frame? When should I hear from you again?"

"Give me two days." He checked his omni. "Given this is early morning, if you haven't heard from me by midnight Thursday, check for other instructions Ducayne may have left you and go from there. I'll try to at least get a message to you sooner."

"Thursday. Ah, what day is today?" All human colonies kept to a seven-days-a-week naming convention, but day lengths varied. Generally, the whole planet would tend to keep to the same time zone as the primary settlement, but ships kept their own time. She was pretty sure she'd landed on a local Tuesday morning, but it didn't hurt to check.

"Still space-lagged?" Burnside grinned. "It's early Wednesday morning. The day is twenty-three hours and ten minutes. At 23:10 the clock changes to midnight."

"Okay, roger that." There would eventually be a leap hour or something to get rid of accumulated errors, but she shouldn't be here long enough to worry about it.

"Right then. I must be off. Thanks for the coffee. And the fix-up. And the shirt. Guess I owe you."

"You do. Let me check the perimeter before you leave." Jackie went forward to check the external cameras and sensors. Certainly nothing had approached the ship; the *Sophie* would have alerted her, but a quick scan of the field wouldn't hurt.

"Looks like it's clear." She opened the inner airlock door. "Be careful out there."

"Always am," Burnside said, stepping into the lock, then he palmed the door close button.

"Yeah, right." Jackie said to herself as she cycled the outer door and Burnside disappeared into the night.

She looked at the clocks, both local time and ship time. She was still transitioning to the former, and she was tired, but the coffee would keep her from getting back to sleep for a while yet. With a sigh, she went back to clean up the galley and reset the traumapod.

PART II: CONVERGENCE

Chapter 29: Convergence

Carson's pod, approaching Tanith

CARSON AWOKE AGAIN, this time knowing where he was, and feeling less disoriented that when he had come out of the coma. That nap had been good advice.

"Computer, status report."

"We are inbound to Tanith at a range of 98,750 kilometers and a speed of approximately 42,000 kilometers per hour. Entry in approximately two hours and fifteen minutes. All systems nominal."

Still 'nominal', good. "Any reason to abort the entry?"

"All systems nominal."

Okay, so not a particularly conversational computer either. Fine.

So, what to do for the next two hours? This is what Roberts would no doubt call the boring part of space travel, although he was thankful he'd slept through the past week-plus. Roberts. Right, he needed to contact her.

"Can you establish a stealth radio link with Captain Roberts and or the *Sophie?*"

"By stealth radio link do you mean one not using normal radio channels?"

"Correct."

"This system is so equipped but establishing a link will depend on whether Roberts and or the *Sophie* is listening, and if they are within range."

Of course it will, you stupid computer, Carson thought but didn't say. "Understood. Please attempt the connection."

"Attempting." A brief pause, then: "A link is established. Voice communication is possible."

"Jackie, greetings! This is Hannibal Carson, can you talk?"

There was a delay of a couple of seconds. Carson didn't know how much of that was lightspeed delay versus Jackie getting over her surprise at hearing from him.

∞ ∞ ∞

Aboard Sophie, *Tanith*

Jackie Roberts had woken again at nearly oh-nine-hundred local time, after finally getting back to sleep after Burnside's nocturnal visit. She sat in the galley eating a light breakfast and working on her third cup of coffee, wondering what to do with the rest of the day. There were always minor maintenance tasks on the ship, but right now there was nothing critical and most tasks could be as easily done with the ship under way.

So much for an easy package pick-up, Jackie thought to herself. Of course, with Ducayne involved, she hadn't really expected it to be easy, but she was starting to get a little tired of the stupid cloak and dagger games. It was bad enough that Vaughan and the *Carcharodon* had been here when she arrived. That made some kind of sense; if they'd been headed to Sol after Zeta Reticuli, Tanith was an obvious refueling stop—but why were they still here?

An alert sounded from the ship's console. That wasn't the standard comm, that was the special secure system that Ducayne's people had installed. *What now?* She stepped over to the panel and keyed it. "This is the *Sophie*. Roberts here."

"*Please hold.*" The voice had a robotic tone to it. Then:

"*Jackie, greetings!*" Carson's voice? "*This is Hannibal Carson, can you talk?*"

Things were just getting weirder. Jackie wasn't sure she wanted to talk, but answered anyway.

"Carson? You're on Tanith? When did you get in? There hasn't been a landing recently."

Even as she said it, she realized that where Carson was involved, landing fields weren't always necessary—he had used improvised explosives to clear a landing zone in the jungle on Verdigris, although she wondered where he'd find another pilot as crazy as she was. Certainly not one of the university ships. And given Ducayne's involvement, it could well be something even stealthier.

Just to confirm that, she asked: "Why are you using one of Ducayne's gadgets rather than your omni?"

"*I'm not quite on planet yet.*"

Aha! she thought, as Carson followed up with a request for her coordinates so he could land nearby. *But not at the spaceport. Interesting.*

She started to ask what was going on, but realized that with a Ducayne connection, he probably wouldn't tell her over a comm link, even a secure one. "All right, call me when you land. I'll let you know then if I can pick you up. I have a couple of things I'm in the middle of. Squawking coordinates." She touched a control on her panel to do just that. There was a delay before Carson responded, probably so he could check them against, well, wherever he was now and however he was planning to get there.

∞ ∞ ∞

Carson's pod, approaching Tanith

The computer screen flashed Jackie's coordinates and a map on the small pod screen.

"Computer, can we land near there?" Carson asked.

"*You* can, but that is the primary spaceport; it is likely you will be observed. These devices have other destinations."

Of course. "Thank you. Pick a landing spot as near there as possible with minimal chance of detection. Make that *acceptable* chance of detection." Otherwise the computer was likely to put him on the other side of the planet. "Specify distance."

"Approximately 47.3 kilometers at a bearing of 137 degrees true," the computer replied.

Okay, he could hike that if he absolutely had to.

"Jackie, got it. I will need a pick up. I may be about fifty clicks out." He repeated what the computer had just told him, and his estimated time of arrival. "Uh, have you happened to pick up a package for Ducayne yet?"

∞ ∞ ∞

Sophie, *planet Tanith*

Jackie was only surprised at how well the timing had worked out. "I should have known that's what this was about. To make a long story short, no." Two could play this 'I've got a secret' game. And it *was* a long story. "I'll fill you in when you get here. And yes, I'll give you a ride."

"Fair enough, thank you. See you then. Carson out."

"Looking forward to it, *Sophie* out." She clicked off, thinking about the conversation she'd just had. A computer had made the connection. Carson was no pilot; was his ship automated? There had been no significant conversation lag except when she'd squawked the data, so he was probably less than half a light-second away. On the other hand, if he knew he'd need a pick-up, he wouldn't leave it too long to contact her. His ETA was several hours from now. With the short days here, it would be near dusk when he arrived.

She didn't expect to hear from Jordan Burnside until tomorrow. Whatever her plans might have been for the rest of the day, they had just changed.

Chapter 30: Vaughan

Harp City

"SO, YOU DON'T have Smith, or Smith's contact, or whatever he was picking up." Vaughan said, more calmly than he felt. "What *do* you have?"

"We think we know where the artifact is, or at least his contact," Mignon said, looking somewhat pleased with himself.

"And how do you know that?"

"We shot him."

"Say again?" Vaughan said, surprised. "You did *what?*"

"We shot him with a tracking dart. Looked like it hit his abdomen. Unfortunately, it didn't stay with him, we found it later in the street, with blood on it. Must have fallen out."

"Or he noticed it and took it out." One of these days, Vaughan decided, he would have to have a serious discussion about subtlety.

"Wouldn't he have destroyed it?" Mignon said, no longer smug.

"Maybe, but that would have confirmed to us that he'd found it. He's probably smarter than that. If he found it, he'd either lead us somewhere else, or he'd warn his contact. Either way we won't know where his contact is."

"Yeah, but if he didn't notice it . . . ."

"Then we might have something." Vaughan didn't think it likely, given the blood, but Smith might have assumed a regular bullet, so he couldn't rule it out. "Okay, worth following up. Where about?"

"A warehouse about a kilometer from the spaceport. One of the older ones, not that anything in this town is old."

"No." Vaughan tapped out a sequence to bring up a map of Harp City on his desk display. "Show me."

Mignon zoomed in the map to the spaceport area, and gestured at a location near it. "Here. Wait a moment." He tapped a command on his wrist omni and a bright blue line, with several turns and zig-zags, appeared on the map. "This is the path we traced from the beacon. We encountered him here—" he pointed to one end of the blue line "—then he went this way, away from the warehouse, circled around a bit to lose us, then back to this building, where he stayed for a while. Then he left and followed this part of the trail, still taking some random turns." He pointed at the other end of the line. "This is where we found the beacon."

Vaughan examined the map. There were other buildings in the area which would have been largely abandoned at night. The place was largely a staging area for goods going to or from the spaceport, although there was also some light manufacturing and the offices and workshops of companies who did ship servicing and the like. Lots of places to hide, and while there were undoubtedly plenty of surveillance cameras, probably very few with the smarts to make real-time decisions about what they were observing. Mostly they would just record for later review, if there was ever any need to. Not a line of investigation worth pursuing, Vaughan decided, although he might want to ensure anything his men had done disappeared from any such recordings. He'd pass that on to his contact with the local police.

Hiding the artifact in the plain sight, in a warehouse full of shipping crates or whatever it held, was clever. It also suggested that Smith's contact had some connection with it, to ensure that the package didn't arouse suspicion. Or perhaps it was clearly labeled and inventoried, but as something else. Like most of the outer worlds, there was little in the way of Customs duties or inspectors here. A few off-world luxury goods that could be taxed were about the only things they might worry about. Anything else was too valuable to a young colony to impede its inward flow, and since Tanith had had no intelligent natives, there were no alien artifacts to smuggle out.

In that case, Vaughan thought, *where did this thing come from? If not from Tanith, why was it brought here?*

He thought about the Zeta Reticuli system. They had encountered some strange things, but his and his crews' memories were fuzzy on just what, and his ship's logs had been tampered with. Of course, those things in themselves suggested a high technology level. Something humans had? Homeworld Security? Vaughan didn't think so. It had to be aliens.

The thought didn't disturb Vaughan. Terraformers aside, he knew there were technologically advanced aliens around T-space somewhere, or had been in the not too distant past. The pair of FTL communicators the Velkaryans had were proof enough, and Vaughan had never bought into the whole religious, Church of Divine Stellar Providence, side of the Velkaryan movement. He just felt that the terraformed planets should belong to those capable of using them, which meant humans. If there were other spacefaring aliens still out there, well, they'd deal with that when the time came. Life had clearly begun on Earth first, at least the life on terraformed planets. If it had begun independently elsewhere, well then, let them find their own damn planets.

"What do you want to do, boss?" Mignon said, interrupting Vaughan's thought process.

"Do? I want you to get that artifact, of course."

"Well, sure. But how?"

That was the question. With his influence on certain people in the local government, could they help? A surprise customs raid on that warehouse? No, it would be too hard to come up with a pretext for that, and there were too few agents anyway. They might get lucky, but more probably it would just tip Vaughan's hand.

"Watch the warehouse and the approaches. Smith may try to reach his contact again tonight. Hack into the warehouse inventory and look for packages that arrived six or seven weeks ago, anything with an indication it's going to be moved out soon— they wouldn't have it buried under another pile of crates if so— and anything where there are just one or two assigned to a specific owner. Anyone importing or exporting enough to need warehouse space will probably be a company, and have a lot."

"Okay, then what?"

"If you find something, let me know. But we're going to want to get hold of it."

"You mean steal it?"

"Steal it, bribe a guard, check it out with forged paperwork, whatever it takes. Use your imagination. Just get it. And keep me posted."

"Got it, boss."

Chapter 31: The Pickup

Aboard the Sophie, *Harp City Spaceport*

ROBERTS BROUGHT UP an aerial view of the surrounding terrain on her main console screen, then overlaid that with a map showing the man-made features. Harp City wasn't much of a city as the name would have suggested, more a town, but a fair size with a population of perhaps thirty thousand or so. That was surprising for a planet this far out, the economy must be good. The system's super-Earths must have some valuable resources in addition to whatever Tanith had. And it had a lot, she realized as she reviewed the data. To the southeast, the direction in which Carson would be landing, was not much. It looked like it bordered a broad swamp, and between that and the town was low scrub and some forest. Most of the surrounding farms were to the east and north. Obviously, Carson, or whoever was piloting his ship, had picked a place where his arrival would be less likely to be detected.

That left Jackie with a problem. Taking up the *Sophie* and flying her out to get him would attract more attention than Carson wanted, given that he wasn't landing at the spaceport. Even if Tanith didn't have the air and space tracking systems to follow her flight—and it did, at least locally—she didn't have a plausible reason for leaving the spaceport just for a joy ride. She studied the map again. There were roads—more likely dirt tracks—in that general direction, but nothing very close. A closer look at the aerial photos revealed the ground to be flat, and the small wooded area was not densely so. Ground transportation it would have to be. In fact, that flat area seemed to blend into what was wetland, a swamp perhaps. Time to modify the bike.

Roberts went back to the *Sophie*'s aft compartment, where she had stowed her bike. It could be rigged with fold-down inflatable pontoons and aquajet propulsion for water work. Sometimes the only flat place to set a ship down was on a lake. Even as an amphibike it was no boat, but it beat swimming. She hardly ever used it. If she was on a charter and carrying passengers, they'd either arrange their own transport at their destination or squeeze a larger ATV into main cargo area. Squeeze being the operative term; Sapphires weren't exactly cavernous.

Either way, the amphibike would do to pick up Carson, so long as he didn't have a lot of luggage, and it would raise fewer questions than flying the *Sophie*. She grabbed a tool-kit and set about attaching the rig to the bike.

∞ ∞ ∞

Carson's pod, entering Tanith's atmosphere

"Pod jettison in twenty seconds," the computer announced. Carson felt the safety straps snug down around his legs and torso, pulling him back against the bed of the pod. He grabbed the handholds on either side of him. He didn't know how rough a ride this was going to be, but those handles had to be there for a reason.

"Ten seconds."

The "message" torpedo he was riding would be just above the atmosphere now, perhaps a hundred kilometers out and coming in fast at an angle, pretending to be a meteor. Carson thought he felt slight the slight tug of initial deceleration. The pod had no window, not that Carson had any influence on what he might have seen out of it anyway. *It's just a fast elevator*, he told himself.

"Five seconds. Four. Three—" The pod blew before the computer announced two; a psychological trick to reduce stress. Or perhaps, to induce stress and give the passenger—Carson felt *victim* might be a better word—an adrenaline jolt so they'd be ready for whatever came next. It certainly did that to him.

The aft hatch of the torpedo blew off with a sharp *bang!* and a jerk that jolted Carson toward the head of the pod. Then *whump!* as the ejection charge at the foot of the pod shoved it clear of the torpedo housing.

Then the relaxing, falling feeling of zero-gee. The computer announced, "Pod is clear. Deploying grid fins."

Carson exhaled a breath he hadn't known he was holding. *Well, that was fun.* The fins, currently folded flat against the side of the pod, would help stabilize the pod, adding drag and pivoting to help guide it. He heard some clunks and whines as they extended, and then quiet, only punctuated by the occasional short hiss of attitude jets. The air outside wasn't thick enough yet for the fins to work.

"Fifteen seconds to entry burn," the computer said.

Here we go again. Carson thought. A small rocket at the base of the pod would fire to reduce his speed and entry heating. About a minute after that, the pod itself would open up and—with any luck—his parachute would open.

∞ ∞ ∞

Southeast of Harp City

Jackie Roberts zipped down the dirt road away from Harp City, after a brief meandering tour through town to mislead anyone who might be watching her. She was beginning to take this spy stuff way too seriously. The feeling of speed was a nice change from the cramped quarters of the Sophie, even though she was barely crawling compared to Sophie's normal flight velocity, let alone warp.

She checked the map display on her omni. The road ran alongside a wooded area now; she should turn off soon. There was a spot. She slowed and turned off the track and into the trees. They were close together, but not so close she couldn't drive between them, and for the most part the branches were high enough above the ground she didn't worry about them. For the others, well, she was glad to be wearing a helmet.

It occurred to her that she'd forgotten to check the guide for possible dangerous animals in the woods or swamp. She hoped that this was still close enough to town to have encouraged such to move away, or been thinned out by the locals. She patted her thigh to reassure herself that she had her sidearm, just in case.

The trees became sparser and more scrubby-looking. The ground here was softer. She must be approaching the edge of the swamp. She brought the bike to a stop and checked her omni again. She was very close to Carson's rendezvous point, although she didn't know how accurate his coordinates were. It was just about time, too.

She moved into a clearing near the edge of a shallow, weed-filled pool and scanned the sky, looking for his ship or landing craft. She didn't imagine he would walk here.

A brief flash and streak caught her eye. Was that a ship entering atmosphere? No, too fast, and at the wrong angle if it wanted to land here.

She was still looking at the sky when, a few seconds later, the streak lit up again some distance farther away, then bloomed into a flash so bright Jackie had to look away. *Wow, that was some bolide.* She idly wondered if any of the meteor would survive to reach the ground.

She blinked away the dazzle and checked her omni again. He should be here. She flipped the omni to telescope mode and held it up against the sky. Maybe Carson's ship had used the meteor as a diversion. No, there was nothing. Wait, what was that? A movement on the screen caught her eye. She increased the contrast and panned around until she found it again. Was that a *parachute?*

It was. And dangling beneath it was . . . *Carson?* Okay, that was unexpected.

She watched him descend, putting the omni away when he was close enough to be seen directly. He was steering the parachute toward the swamp. She realized he was trying to avoid the trees, and might not realize that the flat weedy area was water rather than solid ground. He'd find out soon enough, and it wasn't deep.

She lowered the support arms on the amphibike and began to inflate the pontoons. He might need help. As the pontoons were inflating, she flashed a light at him. He either didn't see it or wanted to concentrate on his landing, because he didn't respond. A few moments later, he hit the water with a splash. Then she heard him cursing.

Chuckling to herself, she mounted the bike and headed out to get him.

∞ ∞ ∞

Carson pulled himself up out of muck, cursing. The water wasn't much more than knee deep, but as instructed, he'd rolled when he touched down, not realizing in the dark that the wonderful clear area he'd steered toward was a swamp. He regretted now opening his visor as he'd descended; water had gotten in and was now trickling down his neck and chest.

He removed his gloves and undid his harness buckles. He gathered up the 'chute then reached up to take off his helmet. Once he lifted it off his head, he heard splashing and the whine of a motor behind him. He turned to see someone on an amphibike headed toward him. Jackie? In the light from the bike, he could see several scattered low mounds amidst the weeds. Nests, perhaps? Of what?

"Hello?" he called to the bike.

"Carson, it's me!" Jackie called to him. "Stay where you are, I'll come and get you."

"I'm fine," he called back, and started to walk toward her.

"Freeze!"

"What? Why?" But he stopped moving. He had a sudden bad feeling about the mounds.

"See those?" she gestured toward them.

"I saw them. What of it?"

"This is a swamp. Those look like alligator nests. I'm guessing this planet has crocodilians." Most terraformed planets did.

He unfastened the flap on the holster strapped across his chest. "You guess? You don't know?"

As the bike approached Carson, he saw several long shapes floating just below the surface of the water. They could be logs, but then one turned of its own accord and start drifting toward him.

Roberts must have seen it too. "I know now," she said. "It has crocs. Are you armed?"

He pulled out his pistol and made sure there was a round in the chamber. "Yes."

"At your seven o'clock, ten meters back. Don't fire unless it rushes you, it might set the others off."

Carson turned to look back over his left shoulder. "Others?"

"Relax, just don't act like a wounded animal."

He wondered what his parachute landing fall had seemed like. But he knew she was right. "This isn't the first time I've dealt with crocodilians," he replied. Although he hadn't actually been in the water that other time.

By now Jackie had brought the amphibike close to him, as he stood carefully still in the knee-deep water. "Do you have bags?" she asked.

"Just what's on my back. Can we get out of here?"

"Okay, come around to the back of the bike, between the pontoons. Great. Now, grab my shoulders and climb on over the back, left foot on the left pontoon first."

"Got it," he said, holstering his pistol.

He put his hands on her shoulders and stepped up as she shifted her weight to the right. "Keep most of your weight on me, centered," she said.

The bike rocked to the left a bit as Carson heaved himself up, then centered as he swung his right leg over the bike and sat on the pillion seat behind her. He took his hands off her shoulders and hesitated, wondering what to do with them.

"Hands around my waist and lean forward," she said. "How are our friends doing?"

The splashing as he had climbed out had attracted their attention. Several more "logs" were drifting closer.

"Like they want to be invited to the party, he said. "Shall we get going?"

"Hang on," she said, and revved the bike. It bucked as the aquajets kicked in, then slid toward the shore. Jackie heard several splashes behind them as the crocs made desperate lunges to catch their fleeing prey, but a few moments later she'd pulled the bike onto dry—well, less wet—land and stopped.

"Okay, off," Jackie said. "I need to retract the pontoons."

And Carson had just been starting to enjoy the ride.

∞ ∞ ∞

"By the way," Carson said, as Jackie prepped the bike for the ride back to her ship. "I like this new look of yours. The tight jump-suit and the leather jacket really work together."

"It's practical."

"Sure. And the Queen of Diamonds motif? That's definitely a new look for you." He grinned.

"That was practical too. I didn't know who Ducayne's con-tact here was, so I had to advertise."

"Okay, but what does the Queen of Di—" and then the connection hit him. "*Oh*. Ha! Wait until he hears about this."

"He'll probably congratulate me for creative thinking. Heck, his message to me was signed Quiche Desjardins."

Carson shook his head, still grinning. "You may be right. In fact, it wouldn't surprise me if he's used it himself at some point." As he said that, he remembered. "Come to think of it, he first suggested Queen Diana as the namesake for an endowment at the university. I take it the biker chick look is not a permanent change?"

She grinned back at him. "I fly a *starship*. What's a biker chick got that I don't? But if you really like the look . . . ." she let that thought trail off with a sly smile.

Carson decided that he did, but just said "I'll keep that in mind. Shouldn't we be getting out of here?"

"Roger that. But you still owe me an explanation of how you happened to be parachuting down into a swamp. And why you're here. I only got in a couple of days ago myself."

"Fair enough. But back at your ship, okay? I want to get out of these wet clothes." He paused, looking around, then slapped at some bloodsucking insect that just landed on his neck. "And away from these damned mosquitoes!"

Chapter 32: Vaughan Recalled

Church of Divine Stellar Providence, Harp City

AS WAS HIS custom, Klaus Vaughan was reviewing reports and the local news feed while sipping coffee, when a message alert popped up. He glanced over at the calendar in a corner of his screen. Another immigration ship was due in soon. If it were in-system, this might be from its data dump. He entered a passphrase and the message opened.

Vaughan read it with increasing consternation. Things were behind schedule on Verdigris, and he was being ordered back there to expedite operations.

"Damn," Vaughan said as he clicked the message closed.

Mignon had been cleaning his small personal arsenal nearby. He looked up at Vaughan's utterance. "Problem, Boss?"

"Orders came in with the *Speedwell*'s email dump. We need to get back to Verdigris. Change in schedule. We leave tomorrow."

"Tomorrow?"

"Things are getting behind. The sooner I get them back on track, the better. Pass the word for everyone to get their gear together and get back to the *Carcharodon*."

"But what about that artifact?" Mignon said. "We've got a line on where it is. Things are set up for a couple of days from now."

Vaughan still wanted that. It might be nothing, but it also might be a significant piece of alien technology, especially if Smith was so interested in it. Standing orders were to collect any of the latter they could. "Move the schedule up. You don't have time to be subtle, just get the crate and bring it to the ship. We *will* leave tomorrow."

"No subtlety. Got it," Mignon said. He began to re-assemble the pistol he'd been cleaning. He was smiling.

Vaughan wondered about that, but it was nice when a man could take pleasure in his work. He said, "Try not to attract any more attention than necessary this time, okay?"

"Got it, Boss."

Chapter 33: Catching Up

Back aboard the Sophie

"WELL, YOU HAVE to admit, landing in the swamp did reduce your risk of detection." Jackie said when she'd heard Carson's explanation for his unconventional arrival.

"Save me from literal-minded robots. I thought I did well to specify within walking distance," Carson growled. His clothes were still soaked from the unexpected splashdown; he had insisted on hot coffee before changing. "I would have been a lot better off if I hadn't done a parachute landing roll. I got soaked."

"At least you didn't land on a croc's nest. Mama might have been angry."

"There is that." Carson downed the last of his coffee and looked at Jackie. "So, you were supposed to pick up a package. You were a bit coy about that on the comm. What's going on?"

"The package wasn't waiting for me when I got here. I managed to make contact with Burnside, Ducayne's man, but he doesn't have it either. He had planned to pick it up yesterday but ran into a problem."

"So, you don't know what's in the package?"

"Do you?"

"Not what it is, but perhaps what it looks like. Ducayne had some pictures."

"What is your interest?"

"There's writing on it. It's alien tech, probably old. Of course I'm interested."

"Burnside thought it might be an FTL communicator."

"Really? Is that possible?"

"A century ago we thought FTL travel of any kind was impossible," she said, "so I'm not going to say no. And we saw some weird stuff in the Reticuli system. But I'm skeptical. Do you have the pictures? I'd like to see what it is I'm supposed to be picking up."

Carson pulled out his omni and tapped in a pass-code sequence, then held it up to his eye so it could do a retina scan.

"Elaborate security," Jackie said.

"Ducayne insisted. Anyway, here's what we've got."

It wasn't much. The first couple of images showed what could have been alien high tech gear, but could also have been a prop from an old sci-fi video series. There was nothing in the images to indicate scale. The next one was better; an omniphone, with a centimeter scale on the screen, rested on it near one of the panels of indicators and what were probably switches on the side of the thing, suggesting that the whole artifact, which was roughly cylindrical, wasn't much more than a meter and a half long and not quite a meter wide. An arrow, added after the picture was taken, pointed to the panel.

The next image was a close-up of what the arrow in the previous picture had been pointing at. There were regular markings on the control panel that did indeed look like a simplified version of cuneiform.

"You're right; those don't look anything like the markings we found in the pyramid on Chara III, or on the disintegrator we found there."

"No, they don't, do they." Carson agreed. "That would tend to rule out any connection to the original, pre-Kesh pyramid builders."

"Let me see those earlier pictures again, of the whole gizmo."

Carson flipped back to one. "Here. Why?"

"Remember the room we found in the pyramid on Verdigris? The one that had been broken into?"

"Sure. There was a dais or bench of some kind, looked like a piece of equipment had been removed."

"Do you see any way this," she gestured at the image, "could have fit into the space where that gear had been?"

Carson looked at it, trying to recall the details of what they'd found on the planet in the Delta Pavonis system. They had discussed whether it might have been an alien signaling device. A Kesh pyramid ship—although they hadn't known what it was then—had shown up very soon after they'd entered the pyramid on Chara III, and they had joked about tripping an alarm.

"The table had a hole for power conductor cables. I don't see anything on this that would have lined up with that. It doesn't look like a good shape for staying put on a table anyway."

"And no cables dangling from it. Do you have pictures of the other side of it?"

"No, that's all I have. If it was from the Verdigris pyramid, or one like it, I don't see it in what we've got. We'd have to look at the whole artifact. No wonder Ducayne wants to get hold of it."

"But if it was a Spacefarer pyramid and device," Roberts said, "there's no reason for it to have Kesh labels."

"I'm becoming increasingly convinced that there's more to the Kesh than meets the eye," Carson said.

"And what has met the eye so far isn't very much. Why do the Kesh have pyramid-shaped ships?"

"No idea. Did we see anything in the Chara museum that would suggest pyramid ships were a good idea?"

"You mean other than the pyramid itself? No. But we were focused on finding a way out. At least I was. You and Marten had lapsed into archeologist mode."

"I don't recall seeing anything either. The Kesh are definitely keeping secrets, but if what Ketzshanass said about their civil war is true, then they probably have good reason," he said. "It sounds like the non-interference faction won that one."

"Well, we won't solve it by sitting around. We need to get that artifact. Burnside is supposed to contact me by tomorrow, otherwise we fall back on plan B."

"What's plan B?"

"No idea."

Carson chuckled at that. "At least I'm here now."

Roberts raised an eyebrow. "You don't think he included that in his plans?"

"Of course n—" Carson stopped in mid-sentence, reviewing how he came to be here. "Damn it, you just might be right."

He shook his head, then continued after a short pause. "You know what? I could use some food. I had some nutrient solution in the pod, but it wasn't very filling."

"I restocked the chef at Tau Ceti, and it's just been me aboard." She gestured around the galley. "Help yourself."

"Thanks." Carson stood and stepped over to the autochef built in to a corner of the galley area, touched a pad and began browsing the menu screen. "You know," he said, "even if that gizmo isn't some kind of FTL communicator, the Kesh still have some interesting technology. Their pyramid ship had anti-gravity and a tractor beam."

"Probably related technologies, but I don't think either of those would fit into something as small as what your pictures showed."

"Well, not the whole thing, but it might tell us something about the technology." He made his selection and waited while the machine prepared it. "On the other hand," he mused, "it could just be the Kesh equivalent of an autochef."

"Well, that *would* be disappointing."

"But more likely. I'd be interested to know the circumstances under which it was found, and where. That can tell a lot about an artifact. If it was found in the alien equivalent of a midden heap, for example, then it's likely to be a piece of broken junk that somebody threw out."

"I'll bet Ducayne and company want to know where it came from too."

The autochef signaled completion and Carson slid its door open, removed his meal—meat and vegetables wrapped in a pastry crust that he could eat by hand—and took it to the table.

He nodded agreement at her comment.

"You're probably right." He took a bite of the hand-meal. It was hot, and spicy, although not like Kakuloan sausage. Something Tau Cetan, he imagined. He chewed thoughtfully. Wouldn't Ducayne have told him everything he knew about the artifact? Maybe not, to avoid biasing Carson to any particular conclusion.

He swallowed his food then said, "You know, I'm getting the feeling I was rushed out here for nothing."

Roberts leaned back against the counter, her arms crossed, looking thoughtful. She shook her head. "That doesn't sound like

Ducayne, though. He's like a chess player. Every move he makes has multiple possibilities for further moves."

Carson had to agree. What *were* the other possible reasons for sending him out here? "Can you pull up the file on Tanith? I'm curious as to what else might be here of archeological interest. If there is something, I can't remember the specifics at the moment. Well, aside from the ancient Carthaginian goddess, but that's usually spelled differently."

"Sure," she said, then raised her voice. "Sophie, galley display, information on planet Tanith, highlight archeology."

"Since when did you start using the ship's voice interface?" Carson asked.

"Since around twenty hours ago when I was rudely awakened, and I asked for coffee. Or whenever I don't feel like going forward to the cockpit or my cabin, where I left my control pad, like now."

"Oh," he said, and took another bite. He skimmed the data on the galley display.

As he'd thought, there wasn't anything of archeological interest here, unless you counted the site of the first landing. If there had ever been intelligent natives here, humans had yet to find any trace of them. He continued reading. There was other information about the 82 Eridani system, and he'd never been here before. An item caught his eye. "That's interesting," he said

"What is?" Roberts asked.

"There are three other Earth-like planets in this system. I'm guessing they're not terraformed?"

"Correct. They're not Earth-like either, the term is 'terrestrial', which just means rocky," she said. "And no, they're all hot and heavy."

"Say what?"

"They're super-Earths, ranging from two-and-a-half to five times Earth mass, and they all orbit the star at or closer than Mercury orbits Sol. Even with 82 Eridani being slightly cooler than Sol, they're all very hot, with high gravity."

"Not exactly tourist spots, then," Carson said.

"No, but there are some outposts, especially near the poles. None of them are tidally locked, they're in a weird spin resonance with each other, so they don't have permanent night sides as such." Jackie looked at him, her head cocked at a slight angle. "What brought that up?"

"Just wondering if the Kesh, or the Spacefarers, would have had any interest in them. Sounds like not."

"They might have had. The planets are all geologically active, so you get ores forming that you wouldn't find in asteroids. Are you thinking that's where the artifact came from?"

"Possible. It would be interesting if there were evidence of old mining operations or the like." Would the Kesh or the Spacefarers have left noticeable evidence of that if they had been here? "What about here? Tanith has been settled for what, fifteen or so years now?"

"Twenty local," Jackie said, "so yes, roughly fifteen Earth years."

"Enough time for some pretty good orbital surveys, but still plenty of ground that hasn't been thoroughly explored. The artifact could well have been found here." Carson didn't think it likely, but what if someone *had* discovered a buried pyramid, or the hidden remains of some alien base? Or perhaps he'd just been reading too many of Brown's UFO files.

"You're wondering if there's more where that came from?"

"Of course," he said. "It would be better if it were on Tanith, I don't relish the idea of tromping around on a hot high-gravity planet."

"That might not even be an option," Jackie said. "I don't know if I have gear suitable, and the third planet may just be too big."

"Too big to land on?"

"Oh, we could *land* on it. Once. I'm not sure the *Sophie* would be able to lift off again. I think the surface gravity is within her specs, but it also depends on the gravity gradient and how thick the atmosphere is. The high temperature doesn't help there; it raises the top of the mesosphere, so orbital altitude is much higher. There are some tricks, but unless there's a good reason, I'd just as soon not try."

"No, I suppose not."

"Let's hope it came from Tanith or one of the in-system moons. But," she continued, "there's no indication of there ever being local sentient life here, and there certainly isn't now.

Haven't the Spacefarer pyramids been limited to planets with local primitives to uplift? Why build one where there aren't any?"

She had a point, but Carson could only guess at alien motives. He shrugged. "As I said, plenty of ground that hasn't been explored. Maybe somebody recently found ruins and hasn't told anyone yet so they can pick the best for private sale. But—"

"Why would anyone buy something from a planet with no reported natives?" Roberts said. "That's a red flag for a scam."

"The find would be announced after tomb raiders have skimmed the best stuff to a warehouse, and then they'll sell it. It wouldn't be the first time." That was a sore point with Carson. Without thinking, he balled his right hand into a fist and pressed it into the palm of his left.

"But there's no evidence sentient life ever developed here, is there?" she asked.

"Not yet. Maybe it just hasn't been discovered. The spearpoint finds on Sawyers World by the first landers was sheer luck. They might have gone undiscovered for decades."

"Okay. You're the archeologist. But there's no pyramid on Sawyers World either."

Carson looked at her. He couldn't keep a wry grin from growing on his face.

"What? Hannibal, why are you looking at me like that?"

"That," he said, his grin broadening, "may turn out not to be the case."

"There *is* a pyramid? Where?"

"It will take some excavating to prove it, but it sounds similar to the Chara pyramid, but partially buried. I had an interesting chat, a few days before leaving for here, with Elizabeth Sawyer. She mentioned something interesting."

"Wait, *the* Elizabeth Sawyer? The *Anderson* expedition? Who the *planet* is named for? That one?"

Carson nodded.

"A pyramid on *Sawyers World?* How?"

"Maybe. I still need to talk to Peter Finley, but Sawyer said that he thought Pete's Peak was a pyramid from the start. It just didn't make any archeological sense. Apparently, it doesn't make much geological sense either, but she and the other geologists dubbed it a volcanic neck and everyone forgot about it."

Roberts brow furrowed as she processed this, then her eyes widened and she looked up at him. "So, the talisman whose star map we thought pointed to Sol might actually point to Alpha Centauri. I'll have to check that. Or . . . maybe the pyramid on Earth just hasn't been found yet."

Carson started to disagree with her, then changed his mind. A Spacefarer pyramid on Earth was unlikely; there were few places it could be and still remain undiscovered. But nor was it clear that the Sol talisman was actually an Alpha Centauri talisman. Instead he said: "I'll tell you what *has* been found on Earth, though. We found out about it after you left with Marten for Taprobane, so maybe you haven't heard."

"I don't recall anything special being found recently on Earth. So, I guess not. What?"

"The remains of a Kesh spaceship."

Roberts jerked upright from her slouch against the counter. "*What?* Where? A pyramid ship? When?"

"No. From the debris, probably a small FTL ship, maybe *Sophie*'s size. It's all broken up, so impossible to tell for sure. It seems it crashed off the Yucatan coast two thousand years ago. Pieces were found by sport divers after a recent hurricane."

"And you think it was Kesh? Why? And how do you know two thousand years? Isn't that a long time in seawater for anything to remain?"

"Isotope dating, and the ancient Greek Antikythera mechanism was underwater just as long. Some of the pieces recovered in Belize have writing on them. It looks like Kesh language."

"That's the second time you've mentioned that. Where did you see Kesh language? I didn't see any signs or the like on the Kesh ship."

"Ketzshanass's communicator panel when we were talking on that moon. You stayed here on the *Sophie*. I caught a look at his panel. Their language looks a bit like cuneiform. Malcolm was trying to translate it when I left."

"You left *that* behind to come here? Hannibal, I'm touched."

Carson grinned. "Sumerian was never my strong suit, and Ducayne can be persuasive." He paused at Jackie's scowl, then his smile widened. "But yes, I wanted to see what you were getting yourself into. Besides, I owe you one."

"Well, not that I don't appreciate it," she said, "but I'm not sure you didn't waste the trip. It should just be a matter of Ducayne's agent here picking up the artifact and me leaving with it."

"You mentioned he doesn't have it yet."

"There was a complication."

"There usually is." Carson wondered what it had been, and looked expectantly at her.

"Somebody didn't want him to connect with his contact," she said. "I'm supposed to hear back from him within the next—" she checked the time "—twenty-five or so hours. Thursday midnight."

"So it's Wednesday night now?"

"Yes, just after twenty-one hundred. Short day; the midnight hour here is only ten min—" Jackie stopped short and looked like she had suddenly remembered something. "Oh."

"What?"

"The Velkaryans are here. The *Carcharodon*, and probably Vaughan. They may have stopped here on the way back from Zeta Reticuli."

"And they're still here?"

"Their ship is parked. Burnside said someone named Vaughan has been getting involved in local politics."

"Damn. A good reason for me to lay low. I had a run in with them—we think it was them—before I left. Vaughan would recognize me. Does he know you're here?"

"He doesn't know me. He wouldn't have gotten a good look at me at Zeta Reticuli. I don't know if he knows the *Sophie*. Plenty of other S-classes on the field, but my landing is public record."

"He didn't hear the name from me." Carson had tried to avoid giving him any information at all. "I wonder what the Kesh did to him. Do you think I should ask him?" he grinned as he said that.

"Sure! His ship is across the field. I can show you. Just walk up and knock on the hatch."

"Ah, maybe tomorrow. Wouldn't be polite to interrupt him in the middle of the night."

"There is that." Roberts grew serious. "Actually, I don't think he's staying aboard ship. Burnside said he was in town."

"Anyway, it's late for me," she continued. "I don't know what time your body clock is set to, but I'm tired. I'm going to hit my bunk. You know the ship, make yourself at home. The aft cabin is available, by the way, since it's not filled with your gear this time."

"Ah, thank you. I'm not really sure what time I think it is. I just came out of a medical coma. I think I'll read up on this place until the coffee wears off. See you in the morning."

"Roger that."

∞ ∞ ∞

Ping-ping. Ping-ping. Roberts came awake, glancing at the time display on the panel beside her bunk. Oh-three-thirty? *Ping-ping!* Dammit. She slapped the comm button. "Yes?"

"Sophie? It's Burnside. On my way there. That okay?"

"Do you have a problem with normal business hours?"

"For me, these are normal business hours."

She sighed. That was probably true. "All right, yes. Will you need patching again? What's your ETA?"

"Not this time. Ten minutes."

"Roger. See you then." She clicked off the comm, lay back on her bunk for a few moments and then said loudly, "Sophie, lights and coffee." The cabin lights came on, and Roberts dragged herself out of bed, pulled on a set of ship's coveralls—loose ones this time—and made her way back to the galley to get her coffee.

She was halfway through the first cup before she was awake enough to fully assess the situation. It must be from being on-planet, she thought. If she'd been awakened in space, she would have been alert and functioning in seconds. Some part of her subconscious must keep track of her environment, and how life-threatening unexpected events were likely to be.

Carson knew about Burnside, because she'd told him. Burnside would have no idea that Carson was here, and she hadn't been awake enough to tell him on the comm. Well, this could be interesting.

Just then Carson's cabin door slid open, and he staggered out, not looking entirely awake himself, and clad only in shorts.

"What's going on?" he said. "It can't be morning already?" There was no window in the cabin, and he obviously wasn't awake enough to have checked the external cameras on the cabin's console.

"It's oh dark thirty. Burnside just called. We're about to have company. You might want to get dressed." She grinned and looked him up and down.

Carson glanced down at himself. "Uh, right. And I'll take some coffee too, please." He stepped back into the cabin, and emerged a minute later in his usual field clothes: tough khaki pants, shirt, and a multi-pocketed vest.

He still looked like he needed coffee, and Roberts handed him a cup. He had just taken his first sip when there was a pounding on the airlock door.

"That should be Burnside," she said, and turned to check the external cameras. It was him, and he was alone. She opened the outer door to let him in.

"Okay, hang back here in the galley for a moment," she told Carson, then went forward to the inner lock door. Burnside rapped on it.

"*It's me, Jackie. Do we have to go through this every time?*"

"I wanted to give you a heads up so you don't overreact. I have company. Carson is here."

"*What? How? Never mind, I think I know. Okay, thanks for the advance notice. Now I won't accidentally shoot him on sight, if that's what you were worried about.*"

She opened the inner door. "The thought *did* cross my mind," she said. "Come on back and meet him. Coffee?"

"Sounds good."

She stepped aside to let him past, then closed the door. She turned to see Burnside just standing in the corridor, hands raised. Carson was aiming a pistol at him.

Chapter 34: Carson and Burnside

Aboard the Sophie

JACKIE STEPPED ACROSS the corridor, clear of the line of fire. "What's going on?"

Almost simultaneously, Burnside and Carson said, "Is he really Carson?" and "Is he really Burnside?"

"Yes and yes. Carson, put your gun down. Burnside, this is Hannibal Carson, archeologist. Hannibal, this is Jordan Burnside, or at least that's the name he's going by when it's not John Smith. My contact here."

Carson lowered his weapon, but didn't holster it. "Sorry, just checking. Tell me something a Velkaryan wouldn't know."

"What? Oh, very well." Burnside paused a moment, then said: "The carpet in Briefing Room Two in the Sawyer City headquarters is a color best described as puke green. There's no number on the door, the carpet is the only way to tell which room it is."

Carson laughed. "Good enough." He slipped his pistol into the holster at the small of his back and held out a hand, which Burnside took and shook.

"No harm done. Good to see you're on the ball. No wonder Jackie here likes you."

"I—" Jackie started to protest, then dropped it. "He has his uses. Although I think his current record is that he's gotten me into trouble more often than he's gotten me out of it."

"Come on, it has to be at least the same. You're not in trouble now." Carson turned to Burnside. "Is she? Are we?"

"Not yet, anyway. I'm surprised to see you here, Carson. There haven't been any ships arrive since the *Sophie*, and there was a bright meteor last night. I'm guessing Ducayne arranged one of his, uh, high speed transports?"

"You know about that?"

"I've heard of it. Never ridden one myself, and I'll admit it's not something I'll be sorry about if I never do."

"The trip wasn't bad. The arrival was . . . interesting."

"I'll bet. Anyway, it's good that you're here. I can use your help. Things have gotten . . . interesting." He made a wry smile and looked at Carson.

"Sit down, gentles," Roberts said, gesturing to the seats at the galley table. "Anyone want anything besides coffee?" At the negative responses, she sat down herself. "Okay, Burnside, what's going on?"

∞ ∞ ∞

Burnside took a sip of his coffee and set the mug back on the table. "I ran into a little snag," he said. "I'm going to need help picking up the cargo. That's set for tomorrow, or rather later this morning. It's too heavy and awkward to carry. If Vaughan knows who I am, and he might, given last night's attack, then me hiring a pick-up to get it to the spaceport will raise a red flag and he'll try to intercept."

"I get it," said Roberts. "Since I'm just some independent cargo hauler, it wouldn't be that unusual for me to pick something up from the warehouse that has just been sitting waiting."

"Exactly. Let's just hope you're not on their radar."

"Yeah. And I'll have to clear it with the port cargo office. Since it's not a small package, me picking it up won't be unusual, but it's customary to report such things. Burden of being an authorized courier. He sees me coming through the spaceport gate with a crate in the back of a pick-up truck, he'll have questions. Like why I didn't ask him where to get a truck, and what's in the crate. I assume its labeled as something mundane?"

"Mineral samples."

"Really?" Carson said. "At only a hundred kilos per cubic meter? I can't think of any mineral that light."

"Machine parts didn't make sense; frontier worlds import those, not export them. And people get finicky about exporting plant products. What else would you label it?"

"Make it collectable mineralogical specimens," Carson said.

"What's the difference?"

"How well they're packed. 'Mineral samples' is just a box of rocks. Mineralogical specimens, especially if intended to be collectible, are carefully selected. They might be delicate crystals, and are probably individually wrapped or in display boxes. With lots of padding. Put the destination as a university or a museum or something."

Burnside was impressed. Carson seemed to know what he was talking about, probably from working at a university. "Huh. Okay, that actually makes sense."

"Uh, there is a local business in exporting mineral specimens, right?" Roberts asked.

"Can't say that I've looked," Burnside said. He assumed that most settled planets would have something like that, as well as exporters of other local natural objects for the collector trade. "Does it matter?"

"We might want a layer of the real thing in the top of the crate, just in case somebody does open it," she said. "Not that I've ever done any smuggling myself."

"Of course not," Burnside said.

"I'd like to keep my courier's license, so no, I really haven't."

Carson coughed loudly at that.

"That I know of," she said, and glared at Carson. "Passengers may have lied to me. Although since Hannibal is a professional archeologist, I'm sure any artifacts he's carried have been cleared by the relevant office of antiquities, if any." Her glare changed to a wide-eyed look of innocence.

Burnside wondered what that was all about, but just said, "Okay then. I'll talk to my contact and arrange for the artifact to be repackaged and camouflaged. Jackie, talk to the port cargo master, arrange for a transport vehicle, and I guess see what other packages he has going to Sol. I'll address the cargo to Earth. Umm, Colorado School of Mines, in Golden. It's near the Denver Spaceport. I know the area."

"That won't work. It can't be Sol."

"Why not. That's in your range, isn't it?"

"It isn't a matter of range. This planet gets, what, on average two-dozen immigrants every two weeks? They're coming from Earth. In ships that go back to Earth. Nobody in their right mind would ship a cargo to the Solar system on a private charter. Those immigration ships go back mostly empty; they'll haul cargo cheaper than I can. Me doing it would raise a red flag."

"Oh." Burnside felt like someone had just burst his balloon. "Well, what's in range that makes sense? Sure, Alpha Centauri, but that's a bit of a red flag too, isn't it? The Velkaryans must know we have a strong presence on Sawyers World."

Jackie ran through the possibilities. "Okay, settled worlds I can reach in one hop are at Alpha Centauri, Tau Ceti, Delta Pavonis, Epsilon Eridani—although I can't imagine anyone wanting to send mineral specimens there—Epsilon Indi, and, well, Zeta Tucanae, but that's not very settled. And you've already ruled out Alpha Centauri."

"So, Skead, Verdigris, or Taprobane," Burnside confirmed, giving the names of the terraformed planets rather than their stars. "Verdigris is in the wrong direction, which doesn't matter since we don't want to actually go there, and it has a strong Velkaryan presence—"

"Tell me about it," said Carson, sympathetically.

"Oh?" Burnside guessed there was a story there somewhere. "Anyway, that might raise a flag, or it might throw them off. Leave that for now. Skead and Taprobane are roughly in the same direction from here, right? With Alpha Centauri a bit farther?"

"Less than ten light years from Taprobane. That's pretty much the way I came. Label the crate for Kangara University at Clarkeville there. We can go by way of Skead and I'll pick up any mail for both places. It fits."

"Excellent. Then we have a plan."

"So much for needing me," Carson said.

Burnside grinned at him. "You don't actually think everything is going to go according to plan, do you? You're part of Plan B."

"Which is what?"

"I'll let you know when I figure that out."

∞ ∞ ∞

Roberts walked in to the port cargo office later that morning, after a too-short nap and a bit of breakfast. She'd been half-hoping for someone else to be staffing the office that morning, but alas, it was the same eager but unhelpful clerk as the first time she'd been in here.

"Good morning! I just thought I would check in and see if you had anything going in the general direction of Tau Ceti or Epsilon Indi. I got a lead on another cargo headed that way."

"Oh? Good for you. I'll take a look, but you know you can access the data online, you with a courier license and all." He turned to a console and began tapping out a query.

"Thanks, that's good to know."

"I'm not seeing anything just yet. We've got something for Sol, but the *Speedwell* will be in later today from Earth, she just entered the system early this morning. They'll be going back directly, so they've got dibs on that cargo."

"Of course, I understand. I do have another question, though?"

"Yes?"

"This other cargo I mentioned. Sounds like it's a bit big and heavy, is there a small flatbed or pickup I can use, or do you know where I could find one?"

"There are a few rental places in town, you can search online. Spaceport has one but it's for spaceport use only, and you'd need to be a port employee to drive it. I might be available after my shift, if you're interested."

Something in his tone made Roberts wonder what he just might be available for, but she wasn't interested. "Thanks, I'll keep that in mind, but I wouldn't want to put you to any trouble."

"Oh, no bother, we could work something out."

Not likely. "Okay, but I'm not even sure I have that cargo yet. Thanks anyway. Talk to you later." She turned to leave.

"Pleased to be of assistance."

She rolled her eyes as she left the office. *And they raised the landing fees for this?* She headed back to her ship, tapping a query into her omni as she went.

"Any luck?" Carson asked her as she came back aboard.

"Yes, all bad," Roberts said. "Spaceport might have a vehicle if I 'work something out' with the port cargo master, but he'd probably have to drive it. He mentioned there might be a rental place. The only one based at the port doesn't really have anything suitable. I'll check in town." She transferred her omni connection over to the console in the galley.

"Huh. You'd think there'd be something at the spaceport other than just cars," Carson said. "What if someone wants to go into the field? See if they have a ground cruiser or something."

"We need something with a flatbed. That doesn't sound like an expedition vehicle."

"Jackie, really. You've seen how much gear I can take along on an expedition. How do think we carry it? The crate's not that big, we can probably throw it on a roof rack."

"Oh. Right. Stowing stuff on the outside of a vehicle is counter-intuitive for us starship captains. Okay, let's see what they have."

She turned to the console, then turned back again. "And by the way, there's an immigration ship due in this afternoon, the *Speedwell*. It's already in-system. It'll be busy around here."

"Oh? We'll have to see if we can turn that to our advantage."

Roberts wasn't sure how. An immigration ship meant thirty or so passengers, most of them having made the trip in hibernation pods to reduce life support and, more importantly, living space requirements. They'd be awakened in batches, keeping families together where applicable, and reconnected with whatever luggage they had. They would all be feeling a little hung over from the hibernation, a little dazed at arriving on a new world, and confused about the whole process, no matter how many briefings they'd had before departure. She was very familiar with the routine; she had been an officer aboard such a ship for most of a standard year before moving on.

Most of the immigrants would already have an idea of where they were going and what they would be doing. There would be ground transportation arriving for them. But there were always a few who chose to wing it, hoping to head out to unsettled land and do some prospecting, or farmsteading, or just disappearing and living off the land. The survival rate of the latter tended to be low. "Terraformed" didn't mean "park"—as the crocodilians in the swamp near town attested.

The space port would be busy with people and vehicles for a while, and cargo handlers and service techs seeing to the *Speedwell*. It didn't make money sitting in port any more than she did. The port was scaled to handle it, since they probably got one of these in every week or two. But all that could make for good cover to get Burnside's package in and loaded. All she had to do was find a way to get it here from the warehouse.

She turned to Carson again. "You know, Hannibal, worst case, we attach handles to the crate and you and Burnside can carry it here."

"Twenty-five kilos each, hand carried rather than a back pack? Won't that be fun." Carson thought about it a moment. "Maybe with a carrying pole or something, or even a dolly. The drawback is if we run into trouble, we can't move very fast, and we wouldn't want to just drop it and run."

"I wasn't being serious."

Carson grinned. "Hey, you never know when you'll need a Plan B."

Chapter 35: Teunar

Harp City, aboard Sophie

"SOPHIE, *EMERGENCY! This is Burnside.*" The watchword "emergency" on the suit-to-ship channel automatically triggered *Sophie*'s comm system to answer and put the comms on speaker.

Roberts answered immediately. "Burnside, what's your emergency? Where are you?" she said, heading toward the cockpit to begin prepping for immediate departure, if needed.

"*Gunshot wounds. Not me, my contact. Critical. Near the warehouse, squawking location.*" There was a brief blip as *Sophie*'s computer intercepted the data and routed it to a map display on the secondary console. "*I can't call local EMT, how soon can you get here?*"

Roberts didn't waste time asking why he couldn't contact the local emergency services. She trusted him to have his reasons. If he wasn't in the middle of town she'd just fly the *Sophie* to him, to get the patient in the traumapod as soon as possible. That wasn't an option here. It was a good thing she'd already picked up the ground cruiser. "Carson!" she yelled back to him. "Grab a first aid kit!" She heard commotion aft. The comm was still on speaker; he'd reacted as soon as he heard. She checked the map. "Three minutes if the road is clear. On the way."

"*Roger that. Burnside out.*"

Roberts rapidly hit the controls to make the *Sophie* safe to leave, but left some systems on standby. They might yet have to make a quick get-a-way. She left her seat to exit the cockpit, yelling again, "Come on Carson, let's go!"

The ground cruiser was parked adjacent to the ship. Carson and Roberts scrambled into it, Roberts in the driver's seat. Being designed for overland expeditions, it had manual overrides as well as the standard autonomous navigation. It was worn—clearly it had seen significant use in the field—but she'd been assured that all the important things worked. She powered it up, ignoring the minor complaints of the self-diagnostics. She eased the vehicle around the *Sophie* toward the spaceport exit and began to accelerate, only to slam on the brakes at the crowd of somewhat bewildered looking civilians, some shouldering packs and bags, with at least one carrying a small child. Passengers from the *Speedwell.*

"Dammit!" To the left was the boarding stair for the *Speedwell.* On the right they straggled off toward a fenced area with a gate that led to the spaceport office. The passengers were either heading to immigration control, such as it was, or waiting for their ground transportation. Or both. What they weren't doing was moving out of the way. She edged toward them, tapping the horn button. It made no sound. Great, broken like half the other things on this vehicle.

Carson threw his door open and jumped from the car, running in front of Roberts, waving his hands, and yelling "Out of the way! Emergency! Coming through! Make way!"

The group got the idea and slowly split into two smaller groups, letting her pull the car forward between them and toward the exit. As she cleared the crowd, Carson quickly scrambled back into the vehicle.

"Thank you, Moses," Roberts said as she floored the speed controller. Shabby as the exterior was, the electric motor still had it where it counted, and the car surged forward with a whine.

∞ ∞ ∞

Jackie didn't know the streets, but the car did. It took care of the navigation while she expressed her urgency with the foot pedal. Three minutes later they were rolling down an alley in the warehouse district, Carson on his omni to let Burnside know they were in the area. A figure stepped out from behind a waste pod and flagged them down. Burnside.

"We were ambushed. She was shot, one in the leg, one in the lower left chest. Bleeding badly. I've been applying pressure."

"I've got quick-clot in the first aid kit," Carson said as they moved back to the pod, where a figure, much smaller than Burnside, lay on the ground, wrapped in a blood-soaked cloak, with blood pooled on the ground.

"So do I, but I didn't want to use it. I don't know how she'd react to it."

"What? Why?"

"She's a timoan."

"*What?*" said Jackie. That raised all sorts of questions, none of which mattered right now.

Carson was just as surprised, but said "Doesn't matter, timoans are okay with it." He flipped open the first aid kit and pulled out a small spray can. "Clear the wounds, it's not good through cloth." He started to peel the cloak back with his left hand while shaking the can in his right.

"Yeah." Burnside had his omni in his hand. He pressed something on its side, and a blade instantly extruded from it. He began cutting the clothing away from the wounds.

"Nice toy," Jackie said.

"It comes in handy."

Carson inverted the can and pressed the nozzle, which squirted a stream of foam into and around the wound.

Carson said something that sounded to Jackie like "*Pravit blacktash babble babble*". He wrapped a sensor cuff around the victim's left arm and fastened it. The timoan's eyes, which had been half closed, widened. She nodded, then closed her eyes.

"What did you say?" Burnside asked.

"I told her we had it under control and we were getting her to a traumapod." He looked around, assessing the situation. "Jackie, pull the cruiser around, we'll slide her into the back."

Roberts was already in the car and moving it as he finished talking. The vehicle had separate seats in the rear as well as the front. The rear cargo area would be the best place to lay the timoan down. She got the car turned around and backed up to them.

As she arrived, Carson said: "Okay, Burnside, you take her left side, I'll take her right. Under her neck and knees."

"Got it."

Jackie opened the back then stepped aside while the two men carefully lifted the timoan female into the vehicle, laying her down gently. It was a good thing timoans were shorter than humans, there was enough space to let her lay flat. Carson climbed in with her and put a pad under her head, then covered her with a reflective, insulating blanket.

Burnside got into the back seat, turning to lean over it and check on his contact.

"Okay, Jackie, let's go."

She floored the pedal.

∞ ∞ ∞

"How is she?" Jackie asked as she drove.

Carson checked the display on the first aid kit, which was picking up the sensor readings from the cuff. He muttered something, and tapped a control on the display. The numbers and lines changed. "Could be worse. She's not in shock. All due speed, but try to avoid bumps or sudden swerves."

"Problem?" asked Burnside.

"The thing was set for humans. I changed it to timoan."

"Ah."

"There's internal damage, obviously, and the bullets are still in there. I don't want them moving around, although the quick-clot will help."

"Field medic? And how do you have a first aid kit that can handle timoans? Let alone *speak* timoan?" Before Carson could answer, Burnside muttered "Now I know why Ducayne sent you."

"Yeah, field training and army reserves in my youth. I have a timoan colleague. I only speak it a little, and only his dialect. But she understood. Who is she?"

"Her name's Tevnar. She found the artifact. Can the *Sophie*'s traumapod also handle timoans, then?"

"It can," Jackie said. "Among others. Mammals have a lot in common, at least as far as trauma surgery goes."

They were nearing the spaceport. Jackie could see that the small crowd had thinned, but with their curiosity already aroused by her hasty exit, she didn't want anyone trying to look in the windows. She turned toward another entrance farther down the field.

"Almost there." As the ground cruiser pulled through the far gate—thankfully there wasn't a lot of concern with security here, and a wave of her omni opened the automatic barrier—she glanced around the field. There was activity near the *Carcharodon*. The ship in front of it was being towed out of the way, and there were people moving about it, perhaps doing a pre-flight inspection. Well, that probably explained who the shooter was, or they were. She gave them as wide a berth as she could without being obvious as she steered toward the *Sophie*.

She parked the car near the starboard entrance, away from the Carcharodon, and keyed the unlock sequence for the airlock.

"We're here, guys. I'll go prep the traumapod. Do you want a stretcher?"

"We're good, she's not heavy," Carson said. Burnside grunted agreement.

Roberts hit the override to let both the inner and outer lock doors open at once, and went back to get the traumapod opened up and configured for timoan anatomy and physiology. Its computer was theoretically smart enough to figure out the species it was treating by itself, but it didn't hurt to give it a strong hint.

Carson and Burnside carried Tevnar from the airlock and laid her gently on the traumapod's patient table. They removed her cloak and further cut away the clothing from her wounds. Her eyes flickered open at that, and she looked around, taken in the surroundings.

"Ship? Whose?" she said in hoarse whisper.

"Mine," Roberts said. "The *Sophie*."

"Ah, female. Good. You have good boys." Her eyes shut.

"All right, get her in and let it do its work," Jackie said.

Carson touched the control to retract the table into the pod, and the pod console lit up with diagnostic information and status lights.

"Is she going to be all right?" Burnside asked, concern clear in his voice.

"The leg shot missed the bone and the femoral artery; that should be fine," Carson said. "Not sure about the chest wound. Breathing seemed okay so it probably missed the lungs. I'm not sure what else is thereabouts on a timoan."

"What was that about female and having good boys?" Burnside asked.

"Timoan society is highly matriarchal. They're descended from a species something like meerkats, so that might have something to do with it. She would know humans better than this, but having a female running the ship with males doing her bidding would seem natural to her. Although usually the males would be mates or offspring."

"Ah. I knew the meerkat thing, but haven't had really any contact with timoans until a few weeks ago."

"Yes, about that . . . ."

There was a beep from the traumapod. Roberts checked the display.

"Trouble?" Burnside asked.

"No. It looks like we got her here in time. She's stable but with considerable blood loss. The pod is working on her leg but still checking her thorax. Nothing else we can do now but wait." She looked up from the pod at the two men. "By the way, it looks like the *Carcharodon* is getting ready to leave. They were moving another ship out of the way and doing a pre-flight."

"Crap," said Burnside, disgusted, "they've got the artifact."

"So, how do we stop them?"

∞ ∞ ∞

Burnside looked at Jackie. From all he'd heard, she was a very good pilot. Good enough? "Ever hear of Jason Curtis?"

The range of emotions that crossed her face was nothing that Burnside had expected. Her eyes widened. Her face paled, revealing freckles he hadn't realized she had. Then she closed down, eyes narrowing, frowning, her face reddening. "No fucking way am I pulling a Curtis Maneuver, especially not with passengers and a patient in the traumapod. And don't *ever* mention that man to me again!"

"Uh, okay, just a thought." *What was that all about?* Burnside wondered. Carson looked as though he really wanted to ask what a Curtis Maneuver was, but held his tongue. The two of them could discuss that later. What other options did he have for stopping Vaughan?

"I've got gadgets for stopping a ship going to warp, but not with me. Damn. Jackie, uh, Captain Roberts, can you check the port's data, see if they've filed a flight plan?"

"Sure," she still sounded angry. "But I'll be surprised if they've filed one. A real one, anyway." She stormed off to the cockpit, shutting the airlock doors on her way, and sealing the cockpit door behind her.

Carson rose and started pacing. He kept punching his right fist into his left hand. His face grew redder. Then he stopped and turned abruptly. "I don spaceport coveralls, get to their ship, grab the crate and run." Carson said, making for the airlock.

Burnside grabbed him by the collar and jerked him back. "Don't be an idiot. You wouldn't get near their ship. You said Vaughan would recognize you. Even if you did, you'd never make it off with the artifact."

Carson pulled himself loose, turning to Burnside, and raised his voice. "Fine. I'll crash the ground cruiser into the *Carcharodon*'s hull. They won't be going anywhere for a while." He turned back and headed for the airlock again.

Burnside had half a mind to let him do it, it would be effective. But Carson was valuable, and likely to get himself shot. The resulting police response would blow their cover and still wouldn't get them the artifact. "That won't end well," he moved to block the airlock, struggling with Carson. "And you'll still get yourself killed." He was shouting now; Carson was crazy. Then Burnside heard himself saying: "I'll do it."

Just then an alarm sounded, an indicator above the airlock turned red, and the cockpit door slid open. Jackie Roberts stood there looking even more angry than before.

"*Knock it off!* Nobody is going anywhere; I've sealed the hatch." She looked ready to hit someone, but pointed back to the galley. "Get back there and sit down! One word out of either of you and *Sophie* will knock you both out."

As if to emphasize that, a robotic female voice announced: "System armed."

Carson looked at her, then back at Burnside, before relaxing and nodding. Burnside let him go, and they filed back to the galley.

∞ ∞ ∞

Captain Roberts stood at the galley table, looking down at both of them, disgusted. "I leave you two alone for two minutes and you're fighting over who gets to kill themselves first. Are you both *insane*? We'll find another way."

They both had the good grace, or good sense, to look sheepish.

"I just don't want them to get away with—" Carson started to explain.

Roberts raised her hand to silence him. "Enough. I know you Carson. You're a smart man with a tendency to do stupid things when someone has pissed you off." She turned to Burnside. "And I'm not sure you're any better."

Burnside started to say something, then thought better of it.

She glared at them both for a while longer. "And if that weren't bad enough, you were fighting on *my ship*. You're lucky I don't make you walk home." The incongruity of that last struck her as she said it, but she bit down and managed to keep a straight face. "Do I make myself clear?"

"Yes, Captain," Burnside said.

"Yes, Ja . . . Ma'am. Sorry about that."

"Good. Now," she continued in a calmer tone, "perhaps you'll be interested to hear where they're going. It turns out they have filed a flight plan."

"What?" Carson and Burnside said, almost simultaneously.

"Yes," Jackie continued, her tone normal now. "Frankly that surprises me. Unless you're a commercial flight, nobody cares if you file or not. They only care if you file a false plan; it confuses things."

Any ship would arrive at its destination long before a copy of the flight plan did, if the ship arrived at all. Periodically, as network traffic was updated by other incoming ships, flight plans would be correlated against recorded arrivals and departures. Flags would be raised if a ship had gone missing, but nobody was going to launch a search party; space was too big. The main point was, if the ship turned up somewhere else, a little more checking would be done to make sure that the ship hadn't changed hands without the agreement of the registered owner. Hijacking didn't happen often, but it wasn't unknown either.

"So, where do they say they're going?"

"Delta Pavonis. Verdigris." She looked at Carson. "The New Toronto spaceport."

"That *has* to be for our benefit," Carson said.

Burnside looked from one to the other. "Why do you think so?"

"Last time we were there," Carson said, "New Toronto refused us landing with a rather lame excuse. Turned out there's a pyramid in the jungle nearby. Someone else had gotten to it first. I assume the Velkaryans were involved; it didn't look like regular tomb raiders."

"Which makes New Toronto a logical place for them to be going," Jackie said.

Burnside nodded. "Okay. Now we get to play the game of 'does he know what you know, and if so, is he really going there because you'll think he won't, or . . . .' Well, you get the idea."

"Does it matter?" Jackie asked. "It's not like we can get there before him, not by much anyway. But we can be close behind them, and figure out a plan on the way." She looked at Burnside. "How soon are you ready to leave?"

The traumapod chose that moment to beep again.

∞ ∞ ∞

Aboard the Carcharodon

"Well, you guys sure drew attention to yourselves," Vaughan said, an edge in his voice. "That was supposed to be a nice quiet operation. With any luck nobody would have noticed the crate was missing for days, but you had to go in shooting."

"It would have been, boss. There wasn't supposed to be anybody there. And then that fuzzball shows up. If it was just her we could have dealt with it, one little timoan ain't much—"

"Don't be so sure. They're fast."

"Whatever. But then that Smith guy shows up and tries to interfere. I guess they planned the pickup for today. Next thing I know, shots are fired, the timoan is lying in a pool of blood, and Smith is behind a pile of crates with weapons free."

"And yet you got out."

"Mignon keeps him there with suppressing fire while I grab the crate. Then I cover him while he gets clear. Once we're out of the way Smith goes to see to the timoan, but he takes a couple of shots at us. Just to keep us moving, he wasn't taking time to aim."

"It's a good thing we were leaving anyway. Staying would have been awkward after the ruckus you raised."

"Come on, boss, we got the crate."

"You did. Okay, stow it for takeoff. Let's head back to Verdigris."

Chapter 36: Divergence

Aboard Sophie

JACKIE STEPPED OVER to the beeping traumapod. The status lights were green, it had finished its surgery, although it was still providing Tevnar with intravenous fluids to stabilize her. It had already discontinued the anesthetic. A question blinked on the display:

"Keep sedated Y/N?"

"We should probably let her rest," Jackie said.

"If she's stable and able, I have questions," Burnside said.

"So do I," added Carson, "but they can wait."

"Let's wake her," Burnside said. "I wasn't there for the whole thing, she may have information."

Jackie weighed that. As captain, everyone aboard, especially anyone in a traumapod, was her responsibility, even if they weren't in space. But Burnside had a point, it might make a difference to their plans. And she had questions of her own. "All right." She touched the *NO* button.

There was no immediate change. She hadn't expected one. The pod terminated the low-level sedative feed and injected just enough volume of an antagonist to neutralize it. Depending on the timoan's constitution, and where she was in her sleep/wake cycle, she would wake up soon.

Sooner than Jackie had thought. Tevnar's eyes flickered, then opened. Jackie thumbed a control and the pod door opened and the patient bed slid out part way.

"How are you feeling?" Jackie asked.

"I've been better," came the reply, her voice stronger than when she'd gone in. "My injuries?"

Jackie skimmed the log screen on the side of the pod. "Bullet in the left thigh," she said, reading aloud, "removed. No bone damage. No major artery or nerve damage. Wound sutured. Dressing applied. Bullet in the—" Jackie paused, and said "oh my" in a low voice.

"What?" Tevnar asked.

Jackie resumed reading. "Bullet in the lower left breast—which explains all the blood—impacted and cracked ninth rib. Bullet removed. Sutured, some tissue loss. Dressing applied."

"No wonder my left side hurts like a son of a bitch. That's going to leave a mark."

Jackie winced. She could only imagine.

"Good thing we're not as fussy about symmetry there as humans are."

"Well," said Burnside, "you're certainly sounding more like your old self. What happened? Vaughan's preparing to leave, I assume he got the crate?"

Tevnar started to laugh, then winced and stopped. "Damn rib. Anyway, I sure hope he did, after all that."

"What do you mean?"

"It doesn't have the real artifact in it. It's a fake. I hope he's halfway to hell or wherever he's going before he realizes."

Jackie choked back a laugh. This sounded familiar.

"A fake?" Burnside exclaimed. "You were selling me a *fake*?"

"Not you. The real one is back at my ship. This one was a decoy, just in case. I hate those guys. Didn't expect to get shot over it though. I think you startled them."

"Me? I . . . crap, I'm sorry."

"I should have let you in on the scheme. I was hoping it wouldn't come to that. You'd pick up me and the fake, and then I'd hitch a ride back to my ship with you. Give you the real one there, nice and isolated."

"Just where is your ship?" Carson asked.

"About five hundred kilometers from here, hidden from view. One of my sisters has a farmstead there. You don't think I was going to land at the spaceport, do you?" She coughed, and winced again. "That is not fun."

"You should get back in there and get some rest," Jackie said. "You *have* just been shot." The sister's farmstead was a surprise, although Jackie had known there were scattered small timoan settlements on several terraformed planets.

"Roger that, captain. Sorry, never asked permission to come aboard."

"Permission granted," Jackie said with a smile. "Now get some rest."

"Wait, so you're sure it's okay for Vaughan to leave?" Carson said.

"Yes, sonny." From outside the ship came the roar of a ship's thrusters throttling up, the higher frequencies muted by the *Sophie*'s hull. "And that might be them leaving now, I hope." She looked up at Roberts. "All right, Captain. You can pop me back in the oven. Please wake me if anything interesting happens."

"Roger that," Roberts said, and let the pod retract and close.

She turned to Burnside, smiling sweetly. Too sweetly. "You were saying," she said, "something about the Curtis Maneuver?"

Burnside again had the grace to look sheepish. "Me? No. Curtis? Never heard of him, it, whatever."

"Right answer," she said.

∞ ∞ ∞

Aboard the Carcharodon, *an hour out of Tanith*

The Velkaryan ship had just gone to warp when Vaughan unstrapped and said, "All right, now that we have gravity back, let's go take a look at what we've got. This artifact better be worth the trouble."

He made his way to the small cabin where they'd stowed the crate for take-off. The captain had the *Carcharodon* under constant acceleration toward where they'd go to warp, so there was fractional gravity.

It wasn't a crate in the nailed-together-boards sense, it was a typical small shipping container, a meter long and maybe seventy centimeters wide and high, molded plastic with built-in handles, a hinged lid, and latches. A standard design that could be manufactured anywhere that had a fabber.

It was locked, of course, but the hinges parted easily under the persuasion of a power wrench.

"Okay, let's see what we've got." Vaughan knelt down and pulled the lid off, revealing a layer of foam padding. He pulled that off and tossed it aside. There was layer of loose plastic film beneath that, part of a large bag wrapping the artifact itself. He peeled that back.

Beneath it lay a metallic-looking cylindrical object with a flat rectangular area, perhaps a display panel. Beside that were smaller rectangles which might have been controls. They were marked with odd linear symbols. The whole thing was nestled in rigid plastic foam which had been molded around it, poured in as a liquid and then left to expand and harden. The rest of the object was hidden by the foam.

"Well, well. That looks interesting." Vaughan had been half expecting just a pile of bricks for the mass, if this whole thing had been some kind of scam the timoan was pulling.

"Now, let's see what all this trouble was about." He began probing around the edges where it was embedded in the foam. It felt odd. It looked like metal, but it was not as cold to the touch as he would have thought. The small rectangles weren't buttons, they didn't depress, but they might just be touch sensitive. It looked in surprisingly good shape, not like something someone had found on a dig. Any power or other connectors must be on the lower side. He began to pry the packing foam away from the cylinder, feeling his way down the sides in case there was a hidden protrusion. He didn't want to accidentally pry anything loose.

Then there was a sharp *crack!* as of something breaking.

"Damn it, what was that?"

"Uh, boss, look at the display."

The rectangular display area had a crack running through it. Worse, the crack extended beyond that and into the body of the cylinder, almost like they were a single unit. That was odd. With a growing suspicion, Vaughan took a knife and scraped at the edge of the crack on the side of the cylinder. It wasn't metal, it was plastic. He rapped on the cylinder's side. The sound was a flat tap, not a ringing sound like metal. In fact, it sounded hollow.

"God damn it!" Vaughan stuck the knife into the crack and pried. The cracked widened and a piece of the plastic shell broke off. Inside was . . . nothing.

"It's a fucking fake! It was a scam after all." On closer examination, the thing had obviously been made on a fabber, with different colored plastic to simulate the display, and some kind of bronze-colored fill on the body.

"Maybe it was a decoy. Shall we go back?"

Vaughan was tempted. It could well have been a decoy. His earlier thought of a couple of bricks made more sense for a scam, although this fake was good enough to have held up to a cursory look if the buyer was rushed. Something this elaborate had to have been modeled on something. A real artifact? If he did go back, they'd grab Smith and the timoan and make them talk. But he also had his orders. Still . . . .

"I hope those shots of yours counted," Vaughan said.

"Blood everywhere, boss."

Vaughan bared his teeth. "Good," he snarled. "We do have to report back to New Toronto. Something big is up. But maybe there's time." There was no telling where Smith and the timoan had got to by now, but if Mignon was right, it might well be the nearest emergency room. Vaughan went back to talk to Captain Stinson.

Chapter 37: Packing It Up

Aboard Sophie, *at the spaceport*

ROBERTS, CARSON, AND Burnside sat around the galley table, considering their next move. The galley was across the corridor from the traumapod; Jackie Roberts was keeping an eye on it, although it would signal if there was a problem.

"So, what's next?" Carson said. "Sooner or later Vaughan is going to discover he doesn't have what he wants, and come back to get the real thing."

"If he even thinks there is a real thing," Jackie said. "He may decide the whole deal was a scam."

"Then he'll come back to finish whatever other business he had here on Tanith," Burnside pointed out. "I don't think that's over."

He was probably right. Jackie nodded. "And if it's sooner rather than later, I'd just as soon not be here. Tevnar said her ship was five hundred kilometers away. We should get out of town."

"Are we ready to leave?" Carson asked.

They weren't yet. In a pinch, Jackie could get the *Sophie* ready to go in a few minutes, she had made sure of that shortly after she landed, but that wasn't the only consideration. "We have a car to return," she said, "and we need to clean the blood out of the back. Jordan, do you have stuff you want from wherever you're staying?"

"Not much. I can abandon it if we have to, but if there's time I'd like to grab it."

"Okay." She thought for a moment, prioritizing. "Okay. We clean the car, drop Jordan where he needs to go, have the car return itself, and then I'll bring him back here on the bike. Wait, Hannibal can clean the car then have it return itself. I'll give Jordan a ride."

"I can drive a bike," Burnside said, "if you don't mind, that is. I can get that done while you take care of the car."

"That makes sense. Hannibal, can you start on the car while I finish prepping the *Sophie* and port paperwork? I want our departure to look as routine as possible. You know where things are stowed."

"Sure," Carson said, and got up to get cleaning supplies from an aft storage locker.

"Okay. Burnside, let's get you the bike."

∞ ∞ ∞

An half-hour later, Jackie Roberts had finished her checks of the *Sophie* and filed a flight plan for Tau Ceti. She could amend it from space before going to warp, if needed. It wouldn't be the first time. She and Carson had finished cleaning the worst of the bloodstains from the interior of the car. It wouldn't pass forensic analysis by a long shot, but it was good enough to get by at the rental return. From the condition of it when she'd got it, they weren't too fussy. Expedition vehicles were expected to get a bit messed up, although usually not in less than a day.

Jackie watched as the car drove itself out of the port, and then Burnside pulled up on her bike, this time wearing a backpack and with a small hard-sided case, more of a utility box, strapped to the rear seat.

"That's it? You do travel light."

"Trick of the trade. Let's get this aboard," Burnside said, dismounting the bike and wheeling it the rear cargo door.

Jackie went on ahead to help secure the bike, then closed the cargo door while Burnside went around to enter via the starboard hatch. With the bike stowed, she went on forward to where Carson and Burnside were sitting at the galley table.

"How's our patient?" she asked Carson.

"Stable and resting. Vital signs look good. Lucky for her, neither bullet hit anything critical; her ribs protected her internal organs."

Jackie wondered about his definition of "critical" considering where the second bullet had hit, but he was technically correct.

"Good. All right then, unless you gentles have a reason not to, I'm going to do a walk-around and then get us out of here."

"No, that sounds good," Burnside said.

Carson nodded agreement, then said "Wait, we don't need to secure for zero gee, do we?"

"Negative, just seat-belts. I'll keep her in atmo for now, just a short hop to get clear of the city." With that she stepped through the airlock door to do her final check.

∞ ∞ ∞

A few minutes later, Jackie was back in the cockpit with the ship buttoned down. She keyed the radio. "*Sophie* to Harp Spaceport Ground, requesting clearance to the active for takeoff."

"*Ah, wait one,* Sophie."

"Roger." That was odd. Maybe the guy in the tower was in the middle of something else. It wasn't like there was enough traffic to justify someone just sitting around twiddling his or her thumbs most of the time. Or maybe there was something more sinister. *Carcharodon* may not have left the system yet. Had they radioed back and asked for a traffic hold? Vaughan might have the local contacts to make that happen. Roberts preferred not to have to blast vertically out of the parking area. Besides putting the *Sophie* on a shit-list that would eventually propagate to other spaceports, it might damage ships parked nearby. But if it came to that . . . .

"*Sophie, this is ground. Sorry about that. I'm sorry, there's a bit of a delay—*"

Crap, Roberts thought. Here it comes.

"*—while the* Speedwell *moves out and clears the pad. Wouldn't want you caught in its downwash. Hold five or so until the active is clear.*"

Jackie felt a release of tension she hadn't known she had. "Roger that, ground. *Sophie* will hold until active is clear. Thank you."

"Problem?" Burnside called from aft.

"We picked the wrong day for all this. The *Speedwell* is about to take off. She has priority, we need to wait until she clears. Five minutes."

It was a long five minutes.

"How are we doing?" Carson said at three.

"Just fine," she called back, an impatient snip in her voice. *This is ridiculous*, she told herself, *I've had longer holds than this.* She set up a sensor diagnostic program on her console, just for something to do.

The radio sounded again. "Sophie, *this is Harp Ground—*"

Jackie's gut clenched. Oh crap, now what?

"*—please continue to hold. Slight problem with the* Speedwell *. . . oh, wait a moment. They've cleared it. False alarm, sorry about that.*"

"Harp, *Sophie.* Roger that," and though she didn't mean it, added, "No problem."

The diagnostic scan was still running when a growing rumble, turning into a roar, came from beyond the ship. *At last.* The *Speedwell* was lifting. The sound reached a crescendo and then faded away. A moment after that the radio sounded again.

"*Sophie, this is Ground. You're cleared to the active, runway two-zero, and departure at your discretion. Report clear.*"

Finally. "Roger ground. *Sophie* is cleared to two-zero and for departure. Will report clear. Thank you."

Two minutes after that, the Sophie lifted from the runway, climbing for the sky. As she passed through a thousand meters, five kilometers from the spaceport, Roberts called back.

"Harp City spaceport, this is the *Sophie* reporting clear, southwest at one thousand meters and climbing, turning to heading niner-five." They would expect the turn if she was going to go for an orbit.

"*Thank you, Sophie. Safe trip. Harp City out.*"

Roberts continued her climb until reaching an altitude of ten thousand meters, where she leveled off. By this point, on the heading she'd been following, they were out over the ocean east of the continent where Harp City had been established. She began a gradual turn back toward the mainland, to a point well south of the city. Her charts showed a broad area of savannah where it would be clear to land . . . just so long as nobody had decided to set up a homestead there since the chart database was last updated. She set the autopilot and went back to talk with the others.

"Well, we're clear. Heading southwest at ten K, keeping it subsonic. There's a nice deserted savannah forty minutes away where we can set down. Then what?"

"Then Tevnar guides us to her ship, we retrieve the artifact, and go on our way, Burnside said.

"Why do I get the feeling it's not going to be that simple?" Jackie said.

"Because it's not," Carson said.

Burnside and Roberts looked at him questioningly.

"I want to know where she found that artifact, if there was anything else nearby, and just how she came to find it. If the site is within range, I'd like to visit it. I'd also like to be sure it wasn't looted from a known site, although I don't think she'd have been so worried about it if it were. Nobody has found high tech artifacts at known sites, except the talismans, and they don't look high tech."

"Nobody that you know of," Burnside pointed out. "The Velkaryans got something from somewhere. Maybe a site unknown to professional archeologists, but not necessarily. I wouldn't be surprised if they had sponsored a few digs of their own, and may well have a few archeologists in their pockets."

"But . . . ." Carson began, then trailed off. "No, okay. Fair enough, that's not impossible. I don't like the idea, but human nature being what it is, I can't rule it out."

"But as far as what we're looking for, we won't know until we ask her. How is she?"

Carson went over to check the traumapod display. "She's in light sleep," he said. "Looks like she's mending well, she should be up and about in a couple of days." Timoans healed quickly, and the humans' rapid action had made a significant difference.

"Let's open the pod," Burnside said. "But let her wake up on her own."

Carson looked at the display again. "No reason why not." He looked over at Jackie. "Captain?"

"Go ahead," she said. She was as curious as the others as to what exactly was going on, and she didn't see any harm.

She watched as Carson activated the controls to open the pod door and slide the bed part way out, but left it at that. Tevnar's eyes flickered. Probably the motion of the bed had roused her. Her eyes opened, and she tilted her head left and right, looking around.

"We're airborne?" she asked. "Too noisy for space."

"That's right. Well clear of Harp City," Jackie answered. "How are you feeling?"

"I've been better. Things still hurt. But I can function. Let me get up."

"You're better off to stay lying down for a bit longer," Jackie said, "but we'd like to talk if you're up to it."

"Sure." Tevnar was obviously familiar with traumapod controls, quickly locating the buttons near her hand that elevated the head rest. She raised it about twenty degrees. "That's better. So, are we going to the *Razgon?* To my ship?"

"We can, if you tell us where it is."

"About five hundred kilometers west-south-west of Harp City." She gave Roberts a set of coordinates. "It's an S-class, a Sandquist—" her accent made it sound more like "sandvich", but Jackie knew what she meant "—not a Sapphire like this. Does the job. Parked it five kilometers from my sister's, in a place not easily visible from above, away from passersby. Last time I checked he was fine."

"He?" asked Jackie.

"Timoans refer to their ships and boats as he," Carson said, "and usually give them male names. Although I don't know what *Razgon* means, if anything."

"A kind of animal, a bit like your flying squirrels," Tevnar said. "You spoke timoan, back there. Badly, but still. You study at Kangara?"

"I have a colleague there. Marten, professor of archeology."

"Ah, I know Marten. Mostly a good boy. Bit of a renegade, but smart, him. My second cousin's kit, precocious. Adolescent boys often run away, but he did it younger and farther."

"He's why we have gear for timoans," Jackie said. "I dropped him off on Taprobane two stops back, before coming here."

"That explains why this place smells familiar."

Carson and Jackie looked at each other. "Smell?" she asked.

"You humans have dead noses. Don't worry, you don't offend. But even with your cleaning and your air scrubbers, I thought there had been a timoan on recently. Family, at that."

"Well, you do tend to large families," Carson said.

"By your standards, I suppose." She looked at Jackie meaningfully.

Jackie wondered if that was intended as something about family, and felt her cheeks warming. Then she remembered how they had gotten onto the subject. "I'll be right back," she said. "I have a new course to set." She started forward to the control cabin.

"So," Carson said, "about this artifact. Where did it come from?"

Jackie paused at the cockpit door to hear the answer.

"That, friend, is a long story."

"I think we have time." He called forward, "Jackie, how long till we land?"

"An hour," she said. "And Tevnar, don't you dare start that story until I'm done here. I want to hear it too."

Chapter 38: Tevnar's Story

Aboard the Sophie

"ALL RIGHT. CAN I get some water? This pod may be keeping me hydrated but my mouth is dry."

"Sure," Carson said, and he unfolded a drinking tube from its stowage area in the interior side of the pod. "Here."

Tevnar took a sip, then a long drink. "Ah, better. Thank you. Now, where shall I begin?"

∞ ∞ ∞

"I was headed out from Epsilon Eridani toward Zeta Tucanae. It's my ship but I do some flying for Kangara University. I had just dropped a team of geologists—mixed human and timoan, a field trip—on Spitzer, and heard that there was a team on Zeta Tucanae that might need a pick-up around the time I could get there."

"I hope they found another ride," Roberts said. "That would have been some time ago, given when we heard about the artifact."

"Hush, I'm telling this. And I haven't been here all that time; I gave them their ride, then came back here."

"That explains the delay getting hold of you," Burnside said. "But why didn't you drop the artifact off when you got back to Taprobane after your pick up?"

"It was here the whole time, in safe keeping. I didn't want it aboard with a shipload of scientists. Now, do you want to hear this or not?"

"Sorry. Please, continue."

"Anyway, I went via Kapteyn's Star, a red dwarf, with known planets. Red dwarfs never have terraformed planets, I guess the original Terraformers didn't think them suitable, so these probably hadn't been explored much if at all. I decided to do a bit of sightseeing as well as refueling."

"So, six-and-a-half boring days later, I came out of warp near Kapteyn's, and did the usual scan to locate myself and the planets. Kapteyn's has two large rocky planets, what you call super-Earths, and a few smaller ones and miscellaneous debris. A lot of junk for a red dwarf.

"The larger one—I don't know if any of them have names, but they don't in my data base, just code designations—is beyond the habitable zone and covered with ice, but it's also seven Earth or Taprobane masses, so on top of the fun of mining the ice, landing, moving around, and taking off would be no treat. I'm not even sure the latter would be possible.

"The inner one, now. The inner super-Earth is much more interesting. It's actually in the habitable zone, and has liquid water. Not a lot, the oceans are small and shallow, but it has it all the same. It also has weather, and rain, and fresh water lakes. Perfect, except for the high gravity. It's roughly five Taprobane masses, a bit less than that in Earth masses, but still much bigger than Skead, say. The crazy planet has a low average density, too, so a big diameter. The escape velocity is high. But it was within my parameters. It doesn't have much of a spin, seems to be in some kind of five-to-two resonance between its sun and the outer planet, so not much equatorial boost, but I'd take what I could get.

"But wanted to find the best place to land to take on fuel, so I spent more than a day scanning it from orbit. I must own the best set of images of the place, at least within fifteen degrees of the equator."

"I take it you spotted something?" Carson said. "What was it."

"Hold your *prag* . . . ah, horses, boy, I'm getting there."
"Sorry."

Tevnar took another sip from her drinking tube, then continued. "As I was saying, I was looking for a good place to land and take off. I found a large lake bed, flat, with a small lake off to one side of the middle of it. Now that might be a lake with a salt flat around it, so a salt lake. If needs be I can refuel with salt water;

I've got the filters. But fresh is preferable." She looked up at Roberts. "Right, Captain?"

"Exactly right. And you can call me Jackie."

"Right. Anyway, I noticed a stream bed leading down from mountains a few kilometers away to the north, then draining the lake to the east before turning south. Wasn't much of a stream, its bed was mostly dry too, probably seasonal. But it was probably good enough to keep the lake fresh. The surrounding lake-bed was flat enough to make a good long runway for landing and takeoff, so I decided to give it a try.

"Turned out I wasn't the only one who had thought that."

"There was another ship?" Carson blurted.

"If you're going to keep interrupting, boy, we'll never get through this."

Carson shut up.

"Anyway, I did my de-orbit burn and began entry. Pretty routine. The atmosphere was thinner than I expected for a planet that size, must have blown off over time. Mostly nitrogen. Anyway, I landed well clear of the lake itself. You can never tell with lake beds; sometimes it's just a thin layer of dry clay over soft mud, and I didn't want to get stuck.

"Turned out to not be a problem. Ground was pretty solid, something between sandstone and clay. Solid enough that even when dry it didn't blow around like sand. Pretty solid where I landed, got a little softer near the water, but not so I'd get stuck in it, even with the higher gravity. One-point-seven gees, approximately; my ship has the exact number. I taxied to twenty-five or thirty meters from the waterline. Not a huge lake, a couple of kilometers across, and there wasn't much wind when I landed. Just a few modest waves, looking kind of strange with the gravity. One-point-seven gee doesn't sound like much, but after a while I felt like I'd been carrying a couple of grown kits around all day. Breathing gear didn't help.

"The atmosphere won't hurt your skin, but you can't breathe it. Partial pressure of oxygen is too low, and carbon-dioxide is too high. Surprised there's not more greenhouse effect. Or maybe there is, and the hab-zone is actually farther in than the planet. Whatever." Tevnar paused, as if collecting her thoughts, then continued.

"I ran my refueling hoses out into the lake and got them set up, then went back inside to lie down for a while."

She took another sip of water.

"How are you doing?" Roberts asked. "Do you need to take a break?"

Carson gave her a look like she was crazy, but he didn't say anything. No doubt he was dying to hear the rest of the story, although he surely understood that Tevnar needed rest too.

"I'm fine. Your boy here looks like he'll pop if I don't keep going. I understand. Marten's like that too, as I recall. Always curious, that one. That's what got him in trouble."

Carson cleared his throat, noisily.

"All right, all right. A while later I woke up from my nap and went out to check on the hoses. My tanks were filling nicely, and nothing was plugging the intakes. There's life on that planet. Nothing fancy, some algae and the like. Probably just enough to keep the oxygen levels where they are. Anyway, I had spotted something odd when landing, so after I checked the hoses, I took a look with binoculars. It was something sticking up out of the ground a half-kilometer away. Didn't look much like a rock. It could have been the remains of a dead tree, but not out in the middle of nowhere like that. At that distance though the thick air it was hard to tell. It was sure out of place on the flat lake-bed. I decided when the refueling was done I would go take a closer look.

"I got the hoses put away, my tanks were topped up. Time to go check out the whatever it was. I wasn't going to walk, not in that gravity.

"Jackie, are you familiar with *Sandvich* class ships?"

"Only a little. I've never flown one, although I did some research before I bought this ship."

"Okay. Then you might know that they have a nice feature; the landing gear wheels are motorized. Means you can taxi around without firing up the thrusters. Saves a bit of fuel, and they're quieter on the ground. Spaceports like them because they don't need a tow vehicle."

"It seemed like an extra complication to me," said Roberts. "Something else that could go wrong."

"There is that, but I never had a problem with them, and the weight isn't worth worrying about.

"Anyway, I just taxied around to where I'd seen the whatever-it-was sticking out of the ground. It was covered in dirt and dried sediment, and worn. Might have been underwater part of the time, when the lake level was high. It had obviously been there a long time. But it was no stone or tree. It was a ship."

"What kind?" Roberts asked.

"Like I said, it had been there a long time. It was considerably damaged, but there was enough there to tell what it was, and what it wasn't. No human built that ship, and for damn sure no timoan did either. I'm no geologist, but it could have been there a thousand years."

Burnside had been listening quietly up until now. He was the first to break the silence that followed Tevnar's revelation. "You are joking with us, right?"

"Where do you think I got the artifact?"

Jackie looked at Carson and raised her eyebrow. Carson nodded. "I take it," she said to Burnside, "you haven't heard about Belize?"

"What about Belize? Some place in Central America, right?"

"Recent news," Carson said, "and I guess it hasn't made it here yet. It's one reason Ducayne sent me. Some divers found old wreckage off the coast of Belize. It's still being kept quiet, but it looks like the remains of an alien spaceship. There's writing on what might be parts of an instrument panel. Ducayne has somebody working on that. It resembles markings on the artifact in the pictures you sent him."

"Well, well. What are the odds? Seems a bit of a coincidence."

"They happen," Carson said. "We're beginning to think that there was a lot of interstellar traffic in the neighborhood up until a century or two ago, maybe even since then. We—Jackie and I—have met one of the civilizations involved. Humans, and timoans, are pushing farther out, and the core of our bubble called T-Space is getting pretty busy. People are bound to start finding things. Ducayne can't keep a lid on it forever."

"Well, it's not just Ducayne, but I see your point. This is going to make our jobs a lot harder."

"How so?"

"People can ignore the Terraformers. However powerful they were, they've been gone for millions of years. High-tech aliens who might still be around? That's something else. What do you think knowledge of that would do to Velkaryan recruiting? A little xenophobia goes a long way."

"The damned Velkaryans again. And they may not even be the biggest problem."

"What do you mean?"

Roberts wondered if Carson would bring up what the Kesh had said about the degkhidesh. She caught his eye and shook her head; Burnside had no need to know.

Carson had either already decided that himself or took her hint. "Ah, not for me to say. Ask Ducayne."

Burnside's eyes narrowed as he looked intently at Carson, then he turned to Roberts with a questioning look. She shrugged.

"Okay, fair enough," Burnside said. "Not your call as to whether I need to know, so I guess I don't right now. I will ask him, though."

"I can neither confirm nor deny that there's anything worth asking about," Carson said, his straight face breaking into a slight wry smile at the end.

"Got it."

"But I would like to ask Tevnar about something, and you'll be interested too."

"What's on your mind, Carson?" the timoan said. At least it wasn't "boy" this time.

"I've got pictures of some of the debris we found on Earth. I'm wondering if anything looks similar to what you may have found. I take it, since you brought something back, you found a way inside?"

"Part way inside. A lot of it was clogged with sediment and crash damage. But let's see what you've got. Wait," she turned her head toward Roberts. "Jackie, how long until we reach my ship?"

Roberts checked a nearby display. "Twenty minutes. How are you holding up?"

"I'm going to need to be awake then to help you find it. It's not visible from the air. Carson, sorry, but I should rest a bit. I'll look at your pictures later. Heh, when we get to my ship, you can see the real artifact."

Carson took it well. "Sure. Get some rest. We'll wake you when we get there."

Tevnar lowered her headrest and closed her eyes. "Go ahead and close the pod," she said, "it's quieter."

"No problem." Jackie touched the control to do just that, and checked the monitor screen. Tevnar's pulse and temperature were elevated, but not worryingly so. Probably just reaction to the exertion.

"What do you think?" Burnside asked Carson.

"That story seems way too elaborate to have been made up, nor can I think of any reason why it would be. Jackie, does what she said about Kapteyn's star and its planets make sense?"

"From what I know, yes. I'll check the data on the planets, but it may not have been explored. We tend to ignore red dwarfs. Probably most of them in tee-space have only been visited once, if that. They're more common than any other kind of star. There are over seventy-five within twenty light-years of Sol, and only a handful have maintained refueling stops."

Carson let out a low whistle. "I didn't realize there were that many."

"What about the wrecked ship?" said Burnside. "I get the impression you know a lot more about that sort of thing than I do."

Carson weighed what to say next. Even if Burnside was Ducayne's man, it wouldn't be appropriate to give him information from a privileged source. But there was something he could talk about.

"I've been going through a lot of historical records of so-called UFO sightings, unidentified flying objects. They were a big deal in the early space age. Most of them were either misinterpretations of natural phenomena, or hoaxes, and so on. There were a few that could not be easily otherwise explained, and might—just *might*, mind you—have been sightings of craft operated by the species we know is out there."

"The Kesh?"

"Okay, so you've heard of them. Yes. The individual I talked to said that some of the descriptions sound similar to Kesh scout craft, but that he wasn't aware of any such scouting in that period. What they may have been doing a thousand or more years before that, we didn't discuss. The Belize find is estimated at two thousand years old."

"So, whatever Tevnar has on her ship, and the wreck at Kapteyn's, could be from a Kesh scout craft?"

"That seems most likely. Or rather, the least improbable, other than an outright hoax."

"But why did the Kesh leave known space? Surely *we* didn't scare them off."

"You'll have to ask them that. They wouldn't even tell me if they came from a terraformed planet or if they evolved independently, although they didn't seem too dissimilar from terrestrial life."

Jackie had heard this before, and Carson was lapsing into lecture mode. She got up to head forward. "Don't mind me, guys, but we're getting near her coordinates. I'm going to go fly the ship and start dropping our altitude."

∞ ∞ ∞

As the Sophie descended on a path toward the coordinates Tevnar had given, it became clear to Roberts why it would be hard to spot from above. An escarpment ran northwest-southeast here, with a height difference of one to two hundred meters. Mostly, the sides were steep but not cliffs, with occasional exceptions. The area toward which they were flying was a series of box canyons, possibly where ancient waterfalls had eroded back the scarp in several areas. The area was dry now, with low grassy scrub and scattered trees. There were more trees closer to the cliffs. There were enough clear areas to land vertically, and with the Sandquist's powered landing gear, it could have taxied under an overhang or beneath some of the scrub growing out around the lower part of the cliffs. From above you wouldn't see it if you didn't know what you were looking for, and maybe not even then. She began circling the area at an altitude of six hundred meters, low enough to check out the ground but high enough not to have to worry about trees or other obstacles on the high side of the escarpment. It was a little bumpy, a breeze from the northeast was kicking up some ridge lift and turbulence.

She used the intercom to call back to the men chatting in the galley. "Somebody want to wake up our guest? I think we're here, but I don't know where I should set down," she said.

"On it."

A few minutes later, Tevnar's voice came over the intercom. "Mind if I join you? It will make it easier to guide you."

"If you feel up to it, sure. Come on forward."

This time Roberts had left the cockpit door open, and a few moments later Tevnar came through, a blanket draped over her shoulders, and took the co-pilot's seat. Carson and Burnside followed behind, hanging back behind the seats. "Where are we?" she asked.

"Circling the coordinates you gave me, a kilometer out." Roberts touched a control, and the screen in front of Tevnar switched to a view of the ground. "Anything look familiar?"

Tevnar studied the screen and glanced at the other views on the windows. "Looks right. Hold on, let me turn on the lights." She retrieved her omni and tapped out a sequence. "Bearing 305, unless your hull is messing with my beacon. Under some trees near a cliff edge to its north. Should be enough poking out to see the port running light."

Roberts banked the Sophie to the given heading. Yes, there was part of a canyon wall ahead of her, and there was a red light shining from a stubby wingtip. "Got it. Where should I set down?"

"Vertical landing a hundred meters away should be fine. The canyon will funnel your down-wash a bit, but there's an open area just outside the canyon entrance, here."

Roberts glanced over to where Tevnar was pointing at the overall view on her screen.

"Right, no problem. Gents, please take your seats, it might be a bit bumpy."

As they did so, Roberts eased the airspeed back and diverted more power to the ventral thrusters, turning their glide into a vertical descent. The wind and turbulence didn't help. It got worse when she lowered the landing gear. She hoped that would let off some when it came time to take-off.

As she dropped down below the crest of the escarpment, the buffeting eased. Jackie checked her ground-proximity radar. Forty meters. Twenty. Ten. Five . . . A wind gust rocked the *Sophie*, threatening to send it toward the trees, and Roberts quickly corrected. She thumbed a switch on her joystick handle. "Brace," she said, and cut power. There was sudden weightlessness as the ship dropped, then weight surged back as the *Sophie*'s thrusters cut in at nearly full power for a fraction of a second before impact. The ship came to rest with a thump.

"Nicely done," said the timoan pilot beside her.

∞ ∞ ∞

Carson watched as Roberts ran through her post-landing checklist and secured the *Sophie*, while Tevnar used the app on her omni to check her own ship's systems and turn off its navigation lights. "Undisturbed, just like the last time I checked," she said.

"Good," said Roberts. "I'm sure the boys are anxious to take a look at what you found."

Carson agreed. "You could say that."

"How are you feeling?" Roberts asked Tevnar.

"Sore." She stood up. "The leg's a little weak. Got something I can use as a crutch?"

Roberts did. "Wait one, I'll go get something." She disappeared into the back of the ship and came back with some construction of metal and plastic tubes which would serve the purpose. Carson had no idea what it really was, and didn't ask.

"All right," Carson said, "let's go."

Chapter 39: The Artifact

The Razgon

SOPHIE HAD LANDED a short distance from the *Razgon*, and as Carson and the others hiked toward it, it was still half concealed under the foliage in the shade of the cliff.

From what Carson could tell, the *Razgon* looked about the same size as the *Sophie*, but where the latter was a deltoid shape with internal warp pods and pivoting aft fins, the *Razgon* had a more cylindrical body with stubby wings mounted toward the rear, the tips of which each held a warp pod. Like the *Sophie*, its surface was adorned with the outlines of hatches and inspection plates, plus the thruster ports.

"Hold up a moment," Tevnar said. She touched a control on her omni and the ship's port-side hatch opened while a short boarding stair extruded from its lower edge. "All right," she said, moving to the stairs, "come on in. Layout's a little different from the *Sophie*. Take a right at the corridor and the galley is on your left. I'm going to check the cockpit."

The others followed her in, taking the right and left turns to the galley area. It was a human-built ship, of course, but with a few customizations for timoans. The lighting was dimmer, and everything felt a bit cozier. The galley chairs and table were slightly lower, timoans' average height being a bit shorter than humans', but not so small as a human child. The seating was adequate.

Tevnar came back from the cockpit. "Can one of you gents give me a hand? That artifact is a bit heavy for me right now."

"How did you get it back to your ship at Kapteyn's?" Carson asked, rising to help her.

"With some difficulty. And a freight dolly."

"Ah."

"Here," she said, pointing to a low storage locker near a door at the aft end of the passageway. She touched a control and the segmented door panel rolled up and folded back into a recess above it. "That's it."

It wasn't in a crate, although there was padding around it to keep it from moving around. A metallic cylinder, a two-thirds of a meter long and a half meter in diameter. There was what looked like a display panel of some kind, and square buttons with markings on them. They looked vaguely cuneiform. Whatever this was, it was nothing like the so-called Maguffin they'd found on Chara III, either in overall appearance or the symbols on it. The symbols looked more like what Carson had seen in the pictures of the Belize wreckage. Bingo!

"Here, bring it back to the galley," Tevnar called. "The others will want to take a look at it."

Carson knelt down and pulled it out of the locker. It was hefty, and a little awkward in the passageway. He was pondering the best way to lift when Burnside came aft from the galley

"Want a hand?" he asked.

"Wouldn't hurt. I'd hate to drop it."

The two of them took it by either end, cradling it—there were no obvious carrying handles—and carried it back to the galley table, where they set it down gently. The under or back side of it had an opening that looked like a panel had been removed, or where it had attached to something. Cables extended through the opening; they were torn as through it had been ripped out. There were traces of corrosion and sediment wedged in to gaps and corners of the device, which fit with Tevnar's story.

"Did you clean it up some?" Carson asked.

"Yep. You're probably horrified, being an archeologist, but I wanted to see what I had. And I wanted a good look at it to scan for fabbing a copy."

"So, the Velkaryans have a copy of this?" Burnside asked.

"A plastic shell that looks a bit like it, yeah. If they can figure anything out from that, more power to them."

"As long as they don't have another like it."

"Why would they?"

"No reason. These markings," Carson pointed to the symbols, "are totally different from what we saw in the pyramid. This is more likely Kesh technology."

"Who or what is Kesh?" Tevnar asked.

"Other spacefarers," Carson said. "We haven't really met them, just seen signs. Speaking of which," Carson reached for his omni; he had remembered the Belize pictures. "Tevnar, you pulled this out of a ship, or wreckage of one. Do these pictures look like anything?"

Most of the pictures didn't show much that was recognizable. There were sections of tubing, some structural beams or hull material, all of it dented, bent and severely worn and corroded. But other pictures showed more of interest, like a rectangular display that might have been dislodged from a control panel or dashboard, with symbols or writing on parts of it, and another section with several pipes and what might have been remotely controlled valves at one time.

"Woo, that's a bit of a mess," Tevnar said. "Some of those symbols match what's on this gizmo." She pointed to several on one of the pictures, then to the corresponding labeled rectangles on the artifact. "Could be numbers or common icons like 'ON' and 'OFF', or 'INCREASE' and 'DECREASE'."

"Good call," said Carson, impressed. "You might be right."

"The rest of this, though . . . ." she flicked through the images again, occasionally pausing and zooming in. "This one," she said, stopping at the picture of the pipes and possible valve. "I've seen this valve before, on the wreck. See this bit sticking out? And this connector? I remember that. Looks like a solenoid-actuated valve, and I remember wondering what it might have controlled. Part of a fuel line or part of the waste management plumbing?" She started to chuckle, then winced. "Ouch," she said, putting a hand to her injured side. "Remind me not to do that for a while."

"Where did you find this thing?" Burnside asked, tapping the cylinder.

"It was on the deck, mixed with some debris. There was what was left of a pedestal sticking up from an instrument panel that might have connected to that opening. Might have ripped loose when it crashed, or enough so that gravity got to it eventually. No clue what it is, of course."

"Do you have an idea where it was mounted relative to the rest of the ship?"

"Hard to say. Could have been the middle of the cabin, but that seems silly. It would always be getting in the way."

"Unless it was something added later," Roberts said. "Experimental gear, perhaps? Some of my charters bring some odd stuff along, and I'm not letting them put it in my cockpit." She hesitated, reddening. "Carson, don't say a word."

"Right. You wouldn't let them put unknown gear in the *Sophie*'s control cabin. I got it." He suppressed a smirk.

"Why not just mount it on a wall, or the floor?"

Roberts shrugged. "No particular reason. Unless . . . ."

"Yes?"

"If you don't bias the warp field for artificial gravity, somewhere in the center would be where the influence of the warp pods balanced out, so that would be a good place for some kind of mass sensor or something. That's assuming the ship *had* warp pods as we know them, and some reason to want to sense mass."

"Might be the only thing you can sense outside a warp field, when you're travelling," Tevnar said.

She had a point. Photons got randomized trying to cross the immense local gravity of a warp bubble boundary; light and radio didn't work. Not that they would have been useful while travelling faster than light anyway. An external gravitational field, however . . . if it were strong enough it might be detectable.

"This thing has to be way too small to detect gravity waves," Roberts objected.

"So far as *we* know," Burnside said. "Didn't you say there was some advanced technology out there?"

Roberts opened her mouth like she was about to protest, but then closed it and sat back in her seat looking thoughtful. "Maybe," she said, "but I'd think the mass of any crewmembers moving around would swamp any outside signal with so short a wavelength."

"So, Mister Smith, or Burnside," Tevnar said, "is this what you wanted?"

"It certainly seems so. What are the chances of getting to Kapteyn's to check out the rest of the wreckage?"

"That will cost extra."

"I expected it to. What do you think, Carson, want to come along?"

"Are you kidding? I wouldn't miss it. Considering what I went through to get here, I want as much out of this trip as possible."

"What's the plan?" Roberts asked. "I'd like to see this too. Whose ship were you planning to take? Or both?"

"It's a heavy planet. We know the *Razgon* can land and take off again. What about the *Sophie*?"

Roberts looked at Tevnar. "What about it?" Jackie asked. "Is it within a Sapphire's limits? I'm based out of Skead."

"Then you know how to do a high gravity take-off. Kapteyn's is heavier. I'll give you the specs, so you can judge for yourself. But probably, yes."

Carson knew Roberts well enough to know that "probably" wasn't going to cut it. She would be running lots of simulations and weight calculations based on the data before committing to a landing. That was fine with him.

"So, two ships?" said Burnside. "Not a bad idea. Is that all right with you, Tevnar?"

"The more the merrier. We just need to decide who is going with whom."

"I think we should get off planet," Roberts said. "We can rendezvous in space and transfer there. Ah, Burnside, do you have a suit? I know I have one that fits Carson, but if I don't have another then I'm afraid it's rescue balls."

"Did you see me pack anything big enough to hold a spacesuit? Tevnar, how are you equipped?"

"I don't think you're going to fit in a timoan-sized suit. Sorry, my human passengers got off at Spitzer. But let me check inventory, I've usually got more junk stowed away than I realize."

"Balls," Burnside said. It sounded like he was swearing, but Carson wasn't sure if he meant the rescue balls or something else.

"I'll check too," Roberts said. "It's surprising how many places there are to stow things even on a small ship. Unless it's something I use regularly, things tend to hide. We *are* going to need breathing gear for everyone who goes out on the surface, but I think I've got that covered."

"All right," said Tevnar, "Burnside can come with me for now. We have things to discuss. But I need to taxi the *Razgon* out from under the trees to where it can lift. Jackie, it would help if you play marshaller for me."

"No problem." The *Razgon* undoubtedly had cameras and screens to give Tevnar a full 360-degree view while she backed out of her parking spot, but an extra pair of eyes some distance back would help. Especially if Tevnar's chest wound made it awkward for her to keep swiveling from one screen to another. The Sandquist class's stubby wings didn't pivot the same way a Sapphire's fins did. She'd want plenty of clearance.

"Thanks." The two of them went forward. On the way, Tevnar grabbed a head-set and handed it to Roberts. "Here. And the light-sabers are stowed in a rack by the hatch."

"Light-sabers?" said Roberts, sounding as mystified as Carson was.

"Marshaling wands. Okay, they are a bit short for light-sabers, but you must admit—"

"Oh, I agree." The illuminated batons were designed to make hand-waving signals easily visible. "I'm just surprised you're familiar with old Earth sci-fi."

"Just some of your classics. Keeps me entertained in deep space."

Roberts chuckled and headed for the airlock.

∞ ∞ ∞

Jackie did a quick walk-around of the *Razgon*, not so much checking the starship as looking for branches, tree trunks or other potential obstacles, then headed to the aft end of the ship and walked back thirty meters, scanning the ground. The trees gave away quickly away from the edge of the cliff, and the ground was clear but for some low scrub.

"Looks good," she told Tevnar over the headset. She raised the wands. "Come on back."

"Moving back."

It was odd seeing the ship backing up under its own power without hearing the whine of air being ducted through the fans. One of the advantages of a Sandquist. As she slowly walked back, gesturing with the marshaling wands while scanning left and right for obstacles, she was reminded of her days as a ramp rat when she was a teenager. Many pilots she knew had done that early in their careers; it was useful experience.

The starboard wingtip was nearing a tree branch. "Hold up," she said while waving the wands. "Tree limb to starboard. Pivot to your right fifteen degrees if your nose is clear." She made the appropriate signal with the wands.

"*Roger that. I have room.*"

The craft started to pivot clockwise, moving its nose closer to the trees and the cliff but swinging the wingtip away from the tree.

"*How am I doing?*"

"Another meter should do it."

There was a brief pause. "*Tight squeeze, but okay.*" The ship yawed a little more, then stopped.

"Okay, that's good. Straight back now." Roberts waved the wands backward.

The *Razgon* rolled a little farther, still turning but straightened up and backed out. Roberts waved it back another thirty meters.

"How's that? Clear forward?" Jackie could see the nose from her position.

"*Yep, and clear above. Thank you, much easier.*"

"No problem." Jackie walked back toward Tevnar's ship, turning off the wands and removing the headset as she went.

"Been a while since I've done that," she said as she reentered the ship and stowed the gear.

"Doesn't look like you've lost your touch. Is there enough clearance to the *Sophie*?" Neither pilot wanted the ships too close to avoid the other's downwash.

"No problem. Let's help you get things stowed for take-off."

"That would be appreciated."

∞ ∞ ∞

With both ships readied for space, Carson and Roberts lifted first in the *Sophie*, climbing vertically on her ventral thrusters until well clear of the top of the escarpment, then transitioning to horizontal flight before pitching up and heading for space. Two minutes later, the *Razgon* executed a similar maneuver and followed the Sophie a few tens of kilometers behind, increasing speed to catch up with her in orbit.

Chapter 40: Meanwhile, Back at the Ranch

Sawyers World, Homeworld Security

"YOU LOOK WORRIED," Malcolm Brown said to Ducayne as they arrived at Briefing Room Two, the one with the puke-green carpet. It was more of a dark greenish chartreuse, but somebody had once referred to it as "puke-green" and the term had stuck.

"Disturbing reports about the Velkaryan political situation," Ducayne said.

"Trouble in Venezuela?"

"Among other places. Verdigris too. It would seem they have a thing for place-names starting with the letter V."

"Velkaryans. But they're also in plenty of other places."

"Sure. Just a random observation." Ducayne said. "Anything new from the UFO files, or the Belize wreckage?"

"Not much on the UFOs," Brown said. "Very few sightings where the observer saw any markings, as in the Sirocco case. Of those, most of the descriptions aren't detailed enough to know what they were describing. At least Zamora drew a diagram."

"Does the symbol match anything on the Belize debris?"

"Not on anything they've recovered so far, at least that my sources are aware of." Brown had a channel to one of the groups on Earth involved in the Belize investigation. Unfortunately, most of what they'd found had been small fragments; the consensus was that the ship had either blown up when it crash-landed or been deliberately scuttled. "That doesn't prove anything, any markings I've found so far are worn and eroded, a lot of them are incomplete. But we've been able to get some detailed analysis done on parts of the debris. Some of the things that look like parts of a control panel, for example. Electron micrography and tomographic scans show evidence of lettering where it has worn down to invisibility to the naked eye. I've been compiling a database of all the symbols found so far, and a concordance of sequences that look like words. The language looks logographic rather than alphabetic. Another possible tie to Sumerian."

"Hmm. Deciphered any of it yet?"

Brown wished they had. "We don't exactly have a Rosetta Stone for it, but some symbols are likely numerals, and we have a few tentative words or word-symbols that appear on some of the controls. Possibly the equivalent of 'OFF' and 'ON', but I have no idea which might be which."

"Well, that's something, anyway," Ducayne said. "And it bears no relationship to the language in the Chara pyramid?"

"Not so far. The Kesh—assuming it was them—probably had some written language of their own before discovering how to get into their pyramid, or far enough into it anyway."

"What about the artifact on Tanith? Does anything correlate with the pictures we got?"

"Yes, some symbols appear on both." It had been an exciting moment when he'd realized that, although there were slight stylistic differences. "Several of those that we think are numerals."

"Interesting. Now I *really* want to get my hands on that gadget."

"Oh? You didn't before?"

"Of course I did. But it's sounding even more interesting. I could use some good news."

Ducayne had mentioned disturbing reports when he'd arrived. "So, what is happening with the Velkaryans?" Brown asked.

"For one, I think they have a starship factory on Verdigris, probably at New Toronto."

Brown didn't think Ducayne meant that quite the way it sounded. Yes, Verdigris had technical infrastructure approaching that of Sawyers World, but even Sawyers wasn't quite up to producing starships without importing a lot of components. "Well, they might make hulls and such, but what about the engines?"

"That's just it," Ducayne said. "I've been analyzing their import lists for the past couple of years—and that's just the stuff we know about, we don't know how much they've smuggled, although we know it must be *some*—and a lot of the equipment that companies there, especially New Toronto companies, have bought is potentially dual-use. Semiconductor fabrication systems, for example. That's expensive equipment and it makes sense to have local places to get spare parts for computers, omnis, ship avionics and what-have-you. However, fabrication of the monolithic subsystems of a warp pod or a fusion engine uses very similar equipment. Not that Earth has many regulations, as such, regarding exporting that gear, except to religious settlements. Most worlds don't have the economy to support it. This planet is one of the exceptions, Verdigris may be another."

Sawyers World did have a small starship industry, which mostly supplied parts to the Kiahuna Shipyards in orbit over Kakuloa, but also built specialty ships for customers who could afford it.

Ducayne continued. "A fabrication line for one could be modified to the other, and in the case of some of the brands and models they imported, it wouldn't be too hard for some skilled engineers to do so."

"And they have those skilled engineers?"

"Yes. They have an active recruitment program, and a good local college. Since there's not much call for arts majors on the frontier worlds, it specializes in technology and engineering."

"That might explain why Carson and Roberts were waved off from landing at New Toronto a few months back. If they are building ships, there would be a lot of them at the spaceport. Do we have reconnaissance photos?"

"No. The damned skyweed season on Verdigris lasts most of the year. New Toronto is hidden under a green blanket most of the time. It's not a problem for radar, but that also announces the transmitter's presence."

The near-permanent layers of floating, almost microscopic, aerophytoplankton—skyweed—that had given Verdigris its name would of course make excellent cover for something wanting to hide from overhead observation without making it obvious that it was trying to. "Do we have assets on the ground?"

"If I had any, I wouldn't be griping so much. In Verdigris City, yes, but that's half a world away from New Toronto, and with not a lot of travel between the two. The reports I *am* getting out of Verdigris City are a little unsettling. More Velkaryan presence in local government, and one of the big biochemical companies there was recently acquired by another with Velkaryan connections.

"Couple that with the apparent missing device from the looted pyramid near New Toronto, and it's pretty obvious that the Velkaryans have a strategic presence there."

"It does sound like it," Brown said. "Speaking of pyramids, did your team find a corresponding room in the Chara pyramid, with a device?"

Ducayne had sent a follow-up team to Chara III when Carson first reported back from there, but they didn't know then about the hidden chamber in the upper part of the similar pyramid on Verdigris. Carson had discovered it during a stopover on Verdigris on the way to Zeta Reticuli, and neither Brown nor Ducayne heard about it until Carson and his team had returned, a few weeks ago.

"I haven't heard back yet." Ducayne said. "Chara is twenty-nine light years away, so at least three weeks in warp each way, plus refueling stops, plus time on the planet. No message torpedo, but if they found something worth coming back with immediately, they could show up in the next week or so."

"Ah. Well, here's hoping," Brown said. He changed the subject. "What's happening in Venezuela?" He had been too focused on UFOs and the Belize find to pay much attention.

"Nothing good. There's the expulsion of extraterrestrials, of course, but there weren't more than a handful. The Venezuela delegation introduced a resolution at the *UdT* Council to grant more autonomy to the colony planets."

"That doesn't sound so bad."

"Except that they've been infiltrating a lot of the local planetary governments. The phrasing of the resolution is subtle, but one take on it is that it would exempt the independent planets from various *Union de Terre* charters unless and until those planets joined the *UdT* as members, and maybe not even then. Which means that *UdT* protections would no longer apply to any local intelligent species—or anything else on the planet for that matter."

"Ugh. I can see where some people might like that. They still gripe about Kakuloa."

"Yeah. Ironically, though, it still wouldn't do anything for the old squidberry plantation owners or the tree-squid reservations. Per the amendments to the Treaty of Alpha Centauri, Kakuloa falls under both *UdT* and Sawyers World protections. And yet they're using that treaty as precedent for granting other worlds independence."

"That's a bit of a stretch," Brown said.

"When has that stopped a lawyer or a diplomat?"

"Point taken. But it's just Venezuela; the resolution won't pass."

Ducayne shook his head no. "There are a surprising number of other countries siding with that point of view, or with other parts of the resolution. Most of them are former colonies or invaded territories themselves, two or three centuries back."

"But the *UdT* is hardly imperial Britain, or France, or Spain, or Japan. It's more like, oh, I don't know," Brown said, casting around for some innocuous trading empire of that era. "The Netherlands, say."

"Bad example. You need to refresh your history. The Dutch East India Company? Indonesia, Malacca, Ceylon, Surinam, Guyana, South Africa—"

Brown raised a hand to interrupt. "You've made your point. You're right; bad example. My point was that the *Union de Terre* is more like the old United Nations and areas under its protection were not under colonial rule."

"Most areas under its protection were either war zones or vast wastelands like Antarctica. Even the *UdT*, which this organization is nominally part of, carries that legacy. We're Homeworld Security, not Humanity's Security. What do you think *UdT*'s first reaction would be if hostile spacefaring aliens landed on, say, Skead? Or, better example, Taprobane? They'd pull in and start building defenses around the Solar System, that's what.

"No, I have nothing against the colony planets having a little more autonomy and certainly the ability to protect themselves. I just don't want them thinking they need to protect themselves against other human or human-friendly planets, let alone accidentally starting a war with the Kesh or whoever else is out there.

And with the Velkaryans, it might not even be accidentally. They are dangerous because they're loose cannons."

"Do the Velkaryans know about the Kesh? Or the degkhidesh?"

"I don't know. They're more likely to know about the Kesh, or at least their flying pyramid spaceships. They encountered one at Zeta Reticuli, according to Carson. We don't know if they've reported that back yet, but I got word that the *Carcharodon* is on 82 Eridani."

"That's where you sent Carson, isn't it? And Jackie Roberts is there?"

"Yes, on both counts. I didn't get word until Roberts was on her way."

"But before Carson left?"

Ducayne nodded. "That's one reason I sent him."

"Does he know that?" Brown asked.

"That may have slipped my mind. He can take care of himself."

Very little slipped Ducayne's mind, Brown thought, wondering what Ducayne was up to. "Indeed. I just hope he doesn't have to."

Chapter 41: Change of Plans

82 Eridani, near Anaid, Tanith's moon

"DOCKING COLLAR soft-docked," Tevnar's voice came over the radio.

"Roger that, *Razgon*. Engaging latches." Jackie Roberts touched a control and, from above and behind, the sound of docking latches locking into place conducted through the *Sophie's* hull. She watched as the circle of indicator lights turned from red to green. "All secure. Hard dock."

"Confirmed, Sophie."

The *Sophie* and *Razgon* had met at the Tanith – Anaid L1 point, far enough away from either that the ships would go unnoticed, yet a convenient reference point for a rendezvous. *Razgon* had extended a docking tube between the two ships, connecting to the docking port above and behind the *Sophie's* cockpit. The docking port in turn connected to overhead of *Sophie's* airlock, through which Burnside and Tevnar now floated to join Roberts and Carson.

"I want to propose a change of plans," Burnside said. "I think we should split up. Much as I'm curious about what Tevnar found at Kapteyn's star, Hannibal here is the one with archeological expertise and, if it is alien, more likely to recognize it for what it's worth."

"What are you going to do?" Carson asked.

"I need to find out what Vaughan is up to on Verdigris. I can't imagine he would leave the system without checking that crate. Tevnar, how long would it take him to realize he had a fake on his hands?"

"Five minutes, if that. It would pass a quick glance in a poorly lit warehouse, but not someone poking at it," the timoan said.

"If he didn't come back, there must be some important reason for him to continue on to Delta Pavonis."

"If that's really where he's going," Roberts said. "Just because he filed a flight plan . . . ."

"Doesn't mean he's going there, right. What time was the flight plan filed?"

"I don't remember," Roberts said. "Let me check." She accessed the *Sophie's* computer—it would have uploaded all the updated public information from the spaceport's systems as a matter of course before departure, to sync with the network at her destination; otherwise there was little point in filing flight plans—and pulled up the record she had checked earlier.

"Oh. They filed it *yesterday*, at 14:37. Early afternoon. Well before stealing the crate and shooting Tevnar."

"And after the *Speedwell* entered the system, so time enough to get any messages it was carrying," Burnside said. "I think maybe Vaughan was recalled."

"He could still have lied on the flight plan, as a matter of course," Carson said.

"Probably not," Roberts said. "The captain filed the plan, not Vaughan, and any ship which routinely filed false flight plans would eventually raise flags in the system. A ship that was reported missing and then showed up elsewhere would be investigated. Neither the captain nor Vaughan would want that. Easier to just not file in the first place."

"She's right," Tevnar said.

Carson had noticed Tevnar's apparent lack of discomfort in the now weightless environment. "Zero-gee doesn't seem to bother you the way it does Marten," he said. "I thought timoans didn't like free-fall?"

"I wouldn't say that I *liked* it either, but I'd be a pretty poor pilot if it distressed me. The first few times were . . . uncomfortable . . . but I got used to it. Not all humans like it either, right?"

"No, you're right. Sorry."

"You learn by asking questions."

"If we could get back to the matter at hand?" Burnside asked.

"Okay," Carson said. "You were talking about splitting up. You go to Verdigris, I go to Kapteyn's star?"

"Exactly."

"Since I have no idea where on Kapteyn's II this wreck is, although I could probably find it from Tevnar's description, I'm guessing you want me to take you to Verdigris?" said Roberts.

"Actually no. You and the *Sophie* are known there. Tevnar said she had detailed scans of the planet, she can give you the details on finding it. Right, Tevnar?"

"I can, but that means you'll want me to take you to Delta Pavonis. If Jackie ran into trouble on Verdigris, am I going to have issues as a timoan? You mentioned a strong Velkaryan presence. Besides, I'm not sure if Jackie, is okay with me stealing her charter."

"My commission was to bring the artifact back. What Burnside does is between him and you. I was refused landing at New Toronto, but had no problem at Verdigris City. You should be okay landing there. Jordan, does that work? Or . . . ."

"Or what?" Burnside asked.

"I located my other suit, or rather *Sophie* did. If you want to emulate Hannibal, I have a retro-pack you can use, if Tevnar doesn't." A retro-pack was a kit with retro-rockets, expandable foam heat shield, and a parachute, used for emergency entry from orbit. If he used it, Burnside would be landing on Verdigris the same way Carson had on Tanith. "But you'd be on your own getting off-planet."

Burnside looked at Carson, who was smiling broadly. "What?" he said.

"It's a lot of fun," Carson said. "You'll love it. Just keep your legs together and steer clear of the trees."

"I'd prefer to land with a ship around me. Verdigris City would be fine, but yes, I'll take the suit and retro-pack just in case. Tevnar, does that work for you?"

"Just as long as I get paid *before* you bail out," she said.

"Of course."

Roberts added "You should charge him extra for the Kapteyn's scan data. As for the wreck, I'm not sure if that's considered salvage or an archeological find."

"We'll work something out," Carson said. "Tevnar, if we get back to Taprobane before you, are you okay with bringing Marten in on this?"

Before Tevnar could answer, Burnside added, "Standard charter rates to Verdigris, plus a bonus if we run into problems, plus the fee for the artifact, and I'm thinking a finder's fee for the wreck if it's interesting? Which it sounds like it is."

Tevnar agreed. "That sounds more than satisfactory."

"We're agreed, then?" Burnside said, bringing the group back into focus. "Carson with Jackie on the *Sophie* to Kapteyn's, me and Tevnar on the *Razgon* to Verdigris, and ultimately back to Sawyers World."

"Can we rendezvous on Taprobane?" Roberts suggested. "*Sophie* has a flight plan filed for there."

"That would work better for me," said Tevnar.

Burnside thought a moment, then nodded to her. "That's not very far out of our way from Verdigris, and would save you a trip if you have no reason to go to Alpha Centauri. Unless Hannibal has an objection, Taprobane it is."

"No, that works for me," Carson said. "We'll need to transfer the artifact from the *Razgon*."

"Jordan," Roberts said, "I'll get you the suit and retro-pack. Return them to me when we meet at Taprobane."

"Of course. Thank you," Burnside said. He looked at the group. "Captains? With your permission, let's get to it."

Chapter 42: Second Divergence

Aboard the Sophie, *deep space*

"HEY, HANNIBAL," Jackie Roberts said, "have you ever watched another ship go to warp?" The *Sophie* and *Razgon* had undocked and secured themselves. Tevnar had just radioed Jackie that she was ready to depart.

"No," Carson said, "I can't say that I have. Is it worth watching?"

"It can be, depending on how hard or soft the local vacuum is. If the warp boundary rips apart enough atoms and molecules, there's a briefly visible ionization trail." And if there were too many, bad things happened. But they were too far out for that. "The *Razgon*'s about to warp out. Want to watch?"

"Sure." Carson joined Jackie in the cockpit. She dimmed the interior lighting and switched the windows to a view of the *Razgon*, about a kilometer away now.

Jackie clicked the radio. "*Sophie* to *Razgon*. We're all clear, Tevnar. Any time."

∞ ∞ ∞

Aboard the Razgon, *deep space*

"Burnside, prepare for gravity. Everything is secure, we're going to warp."

Burnside snugged his seat-belt. "Any time."

Tevnar lifted the safety cover off the ENGAGE WARP switch and flipped it. The switch itself didn't actually do anything but tell the ship's computers it had been flipped, but neither would the computers initiate the warp start-up sequence without that switch *being* flipped. There was something visually and physically satisfying about flipping a mechanical switch that clicking an icon on a screen didn't have.

∞ ∞ ∞

Aboard Sophie

Carson watched the *Razgon* intently, not knowing quite what to expect. He'd been in ships when they activated their warp drives plenty of times, but never seen it from the outside. Inside, it wasn't much. Any view out the window just went away, gravity came back, and sometimes there was a slight tingle which the physicists said had to be imaginary.

As he watched, Tevnar must have activated her warp drive. The *Razgon* just disappeared. One moment it was there, the next not. At the same time, a very faint, deep violet, trail appeared in space, extending from the *Razgon*'s position to as far as he could see, in the direction of a yellow star Carson assumed was Delta Pavonis. Carson was glad he'd seen it, but was underwhelmed.

"That was neat," he said, "but I was expecting something flashier."

"Not much gas out there," she said. "It is flashier closer to a planet. But you don't want it *too* flashy, that's bad."

∞ ∞ ∞

Aboard Razgon

Burnside felt himself settle deeper into the seat cushion as gravity returned. "When do we arrive?"

"It's just over nineteen light years, so three-hundred-thirty-five hours. Fourteen of your days."

"Fourteen days." A long trip, but Vaughan wouldn't get there any faster, give or take. It would give him time to review the files he'd grabbed before he left, start writing a report for Ducayne, and figure out what to do at Verdigris.

"Then whatever it takes to maneuver in the Pavonis system," Tevnar added, "but there's not much debris so we can warp in most of the way. Not long."

"Fair enough. Are you going to be okay? You're still recovering from gunshot wounds." In fact, Tevnar was doing much better than Burnside would have expected. Timoans healed quickly.

"I'll be fine. Although we should eat more, get some protein in me. I know I'm hungry. And I'll spend my sleep cycles in my autodoc. Nothing against Captain Roberts but I think a ship ought to have a full autodoc instead of just a traumapod."

"You may be right," Burnside said. An autodoc was better-equipped to handle illness and disease in addition to the traumatic injuries a 'pod was designed for. "Although, most humans are immunized against any diseases we're likely to encounter, either as youngsters or before we head into space. Medical science isn't quite there with non-human diseases."

"There is that. I just hope you don't run into a disease you haven't been immunized against."

"It takes a while for a germ to adapt to a potential new host. I suppose there's always that chance, but so far the most dangerous thing I've run into is other humans, intent on stealing what they shouldn't have their hands on."

"Raiders." Tevnar made a gesture that was the equivalent of a human spitting in disgust.

"If it's any consolation, the last person—well, before Vaughan—who tried that with me is now dead."

Tevnar smiled her teeth-baring smile. "Good."

Burnside reflected on that. It was interesting, timoans tended to be highly social, and typically generous in their support of each other. But they did not respond well at all to theft. Burnside wondered if Taprobane had ever had tax collectors.

"But that aside," Tevnar said, "I understand you have flown many trips aboard smaller ships?"

"You could say that, yes."

"Good. Then you know better than to mess with the ship's systems."

"Wouldn't dream of it, unless there's something you tell me to do."

"Good. Let me show you what you need to know, like the galley and the fresher. Pretty standard, maybe a little different from the *Sophie*'s. You're travelling light. I'll show you the laundry too."

Burnside was. Most of what he'd grabbed from his apartment had been devices and files that he might need. He'd destroyed the rest. He'd managed to throw one change of clothes into his pack. Not that it would have bothered him much. He'd been a field agent for a long time. Most of what an agent traditionally did—

the boring reviews of data sources and watching people—had been automated for decades. Burnside was used to getting his hands, and the rest of himself, dirty. But yes, clean clothes would be nice. And Tevnar no doubt thought so too. What was that she had said about odor?

∞ ∞ ∞

Aboard Sophie

"Okay Carson," Captain Roberts said, "our turn. If there's nothing left floating around—" she knew there wasn't, they had secured from zero-gee before the Razgon warped out "—then strap in and let's go." She had been rotating the *Sophie* to line up on the dim red Kapteyn's Star as she spoke.

"All set, Captain," Carson said as he tightened his seat straps.

She tapped the control. The windows went dark, and gravity came back. Jackie gave it a minute to be sure everything was functioning properly. She tapped another sequence to bring up a more detailed warp control screen on her console. She wanted to confirm that the sequence of bias adjustments she'd programmed earlier had loaded properly. It looked good. She unbuckled, and told Carson he could do the same.

"I imagine you want to take a closer look at that artifact," she said.

"You've got that right," Carson said. "Don't you?"

"I do, but I also want to go over all the data that Tevnar gave me on Kapteyn's-II. I'd prefer no surprises."

Carson nodded. "I like that in a starship captain."

Jackie wondered what else he liked in a starship captain. The man was impossible to read sometimes. But there was something else. "Speaking of no surprises, things are going to get heavier from now until we reach Kapteyn's. The planet's gravity is 1.7 gees; I've programmed the drive to increase our gravity as we go to help us adapt. We'll get tired more quickly aboard ship, but we'll be thankful when we land."

"Sounds reasonable. When do we get there?"

"Six and a half days, standard."

Chapter 43: Kapteyn's Star

Aboard the Sophie, *near Kapteyn's Star*

"WELL, THIS IS awkward," Roberts said.

"What's the problem?

"Our landing site, near the lake and the wrecked ship. It's in darkness. On the night side."

"Oh," Carson said. He'd been looking forward to getting right at it. "Then we wait. How long is the day here?"

"Nineteen-point-four standard days. Nearly three weeks."

"Oh." Carson said again. "Crap. I don't suppose it will be dawn over the crash site any time soon?"

Roberts checked her console. "About a week. I guess we're doing a night landing."

It wouldn't be the first time Carson had been in a ship doing a night landing, but those had all been at spaceports. Usually off-field landings were done in daylight. Well, there was a first time for everything.

"Are you okay with that?" he asked her.

"Tevnar gave me copies of the camera feeds from her landing, so it's not totally unknown. The area is pretty flat and free from obstacles."

"Except for the occasional wrecked spaceship," Carson said.

"Yes, except for that."

"All right, Captain. She's your ship. I'm just along for the ride."

"Hardly that. But I'll do some radar and infrared scans from orbit first. And don't worry, I have good night vision," she said, and winked.

"I'm not worried," Carson said. *Much,* he mentally added.

∞ ∞ ∞

He really hadn't needed to worry at all. Despite her comment about good night vision, Roberts set the windows to infrared with a radar overlay. Between that and the high-intensity landing lights, she eased the *Sophie* to a landing as smoothly as if it were high noon.

∞ ∞ ∞

"The water level is up a bit compared to Tevnar's data," Roberts said as she let the landing roll out toward the wreck. "It might have rained when night fell; it is cooler out there than what Tevnar's data showed."

"Is that going to be a problem?" Carson asked.

"I don't think so. We can still get to the wreck. I'm going to hold the *Sophie* short of it though. The ground might be softer."

"Okay." Carson began gearing up for the walk. Although the outside air wasn't breathable, there was enough pressure that he wouldn't need a full space suit. In this gravity he was thankful for that. He wore a snug form-fitting coverall to help maintain blood pressure against the gravity, boots, breathing gear with the suit's bubble helmet. Gloves. Carson chuckled to himself. He must look like a character from the cover of a 1940s pulp sci-fi magazine. He looked over at Roberts, similarly suiting up. Yes, she'd fit on the cover too, especially in a bikini. Hardly practical on this planet, though.

What gear should he take? He wished he had one of his full-spectrum recorders with him, but the camera in his omniphone would have to do. He tossed a few other items in a shoulder pack, mindful of the weight and rebreather gear on his back.

Roberts parked the ship forty meters from the wreck. From what Carson could see in the lights from the *Sophie*, it didn't look like much. A mound of sand and silt rose from the ground at the edge of the lake, with several clearly artificial ribs and panels protruding from it. They were worn and bent, but enough had remained intact to make out the partial outlines of a ship of some kind, and there were hollow areas within the sand and debris.

"All right," Roberts said as she finished getting her gear on. "We'll lock out. I don't want to get any more of that cruddy atmosphere in the ship than I need to."

"Understood." They moved into the airlock together. Without full spacesuits it was easily big enough to accommodate the two of them.

"Gear check," Roberts said.

Carson verified that his own breathing system was turned on and his helmet secure, then checked Jackie's. He gave her a thumbs-up. "Checked."

She did the same with his, and gave him a thumbs-up in return. She started the airlock cycle, and the outer hatch opened to reveal darkness, lit only by the beams from the *Sophie*'s lights. She turned off the airlock's interior lighting and switched on a "porch light" over the boarding ramp. "Okay, watch your step. Go ahead and turn on your headlamp when you're on the ground."

"Roger that." Carson grabbed the rope rail, turned, and backed down the ramp. With his gear on, and in this gravity, that was easiest, and why Roberts didn't want his headlamp on and shining into her face.

He reached the ground—it was like firm, packed clay with a thin film of water on it. Roberts was probably right about the rain. They'd have to watch their footing; it would be slippery, and a fall in this gravity would be painful.

"Ground is a little slick. Watch yourself."

"Got it."

Roberts joined him on the surface a moment later. "Well," she said, gesturing toward the wreck. "There it is. Is it what you expected?"

"I didn't know what to expect, but this will certainly do." Carson took a few pictures of it from where they stood. "Let's go check it out."

They plodded toward the crash site. Carson felt like he was hiking with a fifty-kilogram pack. He was glad they had spent the last week adjusting to higher gravity.

When they reached the wreck, Carson pulled a pair of items from his shoulder bag. Portable lights. He set them on the ground, to form a triangle with the wreck as one corner. He pointed the lights up at it. "That should help," he said.

"Good thinking. Here, let's see where Tevnar pulled that cylinder from." She checked an image Tevnar had given her, then guided Carson a third of the way around the pile, where there was an opening in the hull—or rather, where the hull had been torn away entirely—large enough to get into what remained of the structure.

"There. Watch your footing, the deck is slanted thirty degrees and there are pipes and wiring scattered around."

She was right. The level "floor" was accumulated sediment, filling nearly half the interior space he could see, guessing by the shapes of the walls. To one side, what must be deck plating jutted out of the sediment at an angle, connected to a bulkhead and what remained of the hull. There was a layer of grime over everything. Carson thought it was beautiful.

"This is fantastic! It's better preserved than I'd hoped." He took pictures of everything, moving around to cover all angles and photographing sediment-covered panels before carefully wiping away what he could and photographing them again.

He turned to Jackie. "Where did Tevnar find the artifact?"

She checked the image again. "On the floor there," she pointed. "It looks like it might have been attached to this." She turned and showed Carson a rectangular arm angling down from what was probably the overhead when the ship was upright. Indeed, the cross section looked right for the rectangular opening on the back of the artifact he had been puzzling over for much of the last week.

"I'd say you're right." He took several pictures of it, concentrating on the end where it had probably attached. "Hard to say with this mud over everything, but the style looks a bit different from the rest of the ship."

"Like I said, probably added on later."

"Yes," Carson said, his voice weary. The gravity was taking its toll. He could keep going for a while, but it would be wise not to push it. When you were tired was when you started making mistakes.

"I'd like to try excavating a bit, but I need to plan that. I've got enough pictures to look at for now. We should head back and get some rest. I'd like to take another look later."

"Good idea."

On the slog back, Carson turned and looked toward the wreck again. He had left the lights in place; their compact power source could keep them lit for days. He wondered what the Belize wreck had looked like when it crashed. Brown had mentioned some unusual stress patterns in some of the hull fragments, more characteristic of destruction by a high-brisance explosive than just crash or erosion damage.

"Jackie, did you look at the outside of that much?" He himself hadn't really looked at the outer surface of the wreck himself, he had been more curious about inside. He would check that before they left.

"Not really. Mostly dirt-covered anyway. Why?"

"Just wondering if there might be markings or signs of why it crashed. I'll look tomorrow."

They were back at the *Sophie* now, and Carson gestured to the boarding ladder. "After you," he said.

Chapter 44: Toward Delta Pavonis

Aboard the Razgon, *half-way to Delta Pavonis*

"STAND BY FOR zero-gee," Tevnar called back over her shoulder to Burnside. She had strapped herself into her command seat in the cockpit while he finished a cup of coffee in the galley.

"Wait one," he said. She heard him hastily drain his cup, rinse it, and secure the galley for free-fall. He walked forward to the cockpit, holding on to one of the handrails where the wall met the ceiling. "What's going on?"

"Just dropping out of warp for a mid-course position check." Over the nineteen-plus light-years between 82 Eridani and Delta Pavonis, a tiny aiming error could build up to a significant distance. Better to make corrections mid-way, but that couldn't be done while in warp. It would also correct for any stellar drift in the years it had taken for Delta Pavonis's light to reach 82 Eridani.

"Where are we?"

"The middle of nowhere, if nowhere is the space between Tanith and Verdigris. Jackie and Carson should have reached Kapteyn's Star by now."

"I wonder how they're doing," Burnside said.

"Doing well, I'm sure. Jackie's sharp, the *Sophie* is a good ship, and Carson seems like a decent chap. I guess Marten likes him. Are they mated?"

"Who, Marten and Carson?" Burnside sounded confused.

"What? No, Jackie and Carson. They seem an obvious match."

"She said not."

"And you believed her?" For an advanced species, Tevnar thought, humans could sure be stupid. She probably knew more about human females than he did. "Never mind."

Tevnar turned back to her task of triangulating their position against other stars, and then ensuring that the *Razgon* lined up properly on Delta Pavonis. "Got it. It's nine-point-four light years to Delta Pavonis. Prepare for warp; gravity's coming back."

Chapter 45: Kapteyn's II

On the surface of Kapteyn's II

IT HAD BEEN mid-afternoon ship's time when they had first landed, and the constant darkness outside didn't do anything to encourage a change in the schedule, so it was close to three in the morning, or "oh-dark-thirty" as Jackie would put it, when Carson woke up, ready to go out again. By then he had had at least six hours sleep. Walking to the wreck and back had tired him out.

Roberts was still in her cabin. He walked quietly to the galley —his small cabin had no work area—and laid out on the table some of the small specimens he had gathered, then grabbed a protein bar to eat while he worked.

The samples were an odd mix: a few pieces of wire, mostly corroded but for the insulation; some metal fragments in various shapes and states of (poor) preservation; and several chunks of the hardened sediment which had filled the lower part of the cabin and surrounded the wreck. The sediment from inside was finer-grained than the rest, he noted. That made sense. Only smaller, lighter silt grains would easily drift into the wreck. He had photographed each before picking them up. Now he took his omni and, using it as a magnifier, looked at each piece closely, taking additional pictures as he did so, and making short notes about each specimen.

His omni had some sophisticated instruments built into it, and several apps useful in archeology, but they hadn't been intended for working with artifacts of an advanced technological civilization. Forensic software might be better. And without more-detailed knowledge about the seasons on this planet and how often the lake rose and receded, even the sedimentology app wouldn't help much. How long *did* it take for different layers to build up here?

He sighed. He had expected it, but to get the maximum knowledge out of this site, it would be best to leave it until he could come back with an experienced team and a full suite of dig gear. He still wanted a closer look at the outside of it, though. What he had in mind would be exhausting. He should get some more rest.

∞ ∞ ∞

Next ship-day

Roberts and Carson repeated the previous ship day's drill of gearing up and locking out onto the surface, then plodding heavily toward the wreck. The water level didn't seem to have changed; if anything, it was down a little. That would be fine, so long as it was still deep enough at the ship for his purposes.

The lights Carson had set up earlier were still there. There was a breeze blowing, but he'd anchored them in the damp muddy sand, and the higher gravity also helped hold them down. He had brought two more, to set up on the other side of the ship, which he proceeded to do. The water was a bit more than ankle deep at the point the wreck extended furthest into the water. Well, at least at the surface; they had no idea how far below ground it extended, although Carson thought not very far, based on the shapes and angles of what protruded.

"You have the pump?" Carson asked.

"Of course," Roberts said, "right here." She pulled a compact motorized turbopump from her shoulder bag. "Just run the intake hose and filter out into the water, like I did yesterday to refuel. I'll set the pump down here." She gestured at a spot above the waterline where it was relatively dry.

"Okay." Carson ran the hose out to where it stood a chance of pulling in reasonably clear water without a lot of sediment. He wanted to wash as much dried mud and dirt off the wreck as he could, not pour fresh mud onto it. *Although*, he realized, *that might not be a bad idea if we want to try to camouflage it while we're gone*. The intake hose set, Carson picked up the output hose and pointed the nozzle toward the lake.

"Start it up!" he called.

Roberts started the pump, and Carson turned the stream of water to the outside of the wreck's hull. The stream was low-pressure, at least for now, since he didn't want to risk damaging the wreck further. The dirt resisted at first. It had dried to a hard solid over the many years it had been exposed, but some of it started to slake off once it had absorbed enough water. It was tricky working in the dark; the work lights helped but the water stream cast awkward shadows.

The hull had its share of dents and crumples and tears. Carson avoided the latter to minimize the risk of damage. Finally, with the dirt down to a stubborn layer that wasn't rinsing off, he increased the pressure to blast away at a section that looked reasonably free of damage. The grime cleared, revealing the white hull surface beneath. It looked like painted metal or a heat-resistant ceramic of some kind. He only cleared a couple of square meters; he was tiring of holding the spray nozzle against both its own pressure and the heavy gravity. He would be back. He shut off the water flow and signaled Roberts to stop the pump.

With it now quieter, she said to him, "Nice job. I should ask you to give the *Sophie* a wash sometime."

Carson chuckled at that, then leaned in to examine what he had washed clean. The white surface looked almost like eggshell, which it obviously wasn't, but it seemed to have fine pores in its surface. They were probably some side-effect of its construction, and their distribution was uneven, as though the surface had worn more in some areas than others. Which was quite likely, Carson thought.

Toward one edge of the cleared surface, there were a few flecks of red. Paint? Carson rubbed at a spot with his finger. No, it looked more like the color was part of the material. "Turn the pump back on for a moment," he called to Roberts, and then pressure-washed another square meter where the red traces were. There were more of them.

With the pump stopped again, he took another look. There were scattered areas, each some ten to twenty square centimeters, and irregular, of the red surface. Close examination showed the color to be as though something had dyed the material of the hull, the color soaking into the surface but, as a crack in the hull showed, penetrating it only a millimeter or less. The surface had clearly worn unevenly, or perhaps the color tended to burn off during reentry. The gaps were where it had worn more.

He stepped back, sloshing in the shallow water. Did the scattered blotches make a pattern? A few of them had clean edges. There wasn't enough of it to be sure. Maybe a chemical or multifrequency analysis of the surface would reveal traces where the paint or dye had otherwise worn to invisibility. The vague pattern was ambiguous. Carson had the nagging feeling he couldn't rule out what Lonnie Zamora had described as painted on the side of the craft he'd seen landed in the Socorro desert, except that this was much bigger than what Zamora had described.

"You okay?" Roberts asked. "You've been staring at that thing for a while now. Does it have some special significance?"

"It's too faded and irregular to be sure," Carson said. "Could be something I heard described once, but it could be lots of other things too."

"Okay. Come around here, I have something else to show you."

"Oh?" Carson said as he waded out of where he'd been standing in the water and around the side of the shipwreck where she was beckoning. "What have you got?"

"These gaps and marks here," she said, pointing at a gap a few centimeters wide and roughly a meter long, in line with a similar gap farther up the hull. It was not part of the original structure, it had been cut or burned into the hull later. "Do you think it might have something to do with why it crashed?"

The edges of the cuts were eroded away in a peculiar pattern, like it had been partially burnt or dissolved. Again, he couldn't be sure, what with different hull materials and this wreck having been exposed to the elements for so long, but Carson felt his gut tightening and the hair on the back of his neck standing up. It looked familiar.

"Yes, I do." He paused. *Might as well tell her.* "I've seen something like this before," he said, his voice dead. "Not as big."

"Carson? What's wrong? Where have you seen this?"

"On the hull of the *Carcharodon*, after it was hit by an alien particle-beam weapon. I think it's time to leave."

∞ ∞ ∞

Aboard the Sophie

After Carson's disturbing realization, they packed up quickly. There may have been no need to rush, but nor was there a reason to linger. If an automated defense had caused the other ship to crash, it might still be active, even after a thousand years or more. Neither Carson nor Roberts wanted to find out the hard way.

"Get everything stowed," Roberts said as she put the *Sophie* though its pre-flight checks. "Take-off is going to be interesting."

"Working on it." Carson was just getting the last of the loose equipment secured when Roberts began taxiing the ship to where she'd have a good long flat run into the light breeze.

"Everything secure?" she asked him as he came forward and strapped himself in.

"Affirmative. Let's get this show off the ground."

"Rolling," she said, and powered up the thrusters. The Sophie surged forward, and Carson felt himself pressed into the back of his chair.

The craft lumbered forward into the dark, the path in front illuminated by their landing lights. As their speed built, the rumbling from the slight irregularities in the surface rose in pitch but smoothed out. Carson felt his seat vibrating.

Roberts cut in the lifting thrusters as the *Sophie* reached the flying speed of its stubby wings, and the ride smoothed. She pitched up into a twenty-degree climb. The wind had been blowing from the west, so once aloft Roberts gently banked the craft around to face back in the direction they had come, to take advantage of whatever slight rotational speed the planet offered. They were three kilometers above the lake when they passed the wreck site, and Roberts pitched the ship up farther, continuing to accelerate.

"What do we need to make orbit?" Carson asked.

"We're not going to orbit; that's a waste of delta-vee. I'm going to warp as soon as we clear the atmosphere."

Carson remembered Roberts and Tevnar had discussed take-off from high-gravity worlds. As he thought about it, it made sense. The gravity was less than twice Earth's, but the bigger radius meant it tapered off more slowly with distance. The escape velocity here was probably three or four times what it was on Earth.

The sound and buffeting from the ship's passage through atmosphere faded and the ride smoothed, although the roar from the thrusters aft and the continued pressure told him they were still accelerating. The ship was pointed nearly straight up now; with no need to establish an orbit, that was the quickest way to space.

"Standby," Roberts said, then cut the engines.

They were now falling upward on a ballistic trajectory, losing velocity but still gaining altitude. Roberts pitched the *Sophie* over so that it pointed out of the orbital plane of this system, moved a hand to the warp-engage control.

"Going to warp." She activated it, and normal gravity came back.

∞ ∞ ∞

Five minutes later, she warned "Zero-gee again." and turned off the warp.

"What's wrong?" said Carson.

"I have no idea where we're pointed," she said. "I just wanted to make sure we were clear of the system. We should be three hundred AU away. Now to find our next stop." She put the ship in a slow roll so its sensors could get a good look at the stars and identify their position.

"Of course. Well, that was fun."

"No extra charge," Roberts said. She checked a screen on her panel. "Okay, give me a minute to get the *Sophie* lined up, and we'll have gravity again. And I could stand to eat something, all that rushing around in high-gee gave me an appetite."

Five minutes later, they were back in warp, en route to Epsilon Indi. Ten minutes after that they were enjoying brunch in the galley.

∞ ∞ ∞

Aboard Sophie, *deep space*

Carson sat looking over the images he had taken of the wreckage of the alien ship. "Jackie," he said, "how big would you say that ship was originally?"

She looked over his shoulder at the images. "Hard to say, we don't know how much is buried. But just a wild guess from the curves on what we can see, maybe fifteen meters long? A bit smaller than a Sapphire."

That was what Carson would have guessed, although there was too much data missing to have any confidence in that. "And what would the range on that be?"

"Depends on their tech. If they had antimatter—"

"Assume not," Carson said, recalling what she had said about the Kesh reaction when she told them she had antimatter aboard the *Sophie*.

"Okay, then roughly the same as the *Sophie*. Maybe less, maybe a little more depending on the efficiency of their engines. Assuming it was about the same size. So, twenty light years, give or take?"

"How far is it from Zeta Reticuli to Sol, or to Alpha Centauri?"

"Forty-some light-years. You want an exact number?"

"No, that's close enough. So, a Sapphire-class couldn't do that in a single jump?"

"Not even close. Not even with drop tanks. Ditto for a Sandquist or anything else in that size range. Not without antimatter. Why?"

"I'm going to want to check your star charts, if I may."

"No problem, but again, why?"

"Whoever built that ship, if they were on a route I think they may have been, would have needed a refueling stop around here somewhere."

"Here? Kapteyn's? This isn't exactly an ideal refueling spot if you've got a choice."

"No, I meant within a few light years of here. 82 Eridani might work. What else? Delta Pavonis?"

"Depends where you're coming from and where you're going to. For Zeta Reticuli to Sol, Delta Pavonis works if you refuel somewhere like Alpha Mensae first. Not a single jump."

"Fair enough."

"But yes. Possibly Delta Pavonis, or Zeta Tucanae. And definitely yes for 82 Eridani."

There was a pyramid at Delta Pavonis, and he and Marten had found a high-tech artifact at each of Delta Pavonis and Zeta

Tucanae. But those were Spacefarer artifacts, not Kesh. Was there another connection?

"Do you have scans of Tanith?" Carson asked her. It might be worth taking a closer look.

"Nothing special, just the standard database. If you want high resolution scans of Kapteyn's II, there I can help. I have Tevnar's data."

"Never mind. I guess it will keep until I get back to Sawyers World." Carson had a hunch that there was more to the 82 Eridani system, and possibly others, than people suspected.

Chapter 46: Delta Pavonis

New Toronto, Verdigris, Delta Pavonis

THE *CARCHARODON* DESCENDED through the skyweed layer over the port. It was thin today, giving plenty of visibility for Vaughan to see the rows of new ships lined up on the expanded apron beside the runway. It was a fine sight, but there should have been more. They should also be under cover. No wonder he'd been recalled. Just as well they hadn't gone back to Tanith for what might have been a wild goose chase.

Stinson eased the ship down and rolled it smartly off the runway onto an adjacent ramp. Apparently, there was a small reception committee waiting. They must have scrambled when they'd heard the *Carcharodon* was in-system.

Vaughan took a minute to straighten himself up. One of his men opened the hatch and deployed the boarding ramp. A squad of the waiting men formed up in parallel rows, facing each other on either side of a path leading from the foot of the stairs. Vaughan was bemused; somebody must be nervous.

He strode the hatchway and stood there for a moment, surveying the scene, before descending the stairway. The man who seemed to be in charge of the reception came forward to meet him at the foot. Vaughan knew him; he oversaw local operations. The man came to a sharp halt and saluted.

"Commander Vaughan," he said, "we're glad to have you back."

∞ ∞ ∞

Aboard Razgon, *orbiting Verdigris, a day later*

"Well, New Toronto is definitely out for a landing," Jordan Burnside said, staring at the display and seeing the rows of ships parked at the spaceport. "And I think that's the *Carcharodon* down there too."

Tevnar agreed, and said, "We can give Verdigris City a try. Or there should be small towns that have landing fields, if you want," she said. "The only potential problem with that is that they might wonder why we didn't land at one of the cities first. That's the usual routine. Only locals come in direct from space."

"It would attract attention," Burnside agreed. "Maybe you shouldn't land at all."

"That's a long trip for nothing, and I need to refuel."

"Is there somewhere else in-system you can do that? I'm guessing the *Razgon* isn't equipped for a water landing."

"No, he's not. But this ship was never at Harp City, and I don't have to say we came from Tanith."

"It's still a timoan ship. Vaughan would hear about it, and might make the connection. Do you *have* to land?"

"No, the system has a gas giant with ice moons. I can refuel there if I have to."

Burnside decided to clinch the deal. "Bonus for the hassle of doing an off-field refueling," he said.

"Sold. We head back to Taprobane, then?"

"No, I'm getting off here," Burnside said, "then you go back."

"I though you didn't want me to land. Make up your mind."

"I don't. I'm going to jump. Roberts gave the retro-pack, remember?"

Tevnar made a timoan head-gesture that signified rejection, raising her head sharply like a reverse nod. "You humans are crazy. Are you sure?"

Burnside wasn't enthusiastic about it, but it had to be done. The Velkaryans in New Toronto were clearly up to something, and Ducayne would need eyes and boots on the ground. There were other Homeworld Security agents on-planet, but the Velkaryans might well know them; he'd be a wild card. He still had his box of tricks, so he'd be able to make contact with any ship Ducayne sent back here. He told Tevnar, "Better to go now than later, so yes, I'm sure. I'll give you a report you can give to Carson and Roberts to take back to Sawyer's World. This is important."

"How do we do this, then?" Tevnar asked. "Do I just toss you out the airlock?"

"Hah, not quite. First let me get my gear together and suit up. After that, can you kill the *Razgon*'s orbital velocity somewhere above my landing spot? I'll tell you where."

"I can, but the *Razgon* will start to fall and enter the atmosphere."

"Right. It doesn't have to be a full stop; I have the retro-rockets on the pack, and it has a heat shield. I just don't want to push its limits. Once I'm out you can apply maneuvering thrusters until I'm clear, then go to full thrusters or warp out or whatever you think appropriate. That shouldn't take more than a minute."

"It sounds like you've done this before."

"I'm not saying." He hadn't actually, but he had been in a ship that had dropped someone else off that way.

"You and your secrets. Very well. It sounds simple enough."

For Tevnar and the *Razgon*, perhaps. Burnside knew that was when things would start to get interesting for him. But it had to be done. "Then let's get to it."

Chapter 47: Taprobane

Epsilon Indi, planet Taprobane

HANNIBAL CARSON HAD been on Taprobane now for two days, and he was anxious to get back to Sawyers World, but he and Jackie were waiting until Burnside arrived so they could all return in the *Sophie*.

Meanwhile, He and Marten, when Marten wasn't teaching class, had been carefully removing the dirt and impacted sediment from the Kapteyn's artifact. The latter was, for now, kept secured in Marten's office at Kangara University. They were also compiling a list of the different glyphs on the artifact's control panel, if that's what it was, and any such markings on interior components. Marten had already heard about the Belize find through rumors in the archeological community grapevine.

"Do you think the Belize find may have something to do with the feathered serpent legends of the Yucatan?" Marten said.

"It would fit," Carson said. "A Kesh ship crash lands there, the survivor or survivors make an impact on the local culture. Although apparently, not on their written language."

"What about their spoken language?"

"Not if it were just a few individuals and no prolonged contact."

"And yet . . . Give me a minute," Marten said, and turned to his desk console. After a quick search, he turned back to Carson. "Yes, I thought so. The Quichean branch of old Mayan originated sometime around the estimated time of the Belize wreck. It's centered around Belize and Guatemala. Quichean, K'iche', Kaqchikel . . . Kesh? Coincidence?"

"That's a good question. But we know the Kesh were in the Middle East, or at least, Ketzshanass implied as much. Aside from the cuneiform-like script, none of the languages from there sound like that. Not that we heard much Kesh speech, and old Sumerian was logographic."

"Longer ago, and maybe the Kesh priest class didn't speak it to the native riff-raff."

Carson had another thought. "Are there any timoan languages that might be similar?"

"Not that I've heard of," Marten said, "but there are a lot of clans out there. We haven't cataloged everything. But there are no signs that the Kesh, or the Spacefarers, were ever here."

"Which is weird. Why not? But maybe the signs just haven't been found yet."

Carson's omni beeped at him before he could add anything. He glanced at. "Oh, Tevnar and Burnside are here. The *Razgon* is on approach to the spaceport. Let's go meet them."

∞ ∞ ∞

"What do you mean, Burnside stayed on Verdigris. Why?" Contrary to what Carson had assumed, Tevnar had been alone on the *Razgon*.

"He insisted. Said Homeworld Security might need an agent in place, and it would be easier for him to stay than send someone else. Something about parachuting now or having to parachute later. I have his reports for Ducayne."

"I guess Ducayne owes me for a new suit and retro-pack," Jackie said, her tone flat.

She was worried and trying to joke about it, Carson guessed. He ignored it. "But, starships at New Toronto? Do they expect that much traffic?"

"Burnside thinks they expect war," Tevnar said.

"Interstellar war makes no sense. The distances are too great, everything is three-dimensional, there's no front. What is there to fight over?"

Jackie had an answer. "Terraformed worlds. For Terrans," she said, paraphrasing a Velkaryan slogan.

"Oh, those bloody idiots. You may be right." He shook his head.

"Hannibal," she said, "we'd better get those reports back to Sawyers World as soon as possible. The *Sophie* is fueled and ready to go as soon as you're ready."

Chapter 48: Home

Sawyers World, Homeworld Security HQ

JACKIE ROBERTS AND Hannibal Carson were debriefing in Ducayne's office. They'd already discussed the artifact, and Malcolm Brown had eagerly taken Carson's notes and gone off to compare them against what he'd compiled on the Belize artifact. Brown and Carson were convinced they were both of Kesh origin, From scans, the Kapteyn's artifact included something strongly resembling a key component in the latest experimental gravity wave detectors. Jackie still didn't see the point of that in a ship, instead of somewhere isolated from nearby influences.

But now they were talking about Burnside's reports, which Ducayne had partially shared with them. They had both been on Verdigris not that long ago. Tevnar had also briefed them on her experiences with Burnside in that system. Ducayne was worried about the ship-building.

"I don't get it," Ducayne said. "To manufacture warp pods you need some pretty high-tech equipment. Although some of that is dual-use, which they have been importing. We just didn't think they were that far along.

"High-tech equipment like that for making fusors? They use the same sort of massive monolithic integrated circuitry and nanochannels as warp pods" Jackie said. As a starship owner and pilot she understood how both were put together, at least at a high level.

"Exactly like that, yes," Ducayne said.

"Could they re-purpose equipment for manufacturing fusors to make warp units?" Carson asked. His background wasn't as technical as Jackie's or, apparently, Ducayne's.

"To a certain extent, yes. But there are also specialized components and materials, you'd still have to get those from somewhere else," Ducayne said.

"Components for the warp pods, or components for the machines to manufacture them?"

"The former would be easier," Ducayne said. "The parts are small, but the equipment to make them would be a major shipment. Not something you could fit aboard the *Sophie*, for example. A C-class or bigger. But even the small parts . . . well, cargo is inspected."

Jackie knew better. "Not always," she said.

"Well, no, but machinery usually gets at least a cursory check against the manifest."

"What about coffee?" she asked.

"What?" Ducayne looked puzzled. "Sure, let me start the autochef."

"No. I mean shipments of coffee. Roast coffee often skips the quarantine."

Ducayne looked at her sharply. "How is it usually shipped?"

"Crates containing sacks of beans a few kilos each. Sometimes in half-kilo bags for retail. I had a few crates of those on my run from Skead to Tanith. Tau Cetan coffee is easy to find a broker for."

Ducayne frowned. "You could fit a number of sub-assemblies in something the size of a half-kilo coffee bag. Even more interesting things in a twenty-kilo sack."

Roberts suddenly remembered her conversation with David Tefera when he'd delivered the coffee. "The *Cerulean Cloud*," she said.

"The what?"

"Class C cargo hauler. My old co-pilot Andrei Sarsfield and his partner Ben I-forget-his-last-name are the owner-operators. Did a run to 82 Eridani a month or two back, and my coffee dealer on Skead mentioned they would be hauling a load to Verdigris sometime after I left Tau Ceti. You don't suppose . . . ?" Roberts trailed off, wondering just what it was she did or didn't suppose.

"How well do you know him? Or his partner?"

"Andrei and I flew together for about a year, and I'd known him off and on before that. I trusted him. I wouldn't expect him to be involved in anything shady, and have no reason to think he sympathized with the Velkaryans."

"What about his partner? Ben, you said?"

"I only met him the once, and he seemed a little hostile. I assumed it was because he and Andrei were more than just business partners, and that he might be jealous of me. Not that he'd have any reason to be; Andrei was never interested in me that way."

"Hmm. Possibly. Or there may have been some other reason."

Jackie realized something else. "Oh! Do you suppose there could have been contraband in the shipment I took to Tanith?"

"Did you inspect the cargo?"

"The crates were sealed; the documentation was in order. Why would I? It was an on-spec consignment, it wasn't even for delivery to a specific person."

"Tell me how that works," Ducayne said.

"I land, send the docs to the local port authority and invite them to come inspect the cargo before offloading. Then anything I've carried on-spec, meaning I hope I find a buyer for it, gets entered into the net. There's an auction site where brokers can bid on the incoming cargoes, and also offer outgoing on-spec cargoes. It's like any on-line auction, really."

"So, what happened with your cargo?"

"It was roasted beans, so they skipped quarantine. I got a buyer almost as soon as I put the cargo on-line. Some brokers have software that watches for things they're interested in."

Ducayne was still frowning. "Then even though there was no designated recipient, someone in the know might reasonably expect that particular buyer to be ready to pounce on the cargo as soon as it was listed. Is that a fair statement?"

Roberts had to reluctantly concede that it was. She hated the thought that she might have been played. If the cargo had been inspected and contraband found, she'd be protected by both her courier rating and the fact that the crates had been sealed before being brought aboard, although it would have meant an uncomfortable few days to get things cleared up. But . . . "Could they, though? What if more than one person was watching for that kind of cargo?"

"The recipient could have put in a high bid limit, or someone could have hacked the auction software to give them an edge."

"Shit. Shit shit *shit!*" Jackie balled up her fists. "I'm an idiot." She slammed her left fist sideways against the arm of her chair.

"Hey, Jackie, relax," Carson said. "We don't know that you smuggled anything. It could have been just coffee."

"And I thought Tefera was just some space-struck farm-boy with stars in his eyes."

"Maybe he is."

"He knew an awful lot about the business, though."

"He's anxious to learn," Carson said. "Or his folks want him to learn everything he can about the family business. Plenty of innocent explanations."

She looked at him. He had a point, but in her experience with Ducayne, innocent explanations tended to be discounted. "Thanks, Hannibal. I know you're trying to make me feel better." She looked at Ducayne. "You don't really believe that, do you?"

"It's never about what I believe or disbelieve," he said. "It's about what the evidence is and all the different things it could point to."

"That sounds like something you would say."

"Carson would tell you the same thing about his field."

"He's right, I would. Same thing I tell my students."

"Come to that, it's what my flight instructor told me about the instruments," Jackie said. "But I find the connection between David Tefera, coffee shipments, and places where Vaughan and the *Carcharodon* are, to be just a little *too* much of a coincidence."

"Maybe Vaughan just *really* likes his coffee," Ducayne said, but his grim expression and tone said that he also thought it too much of a coincidence.

∞ ∞ ∞

Hannibal Carson thought they were done, but Ducayne turned toward him.

"You have some unfinished business here, too," Ducayne said. "That interview we talked about before you left?"

Carson wondered what he meant, then remembered. "Oh, about Pete's Peak. Right."

Ducayne winced and glanced at Roberts, who hadn't been dismissed.

"Oh," Carson said, realizing his faux pas. "Jackie knows. She's been in both pyramids and met the Kesh too." He fished his memory for the phrasing. "I figured she had a need to know."

Ducayne looked down at his desk and shook his head, then up at the both of them. "No harm done, I suppose. Anyway, I made contact with Doctor Finley. He agreed to a meeting."

"What? How? I thought he was pretty much a recluse, and Sawyer forbade me to mention her."

"I didn't need to. It turns out his daughter, Roberta, is the VP of Sales for Maclaren Arms. We do a lot of business with them; I asked for a favor."

"So, is there a date set for this?" Carson asked. He had a lot of questions he wanted to ask Finley about his peak, or pyramid. No doubt Finely would have a few of his own for Carson. But, "You didn't know when I would be back."

"No, that's why we left it open. Whenever you want, unless he has a prior commitment then."

"Great!" Carson said, then remembered the last time he had visited one of the *Anderson* crew. "But I want a driver. I'm not taking an autocab this time."

Jackie looked at him and, grinning, asked, "How do you feel about bikes?"

Epilogue

Elsewhere, time and location uncertain

RICO OPENED HIS eyes, or thought he did. The darkness didn't change. Rico wondered about that. There had been the firefight at the Denver Spaceport, to give Brown a chance to . . . he *had* gotten away. Rico had seen the ship lift, then everything had gone dim. He'd been shot. Several times. The memory came back all the way and Rico realized where he was. *In a traumapod.* Again.

Crap. While it was just *possible* that the Velkaryans who had been shooting at him had left him for the police to find, Rico had a sinking feeling that it was more likely that it was the Velkaryans who had managed to get him to the traumapod. That wouldn't be for charitable reasons. He wondered if he'd rather be held by the police. Rico groped around the interior of the pod, surprised that there were no restraints on his arms. Perhaps he could open the pod from the inside, get out, and then escape from wherever the pod was, all without being caught.

"Ah, Mr. Lee. Or should I say, Rico?" the voice came over the traumapod's internal speaker. It was not a voice Rico recognized. "I see you're finally awake."

Well, so much for plan A, thought Rico.

∞

The story continues in: *The Centauri Surprise*

Timeline

This lists the chapters in absolute time order, together with the approximate number of days elapsed from the *Sophie* and *Carcharodon* leaving Zeta Reticuli at the end of the previous novel. The Prolog takes place shortly before all this..

Chapter	Title	Days elapsed
2	A Rude Awakening	0.0
5	The *Carcharodon* Arrives	14.0
8	Report Received	35.0
3	Marten's Homecoming	38.9
4	Findings	38.9
6	The White Hart	39.0
7	Cuneiform	39.0
11	Stirring the Pot	42.0
9	Old Records	45.0
20	Operation Jade Ribbon	48.0
10	Planet Skead	48.9
12	Ducayne's Message	48.9
13	Sawyer	48.9

1	Taxi!	49.0
14	Dinner	49.0
15	Going for a Ride	49.0
16	Dessert	49.1
17	Homeworld Security	49.2
18	Departure	49.5
19	Ducayne Has News	50.0
22	A New Artifact	51.0
24	Carson's Other Ride	51.5
21	Approaching Tanith	59.0
23	Harp City	60.0
25	The Whereabouts of Smith	60.3
27	Approaching Convergence	61.0
26	Rendezvous	61.3
28	An Unexpected Caller	61.4
29	Convergence	61.8
30	Vaughan	61.8
31	The Pickup	62.0
32	Vaughan Recalled	62.0
33	Catching Up	62.1
34	Carson and Burnside	62.3
35	Tevnar	63.0
36	Divergence	63.1

37	Packing It Up	63.2
38	Tevnar's Story	63.3
39	The Artifact	63.4
40	Meanwhile, Back at the Ranch	64.0
41	Change of Plans	64.0
42	Second Divergence	64.1
43	Kapteyn's Star	71.0
44	Toward Delta Pavonis	71.1
45	Kapteyn's II	71.5
46	Delta Pavonis	77.0
47	Taprobane	84.0
48	Home	91.0

Glossary

Chara: G type star 27.5 light-years from Earth, also called Beta Canorum Venaticum.

Kakuloa: Alpha Centauri B II - terraformed planet orbiting the second largest star (B) in the Alpha Centauri system.

Kapteyn's Star: a red dwarf star about 12 light-years from Earth. It is known to have at least two planets, each larger than Earth, and orbiting in or near the habitable zone.

Kesh (or kesh): Aliens encountered by Carson, Roberts and Marten at Zeta Reticuli, possessing advanced technology. They neither confirmed nor denied that Zeta Reticuli was their home system, but it is currently (so far as Carson knows) uninhabited.

omni: Short for omniphone - compares to today's smartphones as smartphones compare to walky-talkies. (Look for "Nokia Morph" on YouTube for a nearly-there concept video.)

omniphone: See omni.

parsec: A distance of approximately 3.26 light-years.

Sandquist: A class of small interstellar ship (S-class), capable of sleeping about six if they're close friends, with a range of just over 20 light-years on full tanks.

Sapphire: Another S-class series of small starships, of a different configuration than Sandquist.

Sawyers World: Alpha Centauri A II - second planet orbiting the largest star (A) in the Alpha Centauri system, the first extrasolar planet settled by humans. (See the *Alpha Centauri* series.)

Tanith: 82 Eridani IV - fourth (hypothetical) planet orbiting the star 82 Eridani. In real life, this star is known to have at least three planets, all larger than Earth.

Taprobane: Epsilon Indi III - Third planet orbiting Epsilon Indi, home world of timoans.

thruster: High-efficiency reaction drive, a kind of fusion-powered arc-jet.

timoan: (Analogous to "human") The sentient natives of Taprobane. Descended from the ancestral species of terrestrial mongoose and meerkats the way humans are descended from the ancestral species of monkeys or lemurs.

T-space: Terraformed (or Terraform) space - Usual term for "known space," a spheroid of stars centered on Earth and about 20 parsecs in diameter. So-called because many of the sun-like stars within it were found to have planets that were not merely Earth-like, but deliberately terraformed.

Unholy War: A nuclear war which took place in the first half of the 21st century, involving primarily the smaller nuclear powers, purportedly for religious reasons.

Union de Terre: Union of Earth, the successor to the United Nations formed after the events of and immediately after the Unholy War.

Velkaryans: Church of Divine Stellar Providence. A core belief is that God created the terraformed planets for humans, and, not as loudly stated, specifically for them.

Verdigris: Delta Pavonis III - third planet orbiting the star Delta Pavonis, so named for its greenish hue and the heavy jungle covering the habitable areas.

warp bubble: The thin shell of highly-curved space surrounding a ship in FTL flight. Based on Van Den Broek's lower-energy configuration of an Alcubierre warp metric.

Zeta Reticuli: A pair of G type stars separated by about 0.1 light-year at a distance of 39.2 light-years from Earth. (Technically, Zeta 1 and Zeta 2 Reticuli)

Acknowledgments

NO BOOK REACHES publicationpublication without a lot of work and input from many people. My thanks to the usual suspects (you know who you are) and, especially, to the readers and fans who continue to support my work and have given me valuable feedback. You make it worthwhile.

I also want to acknowledge the largely unsung heroes of the exoplanet community, the scientists, grad students, and even members of the public who help analyze all the data and tease out of it those weak signals showing not only that there *are* planets around other stars (unknown when I was growing up reading science fiction), but that they come in huge numbers and varieties. You guys make my job both harder and more fun. Harder, because I'm scrambling to keep up and incorporate your findings into my stories. More fun, because you're giving me more material to work with. The systems of Tau Ceti, Kapteyn's Star and 82 Eridani in this book are cases in point. Yes, sometimes I also make up a planet, and so, a friendly challenge: prove me wrong.

Also, special thanks to Jessica Hastings for her help in catching and correcting many minor typos and errors in the first printing. Any remaining errors are of course my own . . . or the computer's. A software engineer always blames the hardware. ☺

—*Alastair Mayer, Colorado, 2017, 2018*

Preview: *The Centauri Surprise*

Rico has just woken up in a traumapod, somewhere. Carson is back teaching at his university, waiting to follow up with Peter Finley, one of the legendary first settlers, about what the even more legendary Elizabeth Sawyer has told him. Jackie Roberts is still running her starship charter/courier service. They're all in for some surprises as the tale continues in *The Centauri Surprise*, previewed here.

Talisman

Drake University, Sawyer's World

DR. HANNIBAL CARSON, Professor of Exoarcheology, heaved a sigh and looked up from his desk monitor and gazed at the wall. On the screen was yet another in a stack of virtual papers, the mid-term tests of his Archeology 201 class. They had already been checked and graded by his assistant, but he was the final arbiter and it was his responsibility to enter the grades into the records system. It was mind-numbingly tedious work, and he hated it. It wasn't the tediousness per se, he could be diligent about meticulously excavating a site with a brush and trowel, it was the office he hated. He would much rather be in the field. Even hacking through the jungle on the planet Verdigris, mosquitoes and all, was preferable to this.

He turned his attention back to the mid-term. He updated the student's entry in the grading sheet, closed the file, and opened the next. The knock at his door was a welcome reprieve.

"Come in," he called.

A young woman entered, green-haired, and dressed casually in ship coveralls. "Well, this is different," Jackie Roberts said. "I'm not used to seeing you doing desk work."

"Jackie! I haven't seen you for a while. What are you doing here?"

She held up the small package she was carrying in her left hand and waved it. "Special delivery. It's not really; I saw your name on it and decided to bring it over myself. I just got back from the Solar System and it was among the packages I was carrying."

Jackie Roberts owned and operated a small starship, the *Sophie*, and was a licensed courier.

"Solar System? You were on Earth? I thought you hated the place."

"Technically I was on Luna, I never set foot on Earth. Ducayne asked me to give Regina Elliot a ride, and this package was one of a handful waiting for carriage back here. I got lucky on the timing."

Carson reached for the package, but Roberts pulled it back. "You need to acknowledge receipt."

"Oh, sure." Carson scanned his omniphone over the package, and the two exchanged digital signatures. Somewhere on the network, a database updated to indicate his receipt. Roberts released her hold on the small package. "Who's Regina Elliot?" he asked as he took the package.

"Haven't you met her? She's Ducayne's deputy assistant, or whatever her official title is. His second in command."

"Oh. No, I don't think I have." He looked the package over. It was about fifteen centimeters square and five thick. It could have been a book, except it was unlikely anyone would go to the trouble and expense of shipping a book this far. He wasn't expecting any packages. He examined the shipping label. It was indeed addressed to him, care of the university, but the sender information was a coded address that he couldn't figure out.

"Help me out here, Jackie. Where's this from?"

"I picked it up on Luna," she said, taking it back to read the label. "It had just come in on another flight, I'm not sure where from." With almost no exceptions, any flight coming in from another star landed on Luna first, still technically enforcing the quarantine regulations set down fifty years earlier, although these days that amounted to little more than a document and customs screening and changing to an Earthbound shuttle. Jackie scanned her omni across the package then read something off its screen. "My, my. It's been transshipped a few times, originally it came from—" she scrolled down the display "—Wolf 25, by way of Eta Cassiopeiae. One Doctor Peterson, just care of the spaceport on Wolf 25 II." She handed the package back to him. "Someone you know? Artifacts or something? I better not have just smuggled in something illicit."

He flipped the package over, looking at it curiously. He didn't know any Dr. Peterson that he could recall. "It's still sealed, wouldn't your courier status protect you?"

"It would, and I was joking. The whole cargo was scanned and inspected anyway, so you don't have to worry about that being a bomb, either."

He glanced up at her sharply. He had been running into unsavory characters lately, and had escaped a kidnap attempt not that long ago. Would somebody want him dead that badly? "A bomb?"

Roberts rolled her eyes. "No, I just told you. Lighten up, Carson." She paused, then grinned and added, "But wait until I leave before you open it, okay?"

"Funny. Very funny. Just for that—" he tore the package's plastic wrapper open.

A smaller package, an opaque, padded, specimen bag, fell out of the envelope. There was also a sheet of paper. He unfolded it and read the text printed on it.

"Dr. Hannibal Carson," it read,

"I heard you were looking for things like this. Sorry, but I don't know the provenance of any of them. I inherited these as part of a collection of alien artifacts, most of them probably illegally acquired, which is why I choose to remain anonymous. The rest are going to other archeologists or museums.

Best regards, A Friend."

"What does it say?" Roberts asked.

"Someone is getting rid of a collection of illegal artifacts they inherited, and thought I might be interested in these. We get such things from time to time. Unfortunately, with no provenance it's not going to be very useful. But let's see if I can at least figure out what planet they originally came from." So saying, he opened the specimen bag and slid out a small folded cloth bundle onto his desk. He unfolded it to reveal handful of artifacts.

"Oh, my," Roberts said when she saw them. Carson himself was speechless.

There was an obsidian arrowhead, a woven bracelet with small embedded shells that Carson recognized as coming from a planet orbiting Gliese 68, and a pair of small abstract figurines that looked to be made of fired clay. They were irrelevant. What had caught his attention, and Jackie's, was the largest item in the small collection.

It was about ten centimeters square—if the rounded shape could be called a square—and looked like it was made of stone, with a scattering of embedded cabochon-cut gemstones connected by engraved lines. Carson and Roberts had seen its like before. It was a talisman, just like—except for a different pattern of gems—the one they had used to both locate, and to open, the alien pyramid on the planet St. Jacobs, also known as Chara III.

∞ ∞ ∞

"Is it real?" Roberts asked in a hushed voice. The network-wide search that Carson had run looking for items similar to his original find had turned up several others, a few of them fakes. With a demand for alien artifacts, suppliers weren't above selling a few counterfeits. What could the buyers do, complain to the authorities?

Carson glanced at the other items. They looked real enough, although the best fakes would. He picked up the talisman and hefted it. It was heavier than its stone appearance would suggest. If it were a real Spacefarer talisman, it would have sophisticated circuitry inside powered by a very long-lived technetium battery. This felt like other, real examples he'd held. The pattern of gems and lines—a star map—looked authentic too, but he wasn't the expert on that. He held that up to show Jackie. "What do you think, does this look like a real star map?"

"It does look similar to the real ones. I won't know without running a comparison against my star charts. I wonder where it points to?"

"I wonder where it was originally found," Carson said, "but that's a more difficult question. Anyway, run your analysis against a picture of this one and we'll know where it points to."

"Sure," Jackie said, and used her omni to photograph the talisman from several angles. "Since I'm heading back to the *Sophie*, do you want me to take this one to Ducayne? He's beginning to get quite a collection."

She was right. The partial talisman he'd found on Verdigris, and three others that had turned up in his earlier network search were now in Ducayne's possession at Homeworld Security "for safe keeping". Another, the talisman that Carson and his colleague, Marten, had found on a different dig, was now also in Homeworld Security's care, with the team currently examining the pyramid on Chara III, to which that talisman was a key. It irked Carson that he was getting sidelined from following up on the discoveries he himself had made. He made his decision. "No," he said, "I'd like to examine this one first. In fact, I'd appreciate it if you didn't mention it to Ducayne just yet."

She looked at him and cocked her head, eyes narrowing. "What are you up to, Hannibal?"

"Nothing, yet. I just want a chance to do some investigation of my own, without Ducayne's 'mission priorities' getting in the way. For one thing, these other items might give me a hint as to where this came from." That is, if they were all from the same planet, but as far as he knew, figurines like that did not come from Gliese 68.

She peered at him for a moment, as if trying to read his intentions, and then relaxed and shrugged. "Okay. Not really my business, I'm just the delivery girl. They're your artifacts. But I'm curious, so let me know what you come up with." She grinned, and added, "Especially if you want me to tell you where the map points to."

"Fair trade. I just want to avoid any arguments with Ducayne about who gets to hold onto this," he said, picking up the talisman, "which is easier if he doesn't know about it." He glanced at the time. "Anyway, I have a class to teach soon, and I really should finish up grading these mid-terms." He folded the artifacts back into their cloth, put them into the sample bag, and put it away in a desk drawer. "Thanks for coming by, Jackie. I'd much rather talk to you than do this," he gestured at his monitor, "but duty calls."

"All right," she said. "I need to get back anyway." She opened the door to leave, then turned to him, adding "I'd tell you to stay out of trouble, but I know that's asking too much." She winked at him and, before he could utter a reply, left.

∞ ∞ ∞

The story continues in The Centauri Surprise, *available in hardcover, trade paperback and ebook editions.*

About the Author

Alastair Mayer was born in London, England, and moved to Canada with his family as a young boy. He describes his interest in space flight and science fiction as genetic: his father, Douglas W.F. Mayer, had been an early member of the British Interplanetary Society as well as a science fiction fan (who in fact published some of Arthur C. Clarke's first tales in *Amateur Science Stories*).

Alastair became involved in both the L5 Society (now the National Space Society) and computers, publishing articles in *Byte*, *Final Frontier*, and other magazines, as well as becoming an accomplished scuba diver and a private pilot. In 1989 he moved to Colorado, where he still lives, and where, after working in the computer and satellite networking businesses, he now writes full time.

His short stories have been published in several anthologies and his work has appeared often enough in *Analog Science Fiction* magazine to gain him entry to the "Analog MAFIA" (Members Appear Frequently In *Analog*). Many of his works can be found in e-book format on Amazon, Barnes & Noble, Smashwords, and other e-book vendor sites.

The Eridani Convergence is the third in Mayer's Carson & Roberts series, one of several set in the T-Space universe, which also includes the Alpha Centauri trilogy and the in-progress Kakuloa series.

Visit his web site at www.alastairmayer.org, *which also links to the T-Space Wiki.*

9 781948 188159